TIMEWORM

To Julia!
Make your own future.
Thanks for helping me
pick or you in bless!

JIMMY ADAMS
and
BRENDA HELLER

PAGE PUBLISHING, INC.
New York, NY

First originally published by Page Publishing, Inc. 2017

ISBN 978-1-64027-858-5 (Paperback)
ISBN 978-1-64027-859-2 (Digital)

Printed in the United States of America

CONTENTS

ACKNOWLEDGMENTS

Thank you to our two dedicated high school students, Meg Denis and Michelle Le, who met with us numerous hours at Panera and Starbucks to give us honest feedback. Their continual reminder of how teenagers speak, their reactions to the story, and their love for Murphy and Gracie provided valuable feedback that helped us greatly in creating a novel to capture the readers' hearts and minds.

We offer a special thank you to Tina McCracken. Her eye for detail, her suggestions for polishing the text, and her encouragement were ever flowing and sincere. She is a wordsmith with a shared passion in the art of writing.

Our greatest thanks and recognition go to our spouses, Chelsea Adams and David Heller. The completion of this novel, and the next ones in the series, is greatly due to their sharing of time, resources, and the excitement of this journey. Their support has been an inspiration beyond words and a witness of their desire to help us reach our dreams.

PREFACE

As you become immersed in the pages of this book, we hope the lines between fiction and reality become so blurred, you will feel an insatiable quest to know the actual people, places, and events from history. You will see, dear reader, it is impossible to put a face on evil. The real threat to humanity happens in a culture and in a country when repulsive evil becomes nearly impossible to destroy. We encourage you to enjoy the reading as you learn history and learn to take a stand.

Jimmy and Brenda

PART I

AMERICA 20———

CHAPTER 1

Incident

Run! The darkness suffocated Theo with heaviness as he pushed himself forward. *I ... must ... get ...* He lunged behind a stack of crates piled in the alley. He could feel the blood pulsing through his veins and pounding in his ears.

The darkness—is it my friend or enemy? He muffled his labored panting in the sleeve of his coat. Shadows in the darkness moved the streaks of light as his eyes searched through the slats of the crate. Silence was beginning to deafen him. His breathing fell back to a slower rhythm. His lungs were able to suck down more air.

Where? Theo's thoughts were blunted as the icy touch gripped his throat from behind him.

"DAD!" Theo screamed, jerking upright.

"Theodore, it's time to get up."

Theo could not move in the dark bedroom as he tried to clamp his mind shut to the terrors of the night. Regardless of how many times they happened, he was unnerved by the realness of his dreams.

"Theodore, it's time to get up," a metallic voice repeated.

Theo collapsed back on his pillow, sweating and breathing hard from the reality of the nightmare.

"Theodore ..."

"I KNOW!" Theo yelled into the dark and quiet room. He was safe from his dream, but he needed a minute to bring his heartbeat back to a resting rate. He needed to reassure himself that it was only a dream. "I'm sorry," he barely spoke above a whisper into his wrist-watch, at the same time resting his arm across his forehead. His arm bumped the nub of his earpiece lying on the pillow. Theo took a deep breath and replaced the earbud, promising himself to discuss a new fashion trend in modern earbud technology with his dad when he got a chance.

"Good morning, Theodore. It's a beautiful day out today. The temperature is seventy-five degrees with a slight breeze from the west." The computer maid reported with a crisp voice as it automatically turned on the bedroom lights and lifted the window blinds.

"IRIS, it's too early to get up." The shaggy-haired seventeen-year-old pulled the covers over his head to block out the sunshine and glaring ceiling lights.

"Your father has been trying to link with you for the last twenty-five minutes. He has issued a sleeper code for you, and you know that I am not going to stop bothering you until you are up and out the door," the voice replied coolly.

"Ugh, you are sooooo annoying in the mornings. I hate morning people," Theo mumbled from under the covers.

"Begging your pardon, but I am not a morning person. In fact, I'm not even a person. I am the Integrated Robotic Information System your father designed, and time really has no meaning for me. It could be morning or night. I just understand that it is important for you to be at your father's lab this morning in exactly one hour from now." The voice of IRIS the computer maid filled the room in matter-of-fact detail.

Reluctantly, Theo pulled down the covers as his head emerged from underneath. He slowly opened his eyes, allowing them to adjust to the flood of light coming into his room. *I hate waking up.* "What's for breakfast?"

"I had hoped to get you a nice, hearty breakfast of eggs, bacon, and orange juice, but since you like to sleep in, you may only have time to scarf down a toaster tart on your way to see your father." Theo could detect a hint of annoyance in IRIS's soft robotic voice.

"Fine. I'm up."

"Good morning, Theodore."

"Good morning, IRIS," Theo responded irritably as he sat up and swung his feet over the edge of his bed, feeling blindly for his slippers. He searched with his feet until he found his left slipper and slid his foot into it, but his bare, dangling foot could not find his right.

"Where's my other slipper?"

"It's not by your bed, and no amount of swinging your foot around is going to change that. I do believe you may have more luck finding your slipper if you find Murphy."

"MURPHY!" Theo yelled and waited for a response. Nothing. He waited a few more seconds. Just as he inhaled with the intent to yell again, a plump brown-and-white beagle came plodding on the landing above the steps leading into Theo's bedroom, tail wagging happily and teeth clamped down on a partly chewed slipper.

"Murphy, why do you look like a pudgy ball?" Theo knew it was early morning, but he blinked his eyes to focus, and still his dog looked heavy and out of shape.

Murphy cocked his head sideways and gave a funny little yelp as if to ask, "What do you mean?" The dog stopped and looked at his right flank then his left flank and barked a bit louder. He looked at Theo then started to shake vigorously like he had just been given a bath. The shimmy of the shake began at his head. His ears shook back and forth violently and stretched out a little from his head. Next, his midsection started to vibrate and lift, going from a pudgy belly to a firm stomach. Finally, his legs extended about half an inch in length and muscle rippled from his legs, thighs, and chest. Murphy's body shake slowed to a stop. Almost in a show-off stance, he stood up slightly on his hind legs and gave a loud, powerful growl.

"Man, you're cool." Theo chuckled, watching his best friend morph his appearance. "That's much better!"

Murphy put all four feet on the floor and slowly made his way around the piles of clothes strategically tossed throughout the room, plodding over an empty pizza box, and came to rest at his master's feet, tail wagging even faster.

"Good boy, Murphy, you found my slipper!" Theo scratched the dog behind his long ears. Murphy dropped the slipper at his master's feet and sat down to fully benefit from his morning petting. Theo slid his foot into the slipper and quickly looked down and saw his big toe exposed in the hole that Murphy had chewed. He wiggled his toes and laughed as his big toe moved freely without the restraint of the slipper holding it in place. He looked down at the loving dog and was about to scold him but stopped as Murphy rolled over to his back, exposing his belly for a good rubbing.

"You're such a good boy, Murphy. Yes, you are," Theo cooed affectionately as he got down from his bed and began rubbing his dog's underbelly with both hands, causing Murphy's legs to twitch in happiness. "You know, Murph, sometimes I think if I didn't have you to talk to, I'd flip out and start enjoying talking to IRIS! I was hoping for a puppy, but when Dad brought you home from the lab, I knew we'd be good friends. I just wish I knew how old you are." Murphy jumped up and started a routine of running and stopping in a "Come and get me" stance as Theo laughed and playfully lunged for his dog.

"Oh, I see how it is. You have too much energy! I hope Dad put a locator chip in you so I'll never lose you! Although, who could lose a dog with a blinking blue light collar? Dad made a good choice when he brought you home. Best of buds, huh, Murphy?" With big brown beagle eyes and an out-of-control wagging tail, Murphy did his best to show his master they would be friends forever.

"Sorry to interrupt, Theodore, but you are running a bit late."

"Fine, IRIS. Can you turn on the shower for me—not too hot this time?" Theo slowly stood up from the floor. "Sorry, boy, but I gotta get moving." The big brown eyes looked up to him from the floor.

Theo made his way toward his bathroom, tripping over a pile of clothes and making a mental note to clean up his room. He'd find time after he beat his latest HoloGame, *Death Fortress 4*. He could hear the water in the shower running as he opened the bathroom door. Steam was already filling the small room and fogging up the mirror. He reached in to feel the water and winced as the water hit his hand. "IRIS, can you turn it down a little, please? I'd like to keep my skin from burning off!"

"Of course, Theodore," the stoic voice answered. "The water temperature is now eighty degrees. Will that be sufficient?"

"Fine." Theo stepped into the shower. After a few minutes under the water, he quickly ran the soap over his arms, legs, and chest, ignoring his back and neck as usual. He got out and dried himself off with his warm towel.

"How about some tunes, IRIS!" He grabbed another towel and wiped the steam off the mirror, where he saw an older version of himself staring back.

"Geez, Dad! How many times do I have to ask you not to use this holo-screen? I'd like a little privacy in this house. I mean, I feel like I have no personal space what with IRIS always watching over us."

"Sorry, Theo, but I've been trying to get ahold of you for half an hour or more. I would really like it if you can be here for the first official testing of the TimeWorm."

Theo stared at his father for a minute and noticed for the first time the wrinkles that were starting to form around his eyes and the gray hairs that had somehow taken over as the dominant color in his hair and goatee. He loved his father. They had gotten very close after his mom died a few years back, but lately with his dad's working around the clock, nearing the completion of the TimeWorm, it seemed to him that they had started to drift apart a little.

"Dad, is it actually gonna work this time?" Theo didn't mask the hint of sarcasm in his voice.

"It should. I used some of your suggestions on the power converter to help boost the output. Just in case it doesn't work, the only people who will be present will be me, you, and of course, Viktor."

"Sounds like a plan." Theo reached for his toothbrush. "Dad, all the kids today are getting their earbuds implanted as an earcuff. I'd like to—"

"Theodore, please, we'll talk about it later. For now, just see about getting here!" his dad cut in with his disciplinary voice.

"All right, all right. I'll be there as soon as I can." He reached up, and as his hand got close to the mirror, a control panel appeared. The younger of the two looked at his dad. "See ya in a few." Theo tapped the CLEAR button on the control panel. His dad's image disappeared from the mirror, and he was left looking at himself.

With teeth brushed, hair somewhat combed, and pretty close-to-clean clothes from assorted piles from the floor, Theo slung his backpack over one shoulder and made his way to the kitchen for a quick breakfast. He lurched past the bar in the kitchenette, making a left-handed sweep across the counter as he moved the toaster tart from the plate to his mouth.

"With a quick breakfast, your metabolism will need a boost in a few hours. You need to add a couple of nutrition bars to your backpack."

"Okay, IRIS. Thanks for the health tips." Theo reluctantly grabbed a carton of nutrition bars from the counter and stuffed them into his pack. "Where's my driftboard?" he mumbled, mouth partially full.

"Theodore, please don't talk with your mouth full. It is quite rude," the computer voice responded with discipline in her voice.

"Huh," Theo muttered again as he jammed more breakfast into his mouth. "What does it matter to you! You are a COM–PU–TER, not a human."

"Yes, yes, we've been over this already. I may not be human, but I do have better manners than you do. Besides, your father would not approve of your behavior."

"Sorry, IRIS." Theo did feel somewhat guilty. He really did need to stop harping on her. Although she was only a computer program, he always felt like she was a little human.

"Thank you," IRIS continued in a matter-of-fact tone. "You should find the VX-3000 in the closet by the front door."

"IRIS"—Theo paused, looking up to the ceiling, which was where he usually looked when talking to her—"how do you always know where I leave things?"

"It's simple, really. I pay attention. Most of your electronics give off a power signal."

With that Theo raced up the stairs, shot through the living room, and landed in the small entryway with a closet by the front door. He grabbed his backpack and his driftboard, which looked like a skateboard only about twice as thick to accommodate the two jet-powered thrusters in the bottom. Most driftboards had weak fans that barely kept the rider a float; with a little help from his father, Theo had redesigned the system and enhanced the power.

He stepped outside and into the fresh morning air; he took a deep breath and could taste the ocean. "Time to fly." He dropped the driftboard to the ground, simultaneously igniting its thrusters so that it floated about two inches off the surface of the earth.

"Murphy!" Theo hollered at the muscular beagle that was already running down the stairs so fast it fell and rolled into a compacted ball. "Gotcha!" He swept up the ball with one hand and tucked Murphy into his backpack. "You know, Murphy, you're the first dog that I ever knew could be rolled into a shiny silver ball. I should ask Dad what kind of science he practiced on you!" Theo teased with a "ha" chuckle as he half-zipped the canvas pack and secured a flap over the opening. He checked the shoulder straps of his backpack, clicked the chest strap into place, and stepped down hard on the back of his board, kicking it into the air. He caught the nose of the board in his right hand and started running toward the stairs leading down to the sidewalk. As he reached the first step, he leapt out over the stairs and jumped onto his board. The sidewalk came rushing toward him; he bent his knees, absorbing the force of his board pushing off the ground. Without hesitation, he leaned into the landing and started floating forward, building momentum as he swayed back and forth, generating speed.

Theo pictured himself moving with the velocity of a bullet, zigzagging his way through the morning joggers and commuters, making their way to work. He turned his head once to get a second glance at a particularly cute jogger. *Pink's a good color on her*, he thought to himself with a smile. He performed a quick kick-flip 180. The board kept moving in the direction he was heading, but he gained a better view of the young jogger. He shook his head as she never even glanced his way, obviously not impressed with his board work, yet again. *One of these days, she'll notice me, or I may have to accidentally crash into her*. Theo grinned at the thought. After a month or two of trying to get her to acknowledge that he existed, he was running out of board tricks.

He smoothly turned to face the direction the driftboard was moving and saw a car stop at the intersection directly in front of him. He quickly kicked down on the board, which catapulted him flying like Superman toward the hood of the car. The board continued under the car and coasted to the curb on the other side of the one-way street. Theo hit the hood of the car and rolled the rest of the way across it. He came down with a crash onto the pavement.

"Sorry!" he yelled as he bounced like a cat springing off the ground and back onto his board, moving quickly down the sidewalk. Once he was clear of onlookers and busy morning traffic, he took a second to glance at his watch. "Diagnostic report on VX-3000," he ordered into his watch. The screen quickly switched from the time to a visual of his board.

"No problems detected, other than maybe your board-handling skills," he heard in the earpiece secured in his ear.

"Ha-ha, IRIS, very funny! Are you sure nothing is wrong?"

"All systems are reading 100 percent, full power output," the computer voice reported, void of emotion.

"That was close. Good thing that was a classic car," he said with enthusiasm. "Can you imagine how late I would be to Dad's office if I had to travel on wheels?"

"Correction. That was a classic *muscle* car, which in its day was exceptionally fast. They were built for speed and power, but yes, the use of wheel-operated vehicles does seem quite archaic with the advances society has made." IRIS gave her report in her know-it-all way. In fact, there really was not much the computer maid didn't know, even when Theo couldn't find an answer. She had been programmed by his father, Dr. Luke Marshall, to link with most program networks and always find a reason or an answer for his inquisitive son.

"Dad would be responsible for a lot of those advances, wouldn't he?" Theo asked proudly.

"Quite right. Your father has done a lot to advance modern society, along with the help of Dr. Brack, of course."

"Can't forget old Viktor, can we?"

Theo navigated the rest of the way through the busy neighborhood without further incident. He stopped at the corner of Ocean Avenue and Thirteenth Street and stared at the ocean in the distance, longing to head that way and enjoy the coast for a few hours, but he knew better than to miss his dad's possible big day. With a sigh he turned right and made his way toward the industrial area, which would eventually lead him downtown and to his father's lab in the Brack Towers, owned by his father's best friend and coinventor Dr. Viktor Brack.

A smile crossed his face as he turned the corner where abandoned warehouses and factories worn down from years of no upkeep came into view. He always liked boarding through the old industrial area partly because not too many people traveled this route any more with the installation of the Super Rail. With the serious lack of traffic, he was able to practice on his board and not have to worry about transports or people watching him if he ate it hard on the pavement, which seemed to happen a lot. Also, despite many warnings from his father, he enjoyed exploring the old buildings left over from the Green Revolution, a time when the government passed laws to protect the environment and alternative sources of energy began to replace fossil fuels.

Theo couldn't help but grin as he approached the forbidden zone of dilapidated buildings and pushed the chain-link gate open as wide as the security chain and lock would allow. Setting his pack on the stopped driftboard, he squeezed through the gap in the gate doors. Once through the opening, he reached back and grabbed his backpack and pulled, sliding the driftboard through the opening. The spring-loaded chain slammed the gate shut with a sharp metallic clang just as he tripped backward and landed on his backside.

Theo stood up to get his driftboard when a loud, crisp bark erupted from the motionless backpack and echoed off the abandoned building. The backpack jumped and squirmed around for a second, and then a snout popped out from under the flap. The snout wriggled around and scrunched up as it took in all the new scents from the surrounding area. After a moment of intense sniffing, a paw emerged from the pack. Then the other front paw slipped out from the inside.

"C'mere, boy," Theo ordered with a clap of his hands. "Come on, you must be ready to stretch your legs. Give me just a minute to pick up my driftboard, and then you can sniff all you want as we look around." Murphy's long ears seemed to lift away from his beagle head as Theo tucked the driftboard under his arm and flung the backpack to his back, slipping his arm into the strap.

"Okay, boy. You've been still long enough. We should have time for a quick look around." Kicking bits of crumbled concrete like a game of kicking a rock down a sidewalk, Theo sauntered to the abandoned building and up the steps for a quick look inside. Letting his eyes adjust to the dark interior, he stood at the top, where a staircase should have led down into a long abandoned hallway littered with rusted office supplies, piles of wood, crates, and metal beams. The collapsed stair pieces were lying off to either side of the hallway, probably crumbled during an earth tremor or even from the vibration of a military plane flying too low overhead. The place was also decorated with some really well-done graffiti artwork and some that was not so well done. He found a new piece of graffiti each time he came, but he had never seen another person in the building.

On previous visits, he had spent quite a few hours in this part of the building clearing debris and setting up an obstacle course for himself. He stacked crates at varying heights, laid out a few long rusty beams, and placed old desks and rusted out filing cabinets all along the clearing that he had created. It had taken him a few months to set up the perfect course to hone his driftboard skills. He came up to the beginning of his self-made course and gave the rock one last hard kick, sending it flying out over the ten-foot drop. He watched as the rock disappeared down into the wasteland turned driftboard course. He heard it bounce and ricochet off something down below.

"You ready, boy?" he asked his furry companion. Murphy looked up at him and gave him a little bark and tail wag of encouragement as if to say, "Ready when you are—and I hope this goes better than last time."

INCIDENT

Theo took a deep breath, exhaled slowly, then dropped off the edge of the wall. A huge smiled crossed his face, and he felt the air whip through his hair and the adrenaline course through his veins as he watched the concrete floor come rushing toward him. He shifted his weight to the back of the board and pushed his rear thruster hard toward the floor to level out. Using his outstretched hand to shove off the wall, he started moving his momentum forward. He swayed back and forth, gaining speed as the first obstacle rapidly neared. He squatted down, sliding his back foot to the tail of the board, then popped the back as hard as he could, sending himself and the board up and over the strategically placed filing cabinet. Theo slid his foot forward, leveling himself out, then came down softly on the tail of the board again. He repeated the same ollie over the next few barricades that gained in height. The last pile of crates came into sight; he began to sweat a little as he had yet to clear this without scraping a thruster or two on the top crate. He zigzagged harder and harder trying to build up his speed. Determination replaced the carefree look on his face. He hunkered down lower than before and slammed hard on the tail of the board. He could feel the board rising from the ground as he simultaneously moved the front of the board with his foot, clearing the front edge of the crate pile. He cringed as the back of his board scraped across the top crate and stopped the board just enough to send him flying forward without it under his feet. He landed hard on the ground, tucked, and rolled with the momentum of his fall until he felt his body skid to a stop, sprawled out on the ground.

He didn't move for a moment. He gave the air time to seep back into his lungs and the pain of the fall to start to fade. "Ouch, oh for two today!" he shouted out loud as he pushed himself up to a sitting position beside his board hovering silently beside him. He winced as he stood up and dusted himself off, trying to get rid of any evidence that he (1) crashed and (2) was in one of the old factory buildings. Murphy just watched from where he lay down on the top of the wall that had abandoned its job as floor attached to a stairway.

"Theodore, where are you?" a familiar and stern voice queried. He looked down at his watch and saw his father for the second time already this morning.

"I'll be there in ten minutes, just taking a shortcut," he answered, trying to hide the guilt from his voice while slowly moving his watch down, trying to hide the debris behind him from his father's view. He didn't need his father to see where he was and start lecturing him on the dangers of being in or around those old dilapidated buildings.

"All right, hurry up!"

Theo rode his board to the spring gate, where he scooped Murphy and commanded, "Roll!" just before he dropped the beagle into the backpack.

Theo looked at himself in the colossal mirrored windows that covered the bottom half of the Brack Towers. The three towers seemed to loom over the rest of the city, looking menacing and out of place. The two smaller towers that stood to either side of main research tower only reached to half its height, but each still stood significantly larger than any other city building, and the trio cast a heavy shadow over the entire city block. He started to check himself in the mirrored windows when he noticed his backpack squirming. He chuckled and slipped off the pack. He unzipped the top compartment and pushed the pack over to its side, allowing the shiny silver ball to roll out onto the sidewalk. Just as the ball was about to bump into the door of the tower, it stopped, reversed, then morphed into a muscular brown-and-white beagle, tongue panting and tail wagging.

"Ready?" Theo asked, slipping the pack back over his shoulder. He shivered as a familiarly strange feeling trickled down his spine as it did every time he entered the towers. He didn't know what it was about these monstrosities that made him shudder; he just knew that something didn't seem right about them. If he let his imagination go, he could almost see beast-men in trench coats moving through the shadows. A stench reached his nostrils. A quick glance down at Murphy, who was sniffing the ground beside the mirrored wall, made him wonder if his precognition was more than imagination. *Sometimes I don't like getting messages from the future.* "Come on, Murph." Theo shook the shiver out of his spine.

He straightened out his clothes and tried his best to remove the dirt and debris from his second driftboard accident in the last half hour. Content that he looked the best he was going to, he ran his hand over the door scanner lock and heard the familiar three beeps. With a quick wrist movement, he opened the door and left behind the warmth of the sunshine, entering into the cold, uninspired, and dreary decor of the Brack Tower main entry.

As he made his way across the almost empty room, he imagined the echo of his footsteps shooting rays of ice through the air toward the elevators and toward the lone receptionist sitting at a ridiculously small and out-of-place desk in the foreboding foyer. He wondered who decorated the place and why he or she hadn't been fired immediately. A few pictures of what looked like weird inkblot tests hung from the walls in random places with no set pattern. Spaced between the pictures at odd intervals were peculiar black and silver statues. Theo satisfied his imagination of the gothic decor by assuming the statues were people covered in mud being tortured into weird poses by some unseen demented force.

Theo intentionally moved his sneakers to squeak in his deliberate stomps as he approached the cherrywood desk tucked behind an impressive but cold granite counter. "Hello, Miss Ackermann," he said crisply, enjoying the ringing echo of his voice. Studying the dispassionate face of the receptionist, Theo wondered if her powder-white complexion was a result of too many hours sitting in this dark, unproductive dungeon like a lab rat in an isolated cage. He waited for her to respond, but she either had not heard him or was being her usual not-so-polite self. She typed away on her keyboard, smashing down on the letter keys, each one sending an echo through the foyer. He wondered what the keyboard had done to upset her. He stood there for a few more minutes before he brought his closed fist up to his mouth and cleared his throat as loudly as he could and still no response.

"Helloooooo, Miss Ackermann," Theo introduced himself again, hoping to get her attention this time. He leaned over the countertop, resting his weight on his forearms. He watched as the receptionist bashed down on the helpless keys. "Busy day today?" he asked sarcastically as he looked over to the vacant waiting room with empty chairs and the latest issues of magazines collecting dust. Then he turned back to the ice sculpture sitting behind the reception desk.

After typing a few more notes into her computer, making sure the disgust of being interrupted was evident on her face, she pushed her sparkly horned-rimmed glasses farther up on the bridge of her long, pointy nose. She pulled down on the jacket of her very plain yet modern gray pantsuit, which clashed horribly with her strange choice of 1950s eyewear. Theo just shook his head in disbelief, wondering what anyone else would think of her blatant rudeness. He had thought that receptionists were supposed to be all warm and fuzzy, not cold and prickly. *No wonder she's still a miss.* He let his thoughts wander.

"Hello, Herr Marshall," Ms. Ackermann quipped with bile in her German-accented voice. "Vat do you need?"

"Don't you mean, 'It's great to see you today, Theo. What can I do for ya?'" he said in his mocking, robotic voice while moving his arms in quick sharp motions.

Ms. Ackermann sat motionless in her chair and stared at Theo. She sniffed then turned back to her computer screen and typing.

"Whoa, whoa, whoa, I'm sorry. That was mean," Theo offered his apology. "Can you please buzz me through and let my dad know I'm on my way up?" She didn't budge. "I like your glasses. Are they new? They sure are sparkly."

Her fierce and relentless keyboard typing gradually slowed, letting the young intruder know that his attempt at flattery was having his desired effect. He knew he had to say something else nice and do it quickly before his charm wore off. "I sure wish I could type as fast as you do, Miss Ackermann. I would have already finished typing Mr. Medi's five-page essay on how World War I actually started World War II. All very confusing to a young boy like me." The typing stopped. *Jackpot!* he thought.

"Herr Marshall, Vorld Var I started Vorld Var II because of you greedy Americans poking your noses in places sie do not belong.

Lucky for us, the Führer save our country from your greedy vays. Ten you vonce again interfered vith German progress, fearful dat ve vould surpass you in every vay vith our superior knowledge of technology. Dat is vhy it take American, Russian peoples, and filthy Brits to stop Der Deutsche people. No von could do it by himself! Everybody knows dis."

Theo just stared at the receptionist. He knew he hadn't paid very close attention in world history class most days, but he was sure it really was not America's fault—that in fact both wars were started by the warmongering Germans. "Well not directly," he could see Mr. Medi correcting him while looking over his half-moon reading glasses. "Germany took blame, but did not start the war," he could hear Medi explaining enthusiastically. Man, that guy loved history! Theo didn't get it; sure, he knew the adage, "Those ignorant of history are doomed to repeat it!" How many times had he heard old Medi saying that? But the world had come a long way since 1945. It had been almost a hundred years since that war ended.

"Well, I'll be sure to add that to my conclusion. Thank you, Miss Ackermann."

The familiar buzz of the gate lock releasing resonated throughout the lobby. Theo moved quickly to push the gate open before it locked itself again. He couldn't get away from Ms. Ackermann soon enough. He threw his board down to the ground in front of him and started to jump on it.

"Nein! Not in dis building, Herr Marshall!" the ice queen ordered.

"I forgot, sorry," Theo offered his best sincere fake apology. "Come on, Murphy," he beckoned to the pooch clicking around on the cold tile floors. He kicked down on the board catching the nose in one fluid motion and never stopped running toward the elevators. His footsteps reverberated through the hall and got louder as the walls closed in the closer he got to the elevator station. He pushed the elevator call button a hundred times trying to get one of the six elevator doors to open. Why a place that never had any visitors other than the handful of scientists who worked here needed six elevators was beyond his comprehension.

The elevator up arrow lit in front of him as Theo waited with anticipation for the doors to open so he could be free from the death stare that he knew was coming from behind those bedazzled, ancient horn-rimmed glasses. He slipped his pack off his shoulders and held it in his right hand and his board in his left. He didn't even wait for the door to open completely before he turned sideways and dove into the elevator with Murphy jumping in too, feeling quite at home in the familiar Brack Tower.

With a loud exhale, Theo pushed the fortieth floor button. He shivered and rubbed his arms that had broken out in goosebumps. He shook his head in disbelief as he ran over in his mind the conversation he had just had with Ms. Ackermann. How could she really believe that? What about all those people who had been hurt and killed? He had never liked Ms. Ackermann much, but now he was convinced that she was truly an awful, awful person. Theo popped his head out of the elevator door and yelled down the long hallway, "I am pretty sure everything you said was completely wrong, but it was great talkin' to you as usual!" He ducked his head back just as the shiny silver doors slammed shut. He knew he should have just left well enough alone, but seriously, who thinks like that and even worse, lets people know it.

The lame elevator music started up as the metal box lurched and slowly lifted off the ground level. Anticipating the jolt he knew was about to happen, Theo grabbed ahold of the railing. The sudden thrust had knocked him over the first time he had ridden in the elevator. After a few moans and strange noises, the elevator jerked hard and took off like a rocket, causing his stomach to move up his throat, making him fear that he would see his toaster tarts again. With all the technological advances his dad and Dr. Brack had created, he was still dumbfounded that these elevator rides always felt like they were going to end tragically.

The elevator roared past floor after floor; Theo squeezed the hand railing as hard as he could. Just about the time he thought he was going to lose his breakfast, the elevator began to slow—36 ... 37 ... 38 ... slower ... 39 ... stopped ... 40. "I hate these darn things," Theo mumbled under his breath. The doors opened slowly, revealing the penthouse floor Research and Development facility. He wondered if every floor had the same layout; he had never been on any other floor. Something was different. He noticed how empty of human traffic the entire building was today. Usually, there were twenty or so men and women running around, working on computers, running statistical data for his dad or Dr. Brack. A quick glance at his wrist calendar and it all made sense; today was Sunday. Only his dad, Dr. Brack and, of course, the ice queen would be here on a Sunday.

The Research and Development Division consumed the entire top floor of the Brack Tower and consisted of three separate research facilities. The outer room consisted of six work stations that were spread out in groups of two. The first two were positioned straight ahead of the elevator doors, two more were on the right side of the room, and the last two were on the left side of the room. Each workstation was fully equipped with every sort of high tech gadget, audio/video device, networking station, and large screen monitors on either side of the massive tables. Theo ran his hand over the workstation in front of him as he passed by, and the inset keyboard lit up bright neon orange and moved along the table surface. As his last finger slid off the table, the illuminated keyboard faded, leaving the dark marble surface bare once again.

Theo looked up toward the vaulted ceiling as he made his way to the double glass security doors which lead into the second tier of the Research and Development floor called the Laboratory. He noticed the large industrial ceiling fans were not oscillating, and the main LED lighting system was turned off. The entrance to the inner room was only illuminated with emergency safety lights. He also couldn't hear the familiar buzzing of the super-coolant air conditioner either, which during this time of the year should be blowing lots of cool air into the room filled with machines, keeping the billions of dollars in equipment from overheating and keeping them operating efficiently. He glanced down at Murphy who was unaffected by the quiet as he trotted with his head beside his maser's left shin.

They really plan to use the TimeWorm today. Theo nodded in response to his thoughts. It was the only explanation that made sense to Theo—the only reason for all the main energy-sapping systems to be shut down and operating with as little drain on the power generators as possible. The Brack Towers were on the main public power grid along with the rest of the city, but the Towers did have their own super generators to draw power for most of their experiments and equipment. The city officials had gotten frustrated with the constant power outages over the first few weeks of testing and had threatened to shut off the Towers from city power. Dr. Brack and his dad had quickly put together two giant generators, one located in each of the smaller Towers on either side of the main building.

Theo closed in on the two frosted glass security doors leading into the Laboratory and stood motionless for five seconds while an infrared retinal scanner dropped from its hiding spot in the ceiling, stopping level with his eyes. The orb shaped scanner moved left to right and then back before the light on the door flashed and beeped three times and turned green indicating access was approved. He didn't know why that stupid thing always made him nervous. "It isn't like we wouldn't get the go ahead," he grumbled under his breath as he and Murphy reacted to the green light.

Theo shook off the heebee geebees that the retinal scanner had given him and walked forward. The thick, frosted glass doors opened smoothly without any noise, giving both boy and dog access to the main research and experimentation room. He could see his dad directly ahead of him working on a giant processor, but he didn't see the tall, skinny frame of Dr. Brack. Surely, the other scientist was in the lab; Theo was pretty sure the man never left. Dr. Brack was the only person here more than his father.

He zig-zagged his way around the work stations, processors, and other scientific equipment placed throughout the room. A couple times he almost tripped over power cables and cords lying on the floor. The cords were spread out like an octopus from the center of the room; all power was sent to the control console where his father was working. His dad was squatted down on one knee working on something Theo couldn't see, his dad's white lab coat sticking out like a sore thumb among all the cold metal and black wiring around him.

"It's about time you got here, Theodore," came a stern yet caring voice. "Can you hand me that data tablet over there?" he asked not looking up, only pointing in the general direction of the table next to him littered with his tools. "What took you so long?" he asked before his son could get to the table. "Did you go back to that dangerous obstacle course again?" he asked, not letting Theo get a word out before rightfully accusing him.

"I woke up late, Dad—had a long night of gaming." Guilt was heavy in his words.

"IRIS let me know when you left the house. Plus, she knows where you are at all times, Theodore. Please, don't lie to me, son."

Theo cringed at his dad's words. His dad never had to yell or even raise his voice to get a point across or to express that he was upset. He hated to hear disappointment in his dad's voice, especially because he had done something, knowing full well he shouldn't have. "Sorry, Dad. I just really want to win that race next month at the shore. The winner gets the newest prototype board, the G-1000x. That thing is supposed to handle like it's a part of you."

"That's all fine and well, but you won't win anything if you're grounded for lying to me. Will you?"

"That is an excellent point, oh wise father of mine." Theo tried to lighten the mood a bit.

"Flattery will not keep you from being grounded, but you're not wrong." Luke Marshall showed the same quick wit as his son. He stood up slowly, grunting as his muscles let him know he had been in that position for far too long. The 45-year-old scientist put his hands on his lower back and leaned forward trying to work out the stiffness. He ran his hand through his shaggy, unkempt salt-and-pepper hair. Next, like clockwork, he took off his black framed glasses and wiped them clean with the handkerchief he always kept in his back pocket. "It's that one under the green notebook, right there on the edge of the table."

"Got it!" Theo grabbed the tablet, looked at the flashing screen, and studied the various charts and readings. "Almost there, Dad— 98% power output!"

"Almost," his dad repeated, the annoyance clear in his face. "Viktor won't be happy. I've been racking my brain for days trying to route enough power to get both cylinders up to maximum capacity." He paused for a minute and rubbed his tired eyes, then slipped his glasses back on one temple at a time and wondered why they were always loose on his face. "We can't make the jump without max capacity." He turned, not giving Theo a chance to respond and went back to work on the console, grunting in discomfort as he bent back down.

Theo took a few minutes to organize his father's work table, then picked up the tablet and walked over to the console system to help his dad. He spent a few minutes scanning the information on the tablet. It showed all the areas that had been put on reduced energy output, put on backup power, or shut down completely—all in an attempt to get 2 percent more power to the TimeWorm, hidden away in the core room, the Jump Station.

"Why don't you shut down those stupid elevators for the jump? They've got to use a ton of power considering they rocket you up to this floor like a missile or something." Theo loved the idea of shutting down those death traps for any amount of time.

A loud clang resonated from his dad's direction as he dropped the lock wrench he was using to fasten another power cord to the central command console. It was followed with the familiar grunt of him standing back up. "What did you say?"

"Shut down the elevators. It wouldn't be safe for anyone to be in them when you're using the TimeWorm anyway, so why not cut the power to those too?"

A huge smile spread across Dr. Marshall's weary face. "I think you may have just solved the puzzle, Theo! If this works, you may consider yourself ungrounded for the time being—or until you do something to aggravate me again." His excited voice matched his quick step as he walked toward his son to give him a huge hug and retrieve the data tablet from him.

Theo watched in amazement as his father swiped through ten different screens on the data tablet at a furious pace. "I think that will do it. I'll need a few minutes to run a diagnostic test to see if the additional power from the elevators will be enough to boost the TimeWorm to over maximum capacity needed." Dr. Marshall spoke to his son with hope in his voice. "Theo if this works, it's going to change everything for everyone." Dr. Marshall looked up from the tablet with the joy of a child on Christmas morning on his face only to be replaced by one of equal worry. "Or this thing could destroy everything for everyone."

Theo stared at his dad, not quite understanding the sudden solemn attitude change. He figured his dad would be about ready to explode with excitement as the anticipation of his life's work was about to become reality. "So, Dad, explain to me one more time how this all works because I have read ad nauseam about Kerr Rings and Einstein-Rosen Bridge time-travel theories and can see no way of this actually working. I mean, you would have to go faster than the speed of light to even have the possibility exist." He tried to impress his dad that he knew a little about the science of time travel.

"As you know, light travels at 186,282 miles per second. That would be fast enough to get you around the earth seven and half times in one second. What if we could go just .0000001 faster than light? Then theoretically, we would be traveling faster than time. Time itself would stand still! Problem is, Theo, we need to have a vehicle of some sort that would be able to withstand that type of force." Luke Marshall sounded sure of the science behind time travel, but his furrowed forehead meant he was trying to resolve some problem in a theory.

"I understand that part, Dad, but you're talking about traveling to the future. You know Dr. Brack doesn't want to go into the future. He wants to go backward, the opposite direction!"

"Excellent observation, Theodore, and one you actually helped solve." The teenager twisted around to see Dr. Brack's tall, thin frame standing behind him. It was eerie how Dr. Brack became a part of the conversation when Theo didn't even know he was in the room.

"I did?" Theo's voice broke a little even though he tried to sound like he was involved in a scientific discussion. He was a little shaken with Dr. Brack's unexpected response.

"Yes, yes, you did with your theory on how we could increase the power to the Jump Station's cylinder coil accelerators. That may just give us enough to move both coils in opposite directions at that slight millionth over the speed of light that we have not yet been able to gain." Dr. Brack appeared impressed with Theo's interest in science even though he was only a kid.

"But how does that help you actually travel *back* in time?" Theo questioned out of curiosity, not noticing his dad straighten his back a little and look intently at Dr. Brack.

"It's a simple concept that everyone on earth knows. The stars we see at night, their light, is actually from the past. What if we separate light in its smallest particle and follow it back to its source star, loop around that star, and come back to earth, all at speed faster than light?" Dr. Brack responded with more of a statement than a question.

"Fine. Let's say that we can do all that. How do you move an object or a person that fast without tearing him apart to his smallest particle size?" Theo queried, remembering what his dad had said about the impact on a time-travel vehicle.

Luke Marshall jumped at the chance to further explain. "That's where the cylinder coil comes into play. The inside coil spins slightly faster than the speed of light. The outside coil goes the opposite direction. The resulting force created is basically the opposite of gravity. It will, in fact, pull whatever is in the TimeWorm down to its smallest possible particles." As his dad finished, Theo understood why Dr. Luke Marshall was listed first on the door to the Research and Development Center. He knew his dad had made science his passion and his life.

"How would a person live through that and not just fly into a trillion pieces?" Theo was truly interested.

"Another good question. You are your father's son." Dr. Brack sounded a little terse in his compliment. "The internal coil creates what essentially can be explained as a double vacuum. It will keep everything close enough that it can re-establish its natural state once the traveling at the speed of light slows to the natural speed of the earth's rotation. That gravity will push the person or the object back to its natural form."

"Once the *object*, not the *person*, in the TimeWorm is completely broken down," Dr. Marshall added heatedly as he gave a quick glance in Dr. Brack's direction, "the computer will stop the second cylinder. That will release the outer vacuum, and the force will send the particles straight toward the singularity that will give us the desired time we target in the past."

"So I don't understand how that's a problem." Theo wrinkled his forehead and looked at the workstation.

"Your dad didn't spend his whole life learning and studying just to play around with dangerous experiments!" Luke Marshall exploded.

Everyone fell quiet. Theo gave a puzzled stare at his dad who looked like he was sweating. *Wow,* he thought to himself. *He must be under a lot of pressure. He never talks about himself in third person and NEVER yells.*

"Sorry, Dad." Theo whispered as he reached up and put a hand on his dad's shoulder.

Viktor Brack fixed his icy pale blue eyes on his data tablet to avoid the heated looks that his fellow scientist was throwing at him. Theo shivered as the tension in the room became very thick, and he slowly made his way back to the workstation to put some distance between himself and the scientists. He decided to keep himself busy by reorganizing the desk he had just put in order for his father. He watched as the two men, who on most days laughed and joked with one another like teenagers, now worked side by side in total unnerving silence and never even glanced over at the other.

"Son, come here for a minute, please." His dad broke the silence first.

Theo quickly made his way over to his father and stole a glance or two at Dr. Brack as he tinkered with the Central Time Consol. He noticed Dr. Brack jotted something in an old journal style book then tucked it away on the inside of his stark white lab coat. Now that he thought about it, his father and Dr. Brack were very different men in ideals and features.

He wasn't sure if his dad's lab coat had ever been white, with all the grease and dirt that was smeared all over it from his time spent rolling around underneath the base of the TimeWorm, connecting the power and data cords that would control the main platform and the vacuum cylinders. Dr. Brack was always dressed like he was going to an important business meeting at the White House, and his dad usually just picked up what was handy in his bedroom and gave it the nose test before he put it on.

"What's up, Dad?"

"I need you to go into the Jump Station and tell me what the power sensor and singularity relay detector are reading."

"No problem, Dad." Theo turned and started toward the Jump Station.

"I'm not sure I want your son in there, Luke," came the deep, gravelly voice of Viktor Brack. Theo stopped in his tracks, not knowing what to do. He turned slowly and watched as his dad stood up and turned to face the other scientist.

"Why would that be a problem now, Viktor?" Luke Marshal did not take his eyes off his colleague, and his cold tone of voice suggested displeasure.

"Because there are millions of dollars worth of equipment in that room that I am not sure a teenage boy should be playing around with." Brack's answer was equally terse but his body language of running his hand through his slicked back, thinning white hair suggested a nervousness.

"So now you don't trust my son either?" Dr. Marshall's voice rose louder than Theo would have expected.

"I've told you multiple times—it's not that I don't trust you. It's just that I need to move forward with this project and start getting a return on MY investment!"

Luke Marshall stared at Viktor Brack for a moment then turned his back and walked over to his research table. "All this is about money to you?" He took off his thick rimmed glasses and rubbed the bridge of his nose and remained silent for a few moments. "What has happened to you, Viktor? What happened to the kid I met at University, who didn't care about anything other than the science and discovery of new ideas and theories? Why is it so important to you to send a human being back in time before we have properly tested this machine? Are we sure someone can actually withstand the jump and the molecular breakdown that will occur during the process?"

Luke looked up at his son as he put his glasses back on and grabbed ahold of the table with both hands, arms outstretched, trying to work out the stress in his body. "You are willing to potentially kill someone, for what?" he paused again, "money?"

"That's easy for you to say, Luke. You haven't dumped millions of dollars of your own money into something that hasn't been tested—on something that most people think is an absolute joke and can't believe that we're still trying to create!"

Dr. Marshall hung his head in disgust and shook it in disbelief. "You're right. I haven't spent millions of dollars. But I have given my entire life to this project, and like you, I believe that this *thing* will change the world. *Then* you can recoup your millions—tenfold! *That* should make you happy!" He threw the neatly organized papers and notebooks across the desktop in an unusual display of aggressive, angry emotion.

"So should I go in and get those readings or not?" Theo tried to break off the two men's verbal assault on each other. It worked a little too well as now both men were staring heatedly at him. He put his hands up in surrender. "Just asking."

"That's fine, son. I'm sorry I snapped at you. Your father and I are just having a small difference in opinion on the readiness of the Worm." Dr. Brack's tone apologetically softened.

Theo looked at Dr. Brack for a moment, then over to his father, who had begun shuffling the disheveled paperwork back into somewhat organized piles. Dr. Marshall looked up after hearing Brack's words and nodded. Theo took the cue. He grabbed the data tablet and ran into the Jump Station before anyone could change his mind and retrieved the statistical information for his father.

Theo entered the Jump Station with awe. He had only been in the interior cell a few times, and each time he had his breath taken away by the technology and possibilities that this room held. He looked at the two intertwined cylinder arms sitting in the middle of the small room and the platform where hopefully someday a human being would sit to travel through time. He got goosebumps just thinking about the idea of zooming into the future to see the advances of society or conversely being able to go back and watch the history of the world unfold in front of him.

He stopped and dropped his head for a moment. He knew that he shouldn't be so selfish. He knew that this machine was going to change the lives of millions of people. The medical advances alone would help cure so many deadly diseases, but he couldn't help himself. Why shouldn't he be allowed to use it for a selfish reason? After all, he had helped in a few important areas. If this concept of time travel were ever going to work, then he would be responsible for that in a small percentage. Why couldn't he dream that he could travel back to the one day that had destroyed his family? All the millions of years the earth has been turning but he only wanted to go back a few short years. He could have stopped his mother from getting into the car that day. He could take the medical advances back to when she was injured in the wreck. He could share the technology and science needed to save her life. He could …

"Theo, I need those numbers, son." His father's voice broke his trance. He shook his head and finished walking to the STARS control center. The actual name for the control center was the Singularity Tracker Analyzing Radar System, but Theo had suggested using the much shorter and much quicker acronym. He smiled to himself, yet another way he had helped his father and Dr. Brack.

Theo began recording the power output numbers from the STARS and double checking them with the information he had on the other instruments from the data tablet. As he finished, something caught his eye. He stopped and swiped the screen back to the previous page to the power output readings for each of the individual research tables in the Laboratory. He double and triple checked the power numbers coming from each energy source. He looked at the charts his father had provided showing acceptable power readings. Shocked with the realization of the outcome the numbers predicted, he sprinted to his father.

"DAD!" he yelled at the top of his voice as he made his way out to the waiting scientists. Theo looked down at the tablet as he ran out of the Jump Station, just to check one last time. He did not want to cause any more stress. Something was obviously upsetting the two scientist friends. His discovery could potentially cause more angst by delaying the experimentation timetable for the TimeWorm. "Dad!" he yelled one more time.

"What is it, Theodore? Why are you yelling?"

Theo was panting and trying to take oxygen into his lungs. He handed the data tablet to his father and pointed at the readings coming from his personal workstation. It only took Luke a few seconds to see what his son was trying to show. He swiped through a few screens, typing in security codes and trying to override the system. He looked up to question Dr. Brack. He looked first at his own table then at his fellow scientist's personal research table. He eventually caught a glimpse of Viktor running into his office. He noticed that Murphy's ears had perked up, and he was running behind Brack.

"Viktor, get out here!" Luke Marshall tried for a few more seconds to enter his personal pass codes that should have been good enough to shut down the entire building.

"Viktor!" Luke cursed under his breath then looked at his son. "I can't stop the power surge and heating of the system! Viktor has locked the pass codes! We have to get out of here *now*!"

Theo and his father looked at each other for a moment then both started running for the exit doors. "Why would he do this, Dad?" Theo yelled over his quickened breathing.

"I have no idea, but it can't be for anything good. He's been acting strangely for weeks now. The closer we get to using the Worm, the more distant he has become. I've barely spoken to him the last two weeks." He gestured to his son as they were about to reach the security doors. "Flip over that table while I open the door. I have a bad feeling my security code has been disabled on this too."

Theo could see the absolute terror in his dad's eyes. He pushed all the excess lab equipment to the floor as fast as he could then heaved as the research table proved to be much heavier than he thought it would be.

"Why?" Luke Marshall yelled as he tried and retried his security codes trying to get the exit doors to open. He turned and ran to his son and helped lift the table. "The cables, Theo, we have to cut them." Fear was shaking his voice. "We need to hurry. We can't have more than a few more minutes." Dr. Marshall pulled out his multitool and flipped it around until the wire cutters were sticking out. He furiously began cutting power and data cords that were prohibiting them from flipping the table on its side. He cut through the last one with a grunt of strength and tossed the cutters to his waiting son. "Hurry, son, not much time." He tried to sound calm, but Theo could hear the worry in his dad's voice.

"Why would he do this, Dad? If I hadn't caught the error, you could have been killed. All that power was rerouted to your research table! Why didn't the emergency security system catch the power surge and shut down the whole system?" Theo quickly cut the few remaining cables.

Dr. Marshall looked at his son in silence until he watched the last severed cord fall to the floor. Then with all his might, he pushed the huge table over to its side to protect both of them from the effects of an explosion. "I don't think it was a mistake, Theo. I think Dr. Brack has snapped and doesn't want me standing in his way of using a human subject for the first test. He knows that I will do everything in my power to keep that from happening, and he's the only person with the security clearance to override all my authority throughout the building systems."

"He wants to kill us!" Theo screamed in shock as he squatted behind the overturned table. He picked up the data tablet that was lying next to him and went to the power screen, watching stunned as the screen flashed in silent warning. "He re-routed a lot of electrical power into such a small area. Isn't he afraid of damaging the Worm?"

Dr. Marshall reached for his cell phone and looked at the top of its screen. He threw the phone in frustration. He knew that he had personally set up the security protocols for this floor, and one of the things he had done was jam all outside wireless access. His phone was useless.

"Dad, I'm scared."

"Me too, son," Dr. Marshall admitted, then looked at his son curled up beside him, awaiting the repercussion from the impending explosion. "I'll try the door one last time."

"No, Dad! Don't leave the protection of this table. It isn't safe. That unit is going to explode any minute now."

His dad didn't look back as he jumped to his feet and ran to the door. He used his tool to unscrew the control panel of the key pad. Luke Marshall worked feverishly to remove the panel. He started cutting wires, twisting some of them together. Once he was satisfied with his work, he put the cover back on and punched in his code. The doors creaked and strained then slowly began to open.

"Theo, I did …"

Theo never heard the rest of his dad's statement as he first felt the air around him heat up then felt the table push against him. He looked up just in time to see his dad get launched off his feet, carried with flying debris to the outer room. Theo reached out, then blacked out as the force of the explosion lifted and pushed the table out of the Laboratory, carrying him with incredible force and speed.

CHAPTER 2

Danger in Darkness

The flashing blue emergency lights created strange shadows in the smoke and on the walls that turned the entire facility into a scene straight out of a horror movie. The gigantic fireball from the explosion had set a good majority of the upper floor of Brack Tower on fire, which in turn, set off the sprinkler system. As Theo slowly focused on the table pinning two thirds of his body to the floor, he also noticed that the steady deluge of water spraying from the ceiling was already starting to collect on the floor. His clothes were drenched; his body began to shiver from the icy water. He knew this was the body's natural way of trying to warm itself back up, but it was fighting against the pulsating water.

Theo's body felt as if every nerve had been broken in half, leaving raw ends to send pulses through his battered muscles. The cold sprinkler water was causing his muscles to tighten up and ache from the earlier drift board crashes. Muscles were covered by new bruises from having his body tossed through the air from the force of the explosion. He reached up with his left hand to support his weight as he sluggishly pulled himself out from under the overturned lab table. Slowly straightening his legs into a half stand-half slump position, he held his head with his right hand. He used all the energy he could muster to bring himself into a full upright position, fighting nausea and dizziness as the room spun in his vision. He took one painful step forward but had to stabilize himself against an overturned table before taking another step. He gripped it like a life preserver as the upended table was the only thing keeping him from falling face first into the ice cold water collecting on the floor.

Despite the sprinkler system's best efforts, Theo was aware that items strewn throughout the outer room were still popping and burning in pockets of fire and emitting acrid wisps of smoke that burned the inside of his nose. Mentally fighting his body's urges to collapse and rest, he forced himself to move. He felt the water seeping into his sneakers as he made his way across the room, still holding on to anything that had not been destroyed in the explosion. His shoes sloshed with each step in the ankle deep pools of water amassing on the floor. Theo could hear strange clicking and whirring sounds coming from the far side of the room where the entrances to the Laboratory and Jump Station were located.

"DAD!" Theo yelled. Nothing.

"MURPHY!" He had not seen his robotic best friend since Murphy had chased after Dr. Brack. He scarcely had enough time to get behind the table before the explosion knocked him through the doors of the Laboratory. "Murphy!" He cried out again since he could not hear the light clicks from his dog's mechanical trot. "Focus, Theo, focus!" he breathed, forcing himself to stop to survey the room. The pounding in his head was like a drum beat keeping time as his eyes scanned the room to find both his father and his dog. The smoke and shower from the sprinkler system were creating a very unfriendly environment for finding anything—human or robot.

Discouraged and worried, Theo forced himself to move about the smoke-filled outer room at a quicker pace despite the throbbing and pounding in his head. He had read enough to know the blurred vision and the combination of confusion and pain were signs that he had suffered a concussion, but what could he expect from a blast that hurled him to the hard floor along with the table and debris that had landed on top of him. He was strangely thankful for the heavy table as it deflected the full force of the explosion. A direct hit, and most likely, he would not be moving at all. Trying to suppress the "what ifs" running through his head, his pulse raced with mounting anxiety.

"DAD!" Theo cried out, causing a bolt of pain to course through his body. "Where are you?" He screamed with little care of the quiver in his voice. Defeat began to creep into his thoughts while he fought his reluctant muscles as he flipped and dug through tables, chairs, and pieces of equipment that had been tossed into the outer room by the force of the explosion. He begged his eyes to bore into the piles of papers, microscopes, computer screens, hard drives, and keyboards strewn across the floor in front of him. Even some of the really expensive large screen monitors that doubled as video game televisions had fallen off wall mounts or were left dangling from walls and ceiling, suspended only by cords. In the monitor to the far left, he thought he saw a reflection of movement under an overturned desk.

A spark of hope coursed through his veins and gave him the strength to move across the room kicking debris out of his way and nearly jumping over the larger objects that stood in his path. He could see a pair of brown loafers sticking out from underneath a large pile of papers, books, and overturned office equipment. As he got closer, he noticed the pair of shoes lay motionless. A sudden fear and sadness like he had only felt once in his young life found its way back to his heart. How could this be happening to him twice in such a short time? First, his mother, now his father. How could this be real? This had to be another nightmare.

Deliberately and carefully, Theo slowed his pace as he neared the unmoving shoes. He stopped about a meter from the loafers, took a few deep and slow breaths trying to gain his composure. He gazed around the workshop, taking in the chaos that lay around him. He looked back at the still shoes and knew beyond a doubt that they were his father's. Theo stared intently at the ugly, uncool brown shoes hoping to see one of them move or twitch. If only those shoes would just move a little bit, he could disprove his worst fear and avoid the truth he could not bring himself to face. He took one more heavy, slow breath then closed the distance to his dad in two dreaded steps.

Theo stood just inches away; he didn't even realize he was holding his breath until his lungs screamed at him to inhale. He nudged his father's left foot with the tip of his shoe, expecting a reflex reaction. Nothing happened, nothing at all. A sickening feeling washed over him. He was not sure if no reaction was a horrible thing. "Dad could just be unconscious," he whispered to himself. "That has to be it." He pressed the light button on his watch to illuminate the area where his dad lay. "But what if he's not *just* unconscious? Then what will I do? How will I survive with no parents? People do it every day, but not me. I need my father to be alive and here to take care of me." He looked around the quiet room where the only noise was water falling from sprinklers. "Please, help me. Please, someone." Tears streamed down his face. The more reality began to sink in, the more the tears began to fall.

Theo fell to his knees and sobbed harder than he could remember ever crying before—more than when he got the news about his mother's accident, more than when he watched her casket slowly lowered into a black hole in the ground. He shivered as the memories of those painful days collided head-on with the terror and reality of his father's lifeless feet lying there in front of him. He had a hard time getting air into his lungs. He dropped to his hands and coughed trying to breathe through the heaving sobs that convulsed his entire body.

"Dad," he whispered quietly. "Dad, please don't go."

"DAAAD!" Theo screamed at the top of his lungs, overcome by all the emotions that seemed to be exploding from within him as he jolted up to a sitting position with clenched fists of rage raised up to the sky. Then his body wrenched forward, falling back to his hands. He reached out and put a hand on those hideous shoes, those stupid brown shoes he had made fun of almost every day.

Theo didn't fight the tears as they fell uncontrollably down his face. He sat there with his hand resting on his father's shoes. It wasn't until something bumped into him that he realized he had been sitting there for a long time. He turned to see what had nudged him. A keyboard had floated into him. He quickly looked down and realized that the water level on the floor was elevating at a rapid pace. *Shouldn't it be leaking down the elevator shafts and stairwells?* The water was well past ankle height. *Why aren't the emergency services here yet?* He suppressed a silent panic.

"I gotta get Dad out of this water and find out what's going on." Theo muttered to himself, trying to find courage and strength to move, to do anything other than sit on the floor and wait to drown. He stood up, shook the cobwebs out of his mind, and started looking for anything that hadn't been completely burned or demolished in the explosion.

Searching for something—he didn't know what—Theo determined to save his father. He found a toppled table that was still mostly intact. He dragged it to where his father lay buried in debris, close to being swallowed by the sprinkler water. *Why haven't these things stopped yet? Another problem I need to solve,* he thought as he looked up at the ceiling spouts. He cautiously removed the debris from on top of and around his father's body. He wiped the sprinkler water off his face and put his hand on his chest as if the touch would help him catch his breath and pace his beating heart as he fought against the weight of the research and technology equipment. He bent down and grabbed a large monitor that had fallen onto his father's chest but almost dropped it again when the pile gave a loud, painful groan.

"DAD!" Theo yelled with elation of hearing his father's voice. Energy and hope surged through his veins giving him a renewed strength to throw the monitor a good distance away from his father. "Hang on, Dad. I'll get you out of there," he promised as he cleared away the last few objects.

"Theo," Dr. Marshall whispered weakly. "What water?"

Theo knelt down beside his father and stared at him for a second, overcome once again—this time with excitement. He felt like he had never been happier and that he needed to throw up, all at the same time.

Luke Marshall slowly opened his eyes and saw his teenage son hovering over him like a protective mother hen. "Son, help me up." The scientist exhaled, wincing in pain but awakening to what had happened and the pending situation.

"Are you sure you should move?"

"If you don't help me up, I might drown down here." Luke spoke softly, trying to encourage his son with a slight hint of humor.

"True." Theo hesitated for a moment then started to help his father out of the cold water. He propped the limp body into a sitting position until he could crawl behind his father's back. "Don't worry, Dad," he reassured as he wrapped both arms around his father and pulled upward until he could pull him onto a damaged table.

"Theo … Son, are you okay?"

"What happened, Dad?"

"I honestly don't …" Luke stopped midsentence. They looked at each other as the sound of growling started behind them, quickly crescendoing into a vicious threat.

"Murphy!" Theo yelled in surprise.

Simultaneously, father and son turned to see the robotic dog on an overturned desk, growling and standing on point toward the end of the room near the Laboratory. Theo's heart threatened to beat out of his chest. He pushed himself up to his knees and followed his dog's gaze. "What is it, boy?" The dog did not turn in response to his master's voice but maintained a low growl as he did not lift his eyes from the debris in front of him. "Murphy, what's wrong, boy?"

Murphy paused to look back at Theo and his dad, then turned back around and continued growling and creeping toward the edge of the desk. His ears and tail were upright giving a visual warning sign that he was seeing or sensing something evil, dangerous, or both.

Theo squinted his eyes to locate the source of his dog's alarm. "Wait here, Dad. I'll check it out."

He gave his dad a nod, letting him know he had this. In one motion he pushed away from the table and splashed over to Murphy who was still standing on the desk's edge with a steady stare toward the far side of the Laboratory.

"Use the watch link, Theo."

"Good call, Dad." Theo put a reassuring hand on Murphy. "IRIS, can you patch me into Murphy's optics?"

"One moment, Theodore," through his earbud came the soft, expressionless voice of his computerized assistant. "That should be it. The feed is live."

Theo looked down at his wristwatch/mini-computer and watched as the digital numbers faded and the scenery changed to the first person perspective of his robot companion. He quickly glanced up at his dog, who was intently staring, searching the room. His gaze fell back down to his watch, begging his eyes to find the source of Murphy's unease.

Again, Theo looked up and stared ahead, wanting to see the problem with his own eyes. He shook his head in disgust as he was not able to locate a disturbance. With slow, deliberate steps he started walking toward the Laboratory and the Jump Station, glancing between his own view and Murphy's view showing on his wrist computer.

Murphy let loose a low warning growl from deep down in his belly. Theo took the warning seriously and immediately stopped in his tracks. Frustration began to sink in. "IRIS, can you switch to Murphy's thermal vision?" he asked just above a whisper as he held his watch close to his face.

"I will try, but with multiple heat sources, you may have difficulty isolating and identifying anything specific," she replied with her knowledgeable tone.

Theo kept his eyes glued to his wrist, waiting for the view to be modified. Slowly, the screen altered from a simple vision screen to a mostly black background with a reddish-orange glow from heat radiating around them.

"Looks like you were right, IRIS. This whole screen is glowing from heat sources." He sighed aloud more to himself than to her.

"What do you see, Theo?" his father asked, keeping his voice low.

"*A lot* of red and orange, Dad." Theo paused as he mentally processed the implication from the heat vision. "It looks like either there are still fires in the Jump Station, or someone turned on the TimeWorm." Circumstances had put him into a leadership position, and he wasn't going to disappoint his dad or himself.

"Viktor!"

"What about him, Dad?"

"Where is he?"

"Uh, that's a great question." Theo took a quick glance over his shoulder. "You don't think he turned on the TimeWorm, do you?"

He had become so absorbed with clearing debris that the other scientist had not even crossed his mind.

"Let's hope not, Theodore. This tower probably couldn't withstand another explosion." Worry was thick in Luke's voice.

Theo stared at his watch for a few more seconds, looking for any movement. Not seeing anything of significance, he made up his mind. "Fine, I'll do this the old fashioned way," he mumbled to himself. "C'mon Murphy." He called for his dog with a slap on his hip. Murphy shook his head vigorously, shaking his long ears and resetting his vision to normal as he jumped off the desk, half-swimming, half-trotting until he made his way to Theo's side.

With his pup at his side, Theo's courage grew as he waded ankle-deep through the sea of debris. He cautiously moved from the outer room and made his way toward the inside double glass door entrance to the Laboratory. He knew he would need to cross the demolished room in order to reach the Jump Station and the TimeWorm. He was starting to feel the effects of the day when he strained to move a particularly large monitor out of his way.

The nearer the doors, the more slowly and carefully he began to move, picking each step, trying to hide the sound of his approach just in case Dr. Brack was actually in there. The more he thought about the morning's events, the more the reality of Dr. Brack causing problems started to line up. He hadn't seen the scientist since the explosion, and he had covered a lot of ground looking for his dad and dog. He cringed and stopped midstride as a piece of glass cracked under the weight of his foot, sending a loud snap through the outer room. "Careful," he whispered in quiet reprimand.

Murphy, who had been running point ahead of Theo, stopped at the sound of his master's misstep. He turned with a look that screamed, "Be careful!" Theo retaliated with an "I know!" look and shrug of the shoulders and hands. Murphy turned his attention back to the double glass doors, confident that his master had understood his warning. He again directed his attention to identifying something inside the Laboratory that had heightened his senses. His acutely sensitive nose was having difficulty defining scents due to the heaviness of smoke from smoldering fires. Instinctively, he lifted his head, pointing his nose to the ceiling trying to sense anything out of the ordinary.

Theo and Murphy crept to the edge of the Laboratory. The smoke and shattered lighting made it difficult to see anything through the shadows. The odd noise from earlier had become a constant high-pitch whirring sound, which seemed to be gaining momentum. He looked down at his dog waiting eagerly, tail wagging in anticipation of the first step into the shadowed uncertainty of the next room.

He approached two sliding doors that had resealed after the explosion had ejected father, son, dog, and equipment. The doors had returned to a sealed and locked position. The retina eye scanner had fallen from the ceiling, dangling above the water collecting on the floor. The explosion had dislodged the scanner from its connecting rod, but the power and sensor cables held the scanner like a bobber on the end of a fishing line. Theo stared in astonishment for a moment. He lightly tugged the power cables. He knew he had to check the cords and be wary of any electrical current and possible electrocution if the scanner submerged while connected to the power source. Grasping the scanner, he turned it around in his hands until he found the front; the usually bright red light had faded and seemed to be diminishing. He hoped this worked. He brought the retina scanner up to his eye and waited. Nothing.

He lowered the orb for a minute and planned his next move. After mentally debating for a few moments and feeling out of options, Theo reluctantly slammed the retina scanner with his open palm; the fading red light flickered back to life. He didn't waste any time and quickly brought the scanner to his eye. A familiar beep teased Theo's ears with the sound he would need, but the frosted sliding doors didn't move. He rubbed his forearm against the glass. The icy coating slowly ebbed into clear glass, but he wasn't able to see anything inside except for an occasional spark of electricity or a small flame searching for more to burn. Theo looked down at Murphy. "What do we do now, boy?" he asked as his shoulders dropped in disappointment.

A deep growl bellowed from Murphy as he walked up to the malfunctioning doors, ordering them to open. He pawed at the doors a few times, testing them for his master. He looked back with a frustrated whine, then jumped onto a toppled drafting table and glared at the doors. Theo took a painful step forward, his muscles aching more as the cold water chilled him to the bone. He reached down and rubbed Murphy's ears as he examined the doors, trying to determine what to do. He knew he had to get into the Laboratory and eventually into the interior Jump Station, but those doors weren't going to open manually. He was already sore and exhausted, even though he had only been awake for a few hours. *My day has to get better*, he thought to himself, shaking his head.

Theo moved back from the doors and looked around the outer room where he stood. "It's worth a try," he muttered to himself as he walked over to a monitor that had fallen from a table. He reached down and moaned at the strength it took to lift the monitor out of the water. He clumsily made his way back to the doors and set the screen down for a second to rest his muscles. "Back up, Murph," he commanded, not sure what was going to be the outcome of his plan.

Theo bent over and lifted the monitor. He was about to throw his best shot-put toss at the right sliding door, when Murphy let loose a few warning barks. "What?" He looked back at his dog.

Murphy jumped off the overturned table where he was perched and waded to the window beside the sliding doors. He pawed at the glass then looked back at his master.

"Good idea! How do you do that?" Theo took a few steps to his left and looked at the spider web of cracking in the window. "Back up, boy." He threw the monitor with every ounce of strength he could muster from his sore and battered muscles. The monitor slammed into the glass and bounced back with a splash into the water at Theo's feet, but the window was now completely covered in splintered glass. "One more should do it." He grunted and again cradled the heavy monitor in his arms then let it fly one more time. He almost cried out in joy as it connected with the window and continued through into the Laboratory. Murphy wildly wagged his tail from a perch he had taken on an overturned table.

Theo inhaled a deep breath and bent over placing his hands on his knees, trying to catch his second wind with as much air and as little of the acrid smoke as possible. He stood up exhaling slowly.

He looked through the shattered window into the dark as he wondered what was next. "Watch my back, Murph," he ordered and then stepped into the chaos and darkness.

Theo was hesitant as he crawled through the window into the second room laying in shambles. Small fires were struggling to spread despite the best efforts of the sprinkler system. Flashes of blue electricity sparked all over the room as water hit exposed wires and power cords. He couldn't even recognize it as the room he had just been in with his dad and Dr. Brack before the explosion. The force of the explosion had scattered papers and equipment, cluttering the room with all that had been on and around the workstations.

There was no time to waste. Theo knew he needed to make his way to the TimeWorm. If he didn't find Dr. Brack in the Laboratory or Jump Station, he would check the offices. Emergency lights cast strange shadows adding to the difficulty of seeing or hearing anything. "We need to be careful. He could be anywhere." Murphy heeded his master's warning as he moved stealthily by the boy's side. He realized that danger could be hiding behind any of the overturned equipment or hiding in the shadows. The explosion had created many places a person—a person who had gone mad—could hide and wait for his prey. Flashing lights and shadows challenged him as he navigated the room.

Theo scanned the room slowly. The pitch of the whirring sound indicated an increasing speed which, in turn, increased his heartbeat. In the last hour he had learned his dad's invention worked, survived an explosion, thought he lost his father, and realized that his father's fellow scientist and best friend had changed. That was a lot to take in. He had a sneaking suspicion that his situation was going to get worse before it got better.

As his eyes jumped each time a shadow or spark commanded his attention, Theo realized Murphy was no longer at his side. *Where is that dog now?* "Murphy," he hissed, not wanting to alert Dr. Brack. "C'mon, boy," again barely louder than a whisper, counting on Murphy's enhanced hearing. His robotic dog had superb range that made him a valuable asset right now.

Theo edged his way to the left wall where fewer tables remained. He hoped to get a clearer view before proceeding into the shadows. Something moved in his peripheral vision. He crouched down preparing to launch or flee depending on who or what was coming toward him. He felt around for something to protect himself. His hand scoured the floor until it bumped into a long strip of mangled metal. The rod-shaped metal would serve his defensive needs. As the sound of movement got closer, he tightened his grip, squeezing the rod until his knuckles were white. He pushed himself up from the squatted position, prepared to swing his weapon.

He could sense that whoever was coming was close. His muscles were taut and ready to spring into self-defense. He felt his heart pounding in his temples. He tried to calm himself by taking deep, controlled breaths. Suddenly, he could almost feel the air move. His eyes saw something move behind the overturned workstation in front of him. He lashed out with his mangled steel bat but caught himself with a quick reflex. He dropped the bat to the wet floor and stifled a scream as Murphy's head popped over the desk.

In a huge exhale he hoarsely whispered, "Murphy, you scared the heck out of me!" Murphy cocked his head as if asking who else his master expected. The dog nimbly crawled over the desk and came to his master's side. It wasn't until he was beside his master's feet that Theo noticed Murphy had something clamped in his steel jaw.

"What's that, boy?" Theo reached down to see what the dog had found.

Murphy loosened his grip on a sealed waterproof pouch and gave a panting grin while receiving a quick pat on the head. Theo turned the pouch over in his hands. His first instinct was to give the pouch a toss and disregard it as Murphy's attempt to play fetch. He gave the pouch a quick roll to release some anger with the toss, but with curiosity, he first held the pouch closer to his face to see what was hidden inside. "A book?" He knitted his brow. In school to learn, to play games, and even to tinker with technology, Theo used devices—not paper and pencil. He found books—actually typed on paper and bound—to be an anomaly. He turned the pouch in his hands deciding that opening it would do no harm. After all, everything in the lab had been destroyed. He opened the waterproof covering and removed a leather bound journal. "Whew," Theo gave a low breathy whistle. Murphy glanced at his master and then instinctively turned around to stand guard.

Carefully, Theo opened the book. Even with the limited light, he could tell this book was very old. He turned it over in his hands, inspecting the archaic method of recording one's thoughts. He ran his fingers over the soft leather cover and with his index finger traced the letters of a word he did not recognize, *Societatis*. The faint impression suggested the title had been stamped into the binding a very long time ago. He wondered what the word meant but decided this was no time for figuring out an insignificant book cover. How important could one word really be?

Perhaps a better question was why did Murphy have a book? The explosion had thrown papers and files across the lab. Did Murphy's robotic instincts have purpose in clamping down on this book? Theo decided to take a quick glance through the book before tossing it back down into the rubble. He sat on some boxes smashed in the explosion and leaned toward a ray of light seeping through a darkened window. As soon as he opened the book, he knew he was looking at something that was not meant for his eyes. The inside cover was filled with symbols—some he recognized and some he did not. A swastika was displayed in the middle of the cover. Other symbols grabbed his attention as he scanned the first two pages. The book looked like a strange collection of pentagrams, triquetra, and the sickle and hammer of Communist Russia.

Theo flipped through the book, scanning pages filled with symbols and handwritten words of different languages. The pages held maps, timelines, designs for guns, and page after page of notes. Something caught his eye as he flipped the pages. In the middle of a page in large letters was written *TimeWorm* with the words "back to the beginning—1933" penciled beside it.

"What in the world is …," he started to mumble to himself.

"Give me the book, Theodore! That has nothing for you!" came a harsh voice from the shadows.

Theo jerked his head up as he crammed the leather book into the waterproof pouch and into the pocket of his cargo pants. He bit his lip to promise himself to choose his words wisely as he scanned the dark room. "What in the heck is this, Doc?" he shouted.

"Do yourself a favor and forget everything you just saw. Just wipe it from your mind," the coarse voice ordered. "Drop the book and go tend to your father." A long pause seemed to soften his voice. "I never meant for either of you to get hurt or involved in any of this."

"What's this about, Doc? All these symbols, maps, and designs for weapons?" Theo demanded answers. "Why would you want a book like this?" He reached back midsentence and grabbed the mangled bat, keeping it out of sight at his side. He looked into the smoke-filled room trying to adjust his eyes to the dark and trying to locate the voice. He knew he needed to keep Dr. Brack talking long enough to pinpoint where the doctor was hiding. "My dad is fine, no thanks to you."

Brack's voice again rose in intensity and warning. "Theodore, I told you that I never wanted to hurt you or your father. I didn't say that I wouldn't. The wheels of change are in motion, and neither you nor your dad will stand in my way, not when I'm this close!"

"So close to what, Doc? What could be so important that you blew up your research facility and nearly killed your closest friend?" Theo closed his eyes hoping to zero in on Brack's location. He waited what seemed like an eternity until finally the voice came from a different direction than before. *He's moving to get behind me*, Theo thought and reopened his eyes.

"That's none of your business, young man. I am getting tired of these questions. Give me the blasted book, and I'll let you leave here with your father," he spat angrily, "which is against my better judgement, but you won't be able to interfere."

"Murphy," Theo leaned down to the dog and whispered. Even in the smoke-filled room he could see by the transmitter lights scanning on Murphy's collar that he was still on full alert. Something must be interfering with his heat vision. "Murphy, find him."

Murphy looked back at his master for a moment then leapt into the darkness that had spread throughout the top floor. Theo shivered as his companion disappeared; it was strange how safe Murphy made him feel. He was his very own robotic, four-legged bodyguard. He knew he was in danger; he could hear the anger in the scientist's voice. Without Murphy at his side he was vulnerable in the dark. What happened to his father's friend? Was he losing his mind and his grip on reality?

Theo moved along the wall, away from the last direction of Dr. Brack's voice and deeper into the Laboratory. He kept his left hand on the wall while gripping the mangled mace in his right. He had to stop several times to untangle his feet from power cables and cords that had been ripped from their electrical sockets and hardware lying submerged under the water from the sprinkler system. He covertly scaled desks, work tables, and storage cabinets.

Theo felt the leather book in his cargo pocket, reassuring himself that he had not dropped it into the foot of water covering the floor. Dr. Brack would hunt for him until the book was back in his evil hands. He paused and slowly scanned the room, begging his eyes to identify shapes. The only sound was the strange whirring at a high-pitch velocity indicating a constant speed. The flow of water spraying from the sprinkler system had increased. Theo struggled to see through the showering water.

A flashing yellow light threw a strange glow over the back of the room, making the security door easier to see in the deluge. Theo started sneaking toward the yellow beacon. A piercing scream stopped him in his tracks; by instinct he dropped to a squat. He caught his breath as he had ignored the flooding room and now felt the icy water press against his chest. The commotion continued just beyond the perimeter of the light, deeper into the shadows. The noise grew louder as it moved closer to where he squatted neck-deep in the frigid water.

Theo flattened himself under the water as something came flying through the air through the sparks and sprinklers. Surfacing, he spun around in time to hear a dull thud as Murphy's robotic body bounced off the wall behind him. Forcefully, he waded his way through the rising water to rescue his dog.

"Stop, Theodore!" a voice boomed over the noise. He turned as Dr. Brack made his way, swinging his arms through the water and floating debris.

Murphy let out a small whimper as he lay sprawled on a floating table where he landed after bouncing off the wall.

CHAPTER 3

Jump

Theo watched in horror as the man who had been like a second father to him emerged from the shadows and sparks with a gun aimed at him and with a look in his eyes like he would not hesitate to pull the trigger. "Dr. Brack, what's going on? I ... I'm so confused. My dad needs medical attention. Why do you have a gun?" Theo shouted, stumbling over his words.

Viktor Brack didn't answer; instead, he slowly and cautiously made his way through the wreckage of the aftermath of his well-designed explosion. The closer he got, the more the teen realized that the man he knew wasn't here anymore. He was gone. Theo wondered if the good Dr. Brack really ever existed at all. Maybe this monster with the pistol pointed at his chest was the real man, the manifestation of a real wolf in sheep's clothing.

Theo stood immobile, experiencing every range of emotion that a body and mind could possibly handle. He decided that he liked the way rage felt best and tried his hardest to channel and focus on that sensation the most. Rage for the deception, rage for his father, rage for holding him at gunpoint, and rage for hurting his best friend who lay motionless, a short distance away. "C'mon Doc, at least let me check on Murphy," he pleaded trying to hold his voice steady.

"I hope that dog, thing, or whatever type of devil he is, is dead." Dr. Brack spat words with venom in his voice.

Dr. Brack moved carefully through the floating mess, pistol still pointed directly at Theo although he threw quick glances at the lifeless dog lying on what use to be a table that held productive work. As he lifted his right leg to step over a pile of debris, his pant leg emerged from the water revealing a tear in his slacks exposing a gash along the shin and wrapping around to his calf muscle. Along with being soaked from now nearly a meter of water rising on the lab floor, Theo could also see oily streaks of what he assumed was the scientist's own blood. A smirk worked its way on his face as the understanding of Brack's hostility toward Murphy now made more sense.

"Good boy, Murphy." Theo laughed, trying to hide his fear from the madman who was almost to him now.

"You think this is funny, Theodore?" Brack angrily pointed down at his leg with the pistol.

"Um, yes." His sarcastic and calm response surprised even himself in the face of such turmoil. Maybe in the back of his mind he really didn't believe the doc would actually shoot him. He hoped he was right.

"Hmmph," the doctor snorted and then aimed the gun at Murphy.

"Whoa, what are you doing, Doc?"

"I'll show you how funny it really is, you stupid boy." Brack squeezed the trigger before Theo could respond. The bullet missed its intended target by mere inches but the impact flipped the floating table where Murphy lay, and the lifeless dog slid off of his barge and disappeared into the water.

"Murphy!" Theo screamed and lunged for his companion without any thought for his own well-being. Another shot popped, and Theo ducked and dove in the general area where he had watched Murphy descend into the dark sprinkler water. Shards of the tile wall behind him flew in every direction as the bullet slammed into it well above where his head had just been.

Theo swung his arms through the water as he searched frantically for his dog. After a while his brain and lungs ordered him to surface and take in some much-needed oxygen, but his heart kept him holding his breath and scouring for his best friend. Just as he was about to surface, his hand hit something. He quickly wrapped both hands around the object and exploded to the surface to fill his lungs with air.

He emerged from the cold murky water that was nearly hip deep on him and sucked in more air than his lungs could handle. He coughed violently as he tried to regain his composure and get his lungs back in working order. He stood there dripping in cold water, but he did not feel anything but concern and worry for his dog. He looked down at Murphy's limp body lying in his arms and looked him over as quickly as he could for any obvious damage.

Cradling Murphy in his arms, Theo looked up when he heard a clicking noise only inches away from him. He was now staring at the barrel of Dr. Brack's 1940's German Luger. Theo was first taken aback with having a gun shoved in his face and secondly with the realization of how old the gun must have been. It looked like a replica of a World War II German officer pistol.

As if time froze, Theo's eyes fixated on the gun. Reality blurred as he followed the vision forming in his brain. He could hear sobs coming through words he didn't recognize. He had the sensation of balancing on the rim of an open pit. The sound of a shot pressed against his ears ending the darkness that pressed against the vision that had just flashed through his mind.

"Now!" Brack's screaming voice shook Theo from his trance. He looked from the barrel, to the arm, then up to the face of the man pointing the ancient weapon at him.

"Give me *mein Buch*!" the scientist ordered, losing control of his accent for the first time in front of Theo. Along with his thinning gray hair plastered to his skull from the water and the deranged look in his eye, he looked angrier and scarier than Theo could have ever imagined he might. "Give it to me, now!" he screamed, shaking the Luger in the face of his colleague's son.

"Dr. Brack, please stop this," Theo pleaded almost at the verge of tears. "My dad is hurt. Murphy is injured, and you, you …"

"What, Theodore? What am I?" Brack laughed mockingly at the scared youth.

"You're a fake, a fraud … You're a monster!"

Viktor Brack stood frozen for a moment. An evil smile crossed his face. "You have no idea what I'm capable of. I'm going to change the world. You and your father have helped me, just remember that. Oh, but wait, you won't be able to."

Theo didn't know how to react to Dr. Brack's words. He just stood in silent confusion and disbelief that this was actually happening to him right now. *Maybe I'm just having another nightmare. Maybe IRIS will be opening my window shades and I'll hear her constantly calling my name. I just need to hold out a little longer until she wakes me. Maybe ...* Theo wanted to believe his thoughts, but he was shocked back into reality as he looked down at his injured companion.

"Let's go, Theodore. Turn around and get in the Jump Station."

"I'm not going to be your test dummy, Doc. We have no idea what's gonna happen to us once that thing is turned on. No way!" Theo said defiantly, shaking his head emphatically and stiffening his legs to stand his ground. The thought of being the first human, the first object, to test the time machine and knowing what he knew about the breakdown at the molecular level terrified him.

"Theodore, I'm the one with the gun. Now turn around and get in there." He motioned with his pistol for the boy to lead the way into the Jump Station.

With a look of defeat, Theo readjusted his grip on Murphy and turned and started toward the inner room holding the TimeWorm. As he crossed through the infrared scanner, the door to the Jump Station automatically slid up. As the door lifted, water from the Laboratory poured into the room at the core of the building.

Theo resisted the urge to look down at his arms though he could feel Murphy starting to wiggle. The constant humming of the TimeWorm steadied at a persistent speed. The noise from the machine would have muffled his words, but he didn't want to take any chances. He simply mouthed the words, "not yet." The wiggling stopped, and Murphy lay limp in his arms.

"Give me the book, Theodore."

"My hands are kinda full at the minute." Theo snapped back. He felt braver knowing his secret weapon lay ready in his arms. It also helped that Brack's pistol had dropped down to his side.

"Set that thing over there." Brack spoke with a sinister deepness, looking down at his torn trousers and limping over to the interior control panel. Theo was sure he wouldn't soon forget the chilling change in the scientist's voice.

Theo looked around the Jump Station and noticed that nothing seemed out of place or affected from the explosion. "I remotely closed the door from my office before the explosion." Dr. Brack read the look on Theo's face. "You're smarter than I give you credit, Theodore. You truly are your father's son."

"Well, that answers that question, I guess."

"What question?"

"I had wondered if this was an accident or not. Guess I was hoping you weren't completely evil." Theo struggled to answer unemotionally.

Brack didn't answer right away as he was busy punching information into the Singularity Control Module, which would start searching for light particles from a designated time in history and location he entered into the system.

Theo began mentally ticking off a checklist. *After the computer locks down on the location of the star, it will be just minutes before the TimeWorm starts working its magic.* He smiled; his dad would have corrected him in his best stern voice. "It's science, Theo, not magic!" Theo couldn't help but chuckle slightly, which drew the attention of Brack.

"Something funny, Theodore?"

"Nothing." He carefully set his lifeless dog down on the table next to Brack. He wanted Murphy as close to this jerk as possible. When the time presented itself, he would be able to catch Brack by surprise and somehow get himself and Murphy out of this mess.

"Good, now give me the book or else this time I won't miss that dog or whatever that thing is." The determined scientist never looked up from the screen or stopped punching information into the STARS. He extended his hand toward Theo with his palm facing up. He snapped his fingers and waved his hand impatiently.

Theo reluctantly reached down and pulled the book out of his cargo pocket and placed it on the outstretched hand that clamped shut. He shook his head in disgust and walked to the other side of the small room, putting distance between himself and the evil man.

He watched with irritation as Brack flipped through the pages of the confiscated book with one hand and entered coordinates into the computer system with the other. He glanced from the Luger lying on the table beside the distracted scientist, to his motionless dog, then to the exit.

Theo tried to formulate a plan. *The exit will be the easiest and fastest way to escape. Brack's back is turned since he's focused on entering the data. He might not know if I silently slip out the only door of this Jump Station. But that would mean leaving my best friend behind and allowing Dr. Brack to get away with his insane plan—whatever it is. It must be seriously important. Why else would he try to kill his fellow inventor and best friend, then hold me at gunpoint? Why does Dr. Brack even own a gun from over a hundred years ago?*

He decided to press the scientist and perhaps irritate him enough that he would give up some answers. "What are you going to do when the emergency services start showing up and you have me trapped in here at gunpoint?"

"First of all, I disabled all the outgoing sensors and data relays. So our fine men and women at the fire department will never know about what happened here." Brack looked up at Theo and sneered condescendingly. "Secondly, I won't be here even if they do happen to catch wind of the explosion."

Theo leaned against a table, fuming at Dr. Brack's smugness. He was more worried now that he realized no one was coming to help them. "I'll tell the police what you've done here."

Viktor Brack's methodical key slamming came to an abrupt stop. With one final tap of his index finger, the coordinates were embedded into the computer. Theo heard a feminine computer voice, which sounded very similar to IRIS.

"Thank you, Doctor. The TimeWorm should be ready to send its package shortly."

Brack slowly lowered the notebook to the table then reached over to pick up the pistol. Theo looked from the gun to the notebook then over to Murphy. His robotic buddy lifted his head slightly off the table and opened one eye waiting for his master's command to attack. Theo just shook his head no. Murphy closed his eye, quietly lay his head back down, and resumed his masquerade.

The scientist moved around the console and plodded toward Theo, sloshing his way through the waste deep water that had flooded into the Jump Station when the door opened. "You won't be here either, son."

"I'm not getting in that thing. You'll have to shoot me."

"Well, let me rephrase that. They may find your drowned corpse, but if I run into your mother's grandfather sooner than I have planned, you'll never even exist."

The life was sucked out of Theo almost before Brack had finished speaking. He was stunned by the realization of the threat. He realized that if Brack killed his Great-grandfather Lories, generations, including his mother, would be dissolved before they were even born. He had read about the grandfather effect theory of time travel. One small change in a person's life could change family history. It was one of his father's biggest fears about creating the TimeWorm.

"Wait a minute." Theo reacted as another thought pushed its way through the turmoil going on in his head. "How do you know that getting rid of me and my mother won't directly affect what my dad does with his life? You would run the risk of never meeting the man who was the *real* brains behind building this operation, not just the financier."

"Ouch, Theodore, that hurt." A sarcastic grin broke across Brack's face. "Guess I do forget sometimes you're still just a teenager after all. You forget I have that." He pointed to the notebook lying beside the control console. "I'll have the technology ahead of the time it was invented. I'll be able to create things or push science in the direction I want it to go. I'll be one of the most powerful people in history."

Theo was determined not to let the evil man intimidate him with his words. "I guess you have it all planned. It's a shame that our history will have to depend on you, considering you're only the third smartest mind in this room!"

Theo's words had the desired effect as a grimace replaced the smirk on the scientist's face. Brack lowered his gun and looked down at the water sloshing around his legs. He tipped his head back and raised his voice to the ceiling.

"Computer?"

"Yes, Doctor?"

Viktor Brack hesitated for a moment, carefully thinking his next move. "How long will it take for this Jump Station to be completely flooded when the door is sealed and water sprinklers are started?" He looked around the cylindrical room like he was trying to calculate the answer. He purposely looked at Theo with a sadistic smile on his face.

"One moment, Doctor," the computerized voice spoke without emotion. "At the current rate of water dispersion, the Jump Station will be filled to capacity in precisely 22 minutes 37 seconds."

Again, the scientist did not immediately respond to the computer's calculations. "Very good, Computer. Seal the door—emergency code *Gesperrt*. Oh, so sorry Theodore. I forgot you don't speak German. Well, if you're taking note, the emergency code means *locked down*. Brack spoke as if giving a simple language lesson to a school boy.

"Doctor, are you positive about that directive? My sensor reads that there are currently three life forms in the room."

"Yes, Computer, thank you for your concern." Brack's wrinkled brow proved he had forgotten about the robotic dog. He turned to look at the silent dog on the lab table as he spoke. "Do slow the rate of water dispersion to twenty five percent until after the jump takes place." He paused and raised an index finger as if checking a list. "Oh, also turn on the magnetic field for the table holding that canine. We wouldn't want my furry friend to wake up and decide to get my other leg."

"Yes, Doctor." The dog was pulled down hard onto the smooth metallic table surface. The airtight door slammed shut, locking the three of them together in the Jump Station.

Theo heard Murphy whimper when the table began to resonate with a low hum of the activated magnetic layer. He hung his head, unable to think or react.

"What's wrong, Theodore? Nothing clever to say?"

"Leave me alone." The teen spoke scarcely louder than a whisper. All the fight had vanished from his heart. What was the point? His father was lying in the outer room unable to move his legs, his dog was magnetized to a table, the emergency crews were oblivious due to no fault of their own, and he could no longer think of what to do. He honestly couldn't see a way out of this. If the jump didn't kill him, the water would. He choked back vomit at the idea of fighting for breath. He began to hope that the machine would blow up. At least that way Brack would meet the same fate.

"*Ich werde die Vergangenheit ändern!*" Dr. Brack exclaimed enthusiastically. "Theo, I am going to change the past!" He glanced up to see if his words caused any response. He scoffed as he looked at the defeated teenager.

After a few moments, Theo looked to see what Dr. Brack was doing; then, he put his face in his hands and tried to rub the exhaustion out of his mind. As he rubbed his face, he heard a faint beep in his right ear. He gasped at the sound of the voice coming from his head.

"IRIS?" he muttered as quietly as possible.

"Yes, Theodore. Your ear-link must have gotten damaged or turned off in the blast. I've been trying to make contact with you for nearly thirty minutes. Once I lost connection, I immediately began monitoring the situation without letting Brack's computer system know I am present. It is very smart and might alert him to my presence."

A rush of adrenaline shot through Theo. Tension and soreness coursing through his body seemed to dissipate at the new possibility of escape. He intentionally kept a sour look on his face as he looked up again and scanned the room to think how his IRIS could help him. A newfound energy surged through his veins. The darkness of his hopeless situation seemed a little brighter.

"Can you unlock the door and free Murphy?"

"I am truly sorry, Theodore, but I cannot override Dr. Brack's protocols. The most I can do is record the information that he has put into the Singularity Control Module."

Theo squeezed the table with both hands to keep from slamming his fist to vent his anger. "What good does that do me?"

"There are a myriad of situations where that informa—"

"IRIS, not now!" Theo interrupted her mid explanation. He wasn't in the mood for one of her matter-of-fact statements. "I need out of this room before the Worm is activated!"

"I have run one million test scenarios. I have calculated only a ten percent chance that the TimeWorm will explode and a five percent chance that it will not work at all. That gives you an eighty-five per …"

"I can do the math, IRIS," Theo cut her off again. As much as he was excited to have her in his ear and by his side, he wasn't sure she wouldn't drive him crazier than he already felt. He took a long, deep breath and exhaled slowly just as the voice of the other computer system broke in.

"Doctor, the TimeWorm is fully powered and ready to make the jump."

"*Danke*, Computer." Brack removed his lab coat and revealed a brownish-gray suit that looked like it had been in style during some other era. He secured the leather-bound notebook in an interior jacket pocket and patted it a few times to make sure it was safe. He pulled a black armband from his pocket and worked it up to his bicep on the outside of his coat.

Theo watched as the doctor prepared himself for his jump. He knew something was wrong when he saw Dr. Brack wearing a vintage style suit, but he screamed out in horror as he watched him slip a swastika armband on his right arm. "You're a sick …"

"Watch yourself, boy," Viktor Brack cut off Theo's rant before he could insult him further. "I am tired of your mouth." The scientist picked up the pistol and pointed it at the insolent teenager. "Maybe I should shut it permanently."

Theo stepped away from the table and stood up to his full height and stared straight into Brack's crazed eyes. "Just get it over with." He looked at the armband and gestured toward it with a nod. "You should fit right in there."

"I'll take that as a compliment, Theodore. Armed with my knowledge, I think history is about to work out like it should have in the first place." He smirked as he lowered and holstered the gun. Viktor Brack turned with a stomp and marched to the center of the Jump Station. "Thirty second countdown, Computer." He pulled on the bottom of his suit jacket and smoothed out some of the wrinkles. He paused. "Smile, boy. You're about to witness history being made," he laughed, "then unmade, I guess."

Theo didn't want to acknowledge or even look at him, but his anger got the best of him. "Go to hell!"

"Theodore, may I say something?" A clear voice in his ear took his attention.

"27."

Theo turned his back to the scientist who was busy entering the TimeWorm. "What is it, IRIS?"

"I think you should close your eyes. If my analysis is correct, and it usually is, there is going to be a violent flash of light at the point of molecular breakdown."

"Sure. Thanks."

"23."

"I do have a bit of good news too."

"What could be good now?"

"I should be able to free Murphy once the jump is occurring. Dr. Brack's computer system will be very busy checking on the systems and data at that point."

"19."

"What about the door and sprinkler system?" Theo could feel his pulse increase with anxiety.

"I am sorry, Theodore. I cannot disable that system. Dr. Brack has encrypted it with so many fail safes that I would need a week to disarm it." IRIS almost had a hint of human sorrow in her voice.

"15 seconds. Gravitational arms deploying now." Brack's computer continued the countdown as two titanium spheres emerged from the floor and began spinning vertically and horizontally around the doctor.

Theo's heart was pounding as the sound of the TimeWorm intensified in his ears. He needed someone, anyone, to talk to or he feared he would lose his mind. "Don't go getting soft on me now, IRIS."

"I can't get—"

"I was joking, IRIS. I know you're not human. Um, thanks for helping Murphy ..." His train of thought and chatter were lost as his attention turned wholly to the spheres moving at an incredible speed, hiding the doctor.

"Ten seconds until event horizon."

Theo flinched as he heard Brack scream in sheer pain. He was thankful for the gravitational bars hiding Brack from his view. He wasn't sure he wanted to see what was happening on that platform. The screams got louder and louder until he covered his ears to muffle the blood curdling noise.

"Five." The prism mirror on the ceiling began to throw light down to the prism on top of the gravitational bars.

"Four." The screams had silenced.

"Three."

"Theodore, close your eyes!" IRIS demanded.

"One."

Theo had been so curious and terrified at the same time, he had forgotten IRIS's advice and barely had time to turn and close his eyes. He grabbed the table and ducked in reaction to the chaos.

Silence filled the Jump Station.

"Theodore, Theodore ..." IRIS's computerized voice faded in and out as Theo tried to regain his perspective of the situation.

What am I doing under this table? Despite his best attempts at waking himself from this nightmare, he couldn't make sense of anything. His mind was cloudy and his thoughts were all jumbled into one chaotic mess that he couldn't separate into a single simple idea. *What's going on?*

"Theodore ..."

Sounds were coming in and out of focus all around him. He lifted his head from the safety of his arms and cautiously opened his eyes. Thoughts swirled in and out of his mind making a link between reality and his confusion. *Nothing makes sense. Where am I? How the heck is it raining in the building? Where's Dad? Wait a minute, where did Doctor Brack go?* He spoke aloud to find the only truth he knew. "Murphy?"

"Theo, I need ..."

He rubbed his eyes with the palms of his hands. He slowly crawled out from under the table. As if hearing his own voice would give answers, Theo spoke aloud. "What had happened to Doctor Brack? He was in here, wasn't he?" He looked at the wall in front of him and watched as the rain from the ceiling sprinklers continued to fall. He held out his hands, palms facing up and fingers spread out, and let the water run over them.

"Theodore, are you ..."

He backed away from the table but returned his grip. His legs didn't feel solid enough to support his weight. They were sore and bruised and felt like lead weights. He looked down at his legs for a moment then took a second glance once it registered in his clouded mind that the water level was rising in the tiny Jump Station.

"Theodore, Murphy needs your help."

Murphy, the fog began lifting from his thoughts. *Murphy needs me.* Theo shook his head violently and spun around to locate his best friend. He reached up to his ear and pushed the ear link completely back in so he could clearly hear IRIS. "I'm back, IRIS. What do I need to do?"

"Wait a moment. I am taking a scan of your vitals."

"Why? I'm fine."

"Theodore, you have been unresponsive for fifteen minutes," IRIS reported with almost human concern in her voice. "I am worried that Dr. Brack's time jump may have had some effect on one or more of your systems."

"Time jump?"

"Theodore, Dr. Brack successfully used the TimeWorm. The current situation is not the dream your father visualized, but you should be proud of his work."

"Fifteen minutes? Are you serious? I'm remembering the jump, but it feels like it was just a minute ago." Theo was shocked at the time lapse. "Whadaya think happened?"

"It could be a great many things, but most likely either vasovagal attack or neurally mediated syncope ..." IRIS reverted back to her normal emotionless cybertronic-self.

"What? Can you say that one more time in English, please?"

"You may have had an episode or a gray-out due to any number of psychological or physiological reasons. A person may suffer a simple fainting spell due to things such as anxiety, fear, pain, intense emotional stress, or hunger. However, you shouldn't be hungry. You had breakfast less than two hours ago. A boy your age with your meta ..."

"I don't think I'm hungry, IRIS." Theo was embarrassed that he had been so affected that he passed out. "Pretty sure all the other ones might be the culprit here."

"I agree, Theodore."

Theo rolled his eyes, starting to feel a little more like himself. He tried running over the events of the last few hours. Bit by bit he began to unravel the events in his foggy mind. He recalled that he had crashed hard on his board, been thrown through the air, and had lab equipment crash down on him. He remembered his dad's legs were crushed in an explosion. He remembered wanting to save Murphy right before a threat of being blinded by a bright flash of light. He scanned the room but stopped as his struggling dog came into view. "Murphy! Hang on, buddy!"

"IRIS! How do I turn off the magnetic field on this workstation?" Theo sloshed his way across the Jump Station by moving debris that had floated in from the Laboratory. "I hope you have a plan. Brack's evil computer is going to be hard to trick!"

Theo cleared the distance to Murphy and stroked his struggling companion's ears and chin trying to soothe him. "Take it easy, Murph. Take it easy, boy." He continued running his hand down the length of the beagle's back a few times. Murphy stopped struggling for a minute then licked Theo's face as his master bent down to rub his chin.

"IRIS! What's the plan?" Theo growled impatiently.

"We need to find a way to distract Brack's Integrated Robotic Information System. Murphy needs to see if he can morph into his sphere. With the magnetic currents running through him, I'm not positive that he can, but the smaller surface area should make it easier for you to pull him off the table."

Theo looked hurriedly around the room one more time, scanning for a way to upset the balance to his favor against the evil IRIS. "What about messing with the Central Time Consol and the STARS systems at the same time? Can she stop you at one and me at the other simultaneously?"

"Let's find out. Theodore, I want you to override the door controls. I have a plan for the STARS module."

Theo nodded in silent agreement. He gave Murphy one more long stroke down his back and leaned down to whisper into his dog's ear. Murphy licked his friend in confirmation. Almost immediately, Murphy's eyes became a blank stare as he attempted to morph. A loud growl bellowed from Murphy as he struggled against the magnetic field of the table.

"It's okay, boy. Just keep trying."

Theo moved to the Singularity Tracking Analyzing Radar System and began to review the data that was streaming across the multiple viewing screens. He watched as information flashed across the monitors until he determined which screens he needed for the override process. "I found them, IRIS! Are you ready?"

"Waiting for you, Theodore," she answered matter-of-factly.

"Of course you are," Theo replied slightly annoyed but with a hopeful grin on his face. He couldn't think of another computer program he would want on his side in an event like this. *Evil IRIS better bring her A game,* he thought to himself, his smile fading into a look of determination. He started flipping through the multiple screens on the monitors. He made a mental note of the STARS' time stamp, which was January 3, 1933. He made a mental note to ask IRIS about the significance of that date in history. Right now, though, he needed to distract Brack's computerized bodyguard, so they could get Murphy de-magnetized and open the door.

"Time is of the essence, Theodore."

"I know that!" Theo snapped at IRIS. "I'm trying to think through this pain throbbing in my head and not screw up! Why don't you do your part to mess with the STARS module, and give me time to open the door."

"I'm programmed to watch time, Theodore, and you tend to run a little behind—"

"IRIS! I can't think and talk right now. Just leave me alone!" Theo fought through a tangled mess of fear, anxiety, and anger. He stared harder at the screens trying to focus his thoughts. *I'm a scientist like my dad. I know I can do this. I have watched him work on the systems in the Towers, and I can use my brain to open the door. Think! Think!*

The rising water allowed little time to demagnetize Murphy and open the Jump Station door before they drown. Theo began muttering to himself as he pounded on the keyboard, trying to recall programs that he could identify and use. Just as he opened a cache holding programs for the wiring, Theo heard a pop and sizzle on the right of the work station. The screen in front of him went black. "IRIS, what happened?"

Without anxiety or rush, IRIS reported the incident in her robotic voice. "The water has reached an unsafe level. Although your workstation has a cyber keyboard, the monitor is connected through electricity. The water has shorted the system. The good news is that the magnetism is ineffectual due to the currents being interrupted. Murphy can be lifted from the table. The bad news is that you need to get above the water level to avoid electrocution until I can shut off all electricity to the Jump Station."

Theo used his powerful leg muscles to jump onto the slate workstation and balance on one foot to keep from making contact with the electrified monitor. With the instinct of an animal and the reasoning of a man, he moved cautiously across furniture to the table where Murphy had recoiled and lay confused after the magnetic power suddenly released him. He swooped Murphy into his arms and stood on the table as it began to buoy in the water.

"Hurry, IRIS! I can't stand here all day!"

"One minute more. I process, Theodore. I don't hurry."

"IRIS, you're the one always harping about the time, so you should just ..."

"All electricity has been shut off for the Tower. You are safe to travel about the room. Attempt to open the Jump Station door has aborted," the computer added to the report.

Theo dropped to his knees on the demagnetized table and swallowed hard to fight emotions of hatred and defeat. He couldn't resist the urge to pull Murphy close to his chest and put his nose on his dog's big wet snout. The idea of drowning was terrifying. Just sitting on the desk waiting for his last breaths of air to come was an excruciating way to live his last moments. He would have rather been vaporized by the TimeWorm. Tears began to roll down his cheeks. What was the point of holding them in anymore? He wasn't ashamed of being scared. Who wouldn't be terrified in this situation? Who could sit calmly and just wait for the inevitable?

"Theodore, I am sorry. I have never failed at a task before. I am still currently running passcodes and trying to override the security system." IRIS spoke quietly in his ear. "Unfortunately, if my calculations are correct, I will not have enough time to run every sequence possible before the lab is filled to capacity."

"IRIS, please don't blame yourself. I ... I ... I'm just scared. Brack fooled all of us. It's not even his computer system's fault." He paused to wipe the steady flow of tears. "The stupid machine just did what it was told to do." Theo whispered, too tired and exhausted to speak any louder as he buried his head into Murphy's soft fur.

Murphy responded to his master's grief with a low whine of his own and a few licks of salty tears from his friend's cheeks. The dog nuzzled his master then closed his eyes. His low, soft howl broke the monotony of the sprinkler water pinging off the computers and metal in the room.

"How much time do I have, IRIS?"

"You have approximately ..."

"Never mind. That was a stupid question. I don't want to know." He looked up at the ceiling; the water splashed on his face and erased the evidence of his tears. "Not sure why I asked."

"There is one thing we have not ..."

A loud thud from the door startled them. "What was that?" Theo interrupted IRIS. Murphy squirmed out of the teen's arms and stood on the nearly submerged table. Theo hopped to the floor hidden by the rising water. He swung his arms to fight exhaustion as he waded through the waist high water. Another loud thud on the door reverberated in the room. Two more solid raps from the outside gave him a strong sense of urgency. Theo pushed his body as hard as he still could. He didn't need to save any energy for anything else.

"THEO!" a voice penetrated the thick door.

"DAD!" Theo cried out with as much force as his lungs allowed. "Dad! I'm trapped! Brack is a ..."

"Theo, can IRIS override the door lock?" Luke Marshall's voice was muffled through the solid door.

Theo took a deep breath then slowly exhaled. "No, Dad. She can't get around Brack's system. He has somehow encrypted the system. We were barely able to get Murphy free, and I—"

"Theo, I'm sorry about this. Had I realized what Viktor was planning—"

Theo pulled a floating table beside the door. The ceiling sprinklers were spraying water at a steady pace, turning the small Jump Station into a giant fish tank. The impending doom loomed in his thoughts. Survival meant finding a way out. He climbed onto the table and looked through a narrow window at the top of the door— the only window in the lab. He saw his dad had propped himself up on a few pieces of lab equipment to keep himself out of the water. "How could anyone know what that monster had planned? Dad, you worked side-by-side with Dr. Brack for over twenty years, but he was so full of secrets, no one knew what he was capable of doing. It's not your fault, Dad."

Dr. Marshall pulled himself a little higher on the mountain of mangled equipment, dragging his limp legs up out of the water.

"Theo, has IRIS come up with another option? Emergency services should be here any minute. They should have been here already." Silently, Luke wondered why they hadn't already arrived at the Towers.

"No one's coming, Dad. Brack disabled all the alarms. He really was thorough in his scheming and preparation." Defeat was thick in Theo's voice. He watched his dad pull his motionless legs up out of the water. He didn't think he could be any angrier at Brack, but watching his paralyzed father was pushing him to a level of rage he'd never felt before. "Dad, he's going after Great-grandpa Lories. He wants to make sure you never meet mom and never find or stop him."

Luke didn't respond right away, which made his son even more anxious. He painstakingly repositioned himself into an upright sitting position against the door. "Do you think my codes could still work? I don't think he planned on my surviving the explosion and still being a threat." He spoke to himself as well as yelling for Theo to hear. He needed to hold on to any miniscule sliver of hope.

"IRIS tried all the codes you've ever created. I've never seen her stumped like this."

"I am truly sorry, Dr. Marshall." IRIS broke her silence with her sincerest robotic apology.

"It's not your fault, IRIS. Brack was always a better programmer than I was." Luke tried to ease the computer's admission of defeat, knowing full well that she wasn't programmed to care, but she had become a huge part of their lives, almost like a member of the family.

"Where did Brack go, IRIS?" Luke needed to hear the facts.

"From what I was able to get from the STARS before his system blocked me, he went somewhere in Europe."

"Yeah, it was 1933!" Theo chimed into the conversation. He racked his brain going through all of Mr. Medi's history lessons, but nothing about the date was jumping out at him. "What happened in Europe in 1933 that he would want to be a part of?"

"World War II didn't start until almost 1940, so that can't be the reason. Your great-grandfather won't be there until almost the end of the War in 1945. That's a long time to be waiting to find someone." Dr. Marshall puzzled over the dates, trying to unlock the significance.

"I have a suggestion," IRIS announced, "but it might be a long shot."

"What's your idea, IRIS?" Theo jumped at any way to escape his inevitable fate.

"Use the TimeWorm and send Theo back to this morning before he came into the lab—maybe even yesterday evening. Then he could warn me!" Luke interjected before IRIS had the opportunity to respond.

"That was my first hypothesis, but Brack's system has locked the STARS module onto a fixed set of coordinates. I will be unable to change the location or the time for another jump, but I can make the TimeWorm send Theo to follow Brack back into history."

"You want to send Theo to an unknown location in Europe, to an unknown time?" Luke was exasperated at the idea of sending his seventeen-year-old son to unknown time and place. "What if he ends up in the middle of a battle zone or ocean or worse?"

"Dad, she's right."

"No, Theo! I'll get you out!" Luke reached for the handle of the door behind him to pull himself up. He was nearly in a standing position, but his hands slipped from the wet metal, and he fell down hard onto the debris of equipment.

"Dad!" Theo cried out at the sound of his father crashing back to the floor. "Dad, are you okay, Dad?"

"I'm fine." Frustration with the entire situation was too much for the doctor to handle. The inability to help his son, the loss of his legs, and the outright betrayal of a man he had considered a brother was overwhelming.

"Dad, I don't have any other options. I'll drown if I stay in this Jump Station much longer." Theo raised his voice again after a pause. "Dad, I'm scared."

"I am too, Theo. I am too."

"Dad, I can do this." Theo bolstered his voice to assure his dad and suppress his own doubts.

"I don't mean to interrupt, Dr. Marshall, but we only have a small window of time left to use the TimeWorm before the rising water will render it inoperable."

"How long to restart the system and have the power to make another jump?"

"Sorry, Sir, but I have already started the process without your directive."

"Good work, IRIS," Theo offered his praise then looked back through the window. "I'll take Murphy with me. He can get me through anything." He could see the anguish in his father's face.

Luke maneuvered himself around until he could grasp the door handle and extend his arm to reach for the window frame.

"Be careful!" Theo ordered as he watched his father's face turn bright red with the strain and energy it took to support himself with only his arms. "Dad, please be careful."

"It's not like I can fall and be paralyzed from the waist down a second time today," Luke quipped jokingly.

Theo just stared at his father as he yelled back through the glass, "Seriously, Dad?"

"Well, just focus on yourself right now."

Luke held himself steady against the wall, keeping his face close to the window so his son could hear every word. "But seriously, we need to talk."

"Might I suggest you talk quickly?" IRIS's robotic voice seemed to contradict her message of urgency. "I estimate that Theo has roughly seven minutes before the TimeWorm will cease to function."

"Do we need to distract Brack's system?" Theo had begun a mental checklist. He didn't want the evil computer to run interference on his only slim hope of survival.

"I've been able to turn its attention to a fake program attacking its own system structures. By the time it realizes we are about to fire off the TimeWorm, interference will no longer be possible."

"Good work," both responded.

"Thank you. It is the least I can do."

"Was that a joke, IRIS?"

"Impossible, Theodore. I am not programmed to be funny."

Father and son smiled at each other through the glass at the computer system's denial of being funny.

Slowly, Luke's smile faded as his face showed stern and worried emotions. "Theo, do you understand fully what you are about to do?"

"I think so. I'm apparently about to put myself through a very painful experience if Viktor's screaming was any indication of how a time jump feels."

"I'm not talking about the time-travel experience itself. I'm talking about the end result of the jump." He warned his son. "You will be a foreigner in a strange land. You won't speak the language, understand the customs, or even know how the people of that time think and feel about outsiders."

"Well, when you put it that way, I guess the jump isn't the only thing making me face my fears. I thought drowning sounded scary," Theo added a little under his breath.

"Murphy should be able to help with the language barrier. You will need to find a place to hide and stay away from people. I'll get this mess straightened out and with IRIS's help get the Worm up and running again. I should be able to locate you and eventually bring you back."

"How long do you think it will take to fix the Worm and bring me back?" Theo gave his best attempt at sounding like a scientist in conversation, not a 17-year-old who, just this morning, had thought adventure was reaching the next level of Holo-Games' *Death Fortress 4* or landing a jump on his driftboard.

"I honestly don't know, Theo. It will depend on how much damage the flooding does to the systems. I'll need time to repair the re-locator."

Theo scolded himself mentally to show no emotion.

"I suggest trying to get to somewhere in Switzerland. It should be the safest place since you will be arriving some time in the 1930s. Dr. Brack has only been gone a short time for us, but the singularity particles will send you back as a few years have passed," IRIS offered.

"Avoid him, Theo! Do not go looking for Viktor or anything else that could expose who and what you are to those people!" Luke emphatically warned his son.

"A tourist?" Theo asked sarcastically, trying to lighten his father's intense mood.

"An alien time traveler, Theo. If people figure out when and where you're from, they will not react mildly. Their superstition and fears will make them behave irrationally—even if you are just a kid," his father explained ignoring his son's poor attempt at being funny.

IRIS's voice fell between the father and son who looked at each other through the glass. "Theodore, you and Murphy should enter the Jump Zone now. The STARS will be activated in thirty ... twenty-nine ... twenty-eight ..."

Theo was glad he had not removed his backpack as he commanded, "Roll, Murphy!" and tucked the silver ball into the pack. With a tap on the glass to assure his father, he began to jump from table to table to quickly move inside the Jump Zone before he had time to think or become frightened.

"Twenty-two."

Luke Marshall let his body fall back to the pile of equipment once used to fulfil hopes and dreams as he lifted his head and cried for his losses—his wife, his mobility, and his scientist friend—and as he prayed for Theo's survival. He closed his eyes to block what he would hear as his son made the jump.

He could not prepare his heart and mind for the screams.

PART II

GERMANY, WINTER 1935

CHAPTER 4

Flight

The armored tank moved like unsatisfied wildfire, destroying anything in its path. The night screamed with the squeal of the steel track as it wove around the road wheels. Snowpacked roads through town were shredded and left in shards of ice and mud. So what if the turret swung too far and caught the post between porch and roof of a storefront. No man stopped to survey damage. No man looked back through the periscope with regret. Unheard to ears in the outside world, destruction caused by the tanks encouraged laughs and guffaws from inside the metal beasts. Cruelest of all was the intentional aim, the unstoppable bearing down and crushing of any man, any soul in the Romani ghetto who unsuspecting fell into the path of the destroyer driven by men with an insatiable thirst to kill any who failed to be born Aryan.

Grey Cooper ran in the shadows. Earlier he had been in town and had heard the rumor and had seen the tanks deployed with the military directive. The executive order of the Führer was clear. By November, the Nuremberg Laws that targeted Jews had been defined to include anyone not deemed pure Aryan, including blacks and gypsies.

Ghettos that had once been segregated to allow cultures to "live with their own," raising families in the life they knew and loved were no longer threatened for their differences but were razed to the ground to annihilate those whom the Reich deemed unworthy.

For miles he had run until Grey feared the heavy panting would tear his lungs from his heaving chest. He couldn't stop. He ran. He ran from the tanks of destruction, but he ran for more than himself. The shadows covered the man with the black skin, but the shadows would dissipate with the dawn and the tanks would open to unleash the brutes of the Reich who would go door to door to destroy.

He ran because he had to beat the night. Grey had two loves, his wife and his child. He ran to warn them of the oncoming onslaught. He ran to reach them while the night still hung in the clouds to cover a Jewish woman who would also run in the cover of the night.

He ran to save them.

"Gracie, we must go." Grey's voice was tense and low.

"But, Papa! Where's Mama? Why can she not go too?"

"Please, my Gracie. I need you to stay with a friend of mine for a while." Without saying more, he clutched his daughter's hand and led her out the door of the small apartment they shared with two other families who kept to their separate rooms. Gracie did not argue further as she knew by her papa's stern brow that this was not a time to question or cause problems. She saw her papa's sad eyes. She noted how his hand lingered on the door knob even after the click of the latch had echoed in the dark hall beside the stairwell.

"I'm sorry, Papa, but I didn't get to tell Mama that I will see her when she returns tomorrow. She left so quickly and you were gone!"

"Hush, Gracie. We'll talk later. For now, you must trust me and not disappoint me by causing me problems!" Her papa's voice seemed to intensify and speak with a harsh tone.

"I understand," Gracie uttered just above a whisper. But she didn't understand. She didn't understand why her mother was gone when she awoke this morning. She didn't understand why Papa was taking her to meet a friend tonight. It was already dark with no visible moon. It would be chilly in the dark alleys and streets. She didn't understand what was upsetting Papa. She didn't understand why her papa insisted she pack a bindle of clothes.

By the end of a half hour of brisk walking in shadows and periodic quick stops to step behind a pillar or a bush, Gracie was beginning to enjoy the chance to pretend an adventuresome game with Papa. Perhaps the situation had more gloom than she wanted to invite into her imagination at the time, but the thrill of "hide and seek" as she and Papa escaped and outwitted the shadows of the night helped her remember to stay quiet. Gracie became caught up in her game of shadows even though Papa didn't realize the fifteen-year-old was passing the time and journey by playing a mental game.

She remembered several years ago when Papa and Mama would play games with her, and they would all roll with laughter until the tears came from their eyes. She promised herself that when morning broke, she would beg Papa to laugh loudly with his laughter that seemed to bubble up from deep inside and explode out into the room. Even in the dark, Gracie realized the plan had put a smile on her face. She looked up at Papa to see if he too was enjoying the silent game of the night. Even without a moon, she could see his dark skin with light falling in streaks across his handsome face. Mama always called him her beautiful dark knight, and Papa would smile until his eyes narrowed into a wink at Mama.

Somewhere between the time the clock in the Munich square had chimed eleven and twelve, Papa pulled Gracie to a doorway on a side street where his knuckles rapped a hard but muffled sound on the wooden door. Gracie was surprised to see Papa's patience in waiting silently in the doorway after hurrying so quickly through the night. Minutes passed and again Papa raised a clenched fist to hit three separate pounds against the wooden door with the side of his curled hand. He muttered something under his breath that Gracie could not hear clearly, but as she looked up and saw his eyes scanning the dark and his back flatten against the door, she understood that he was not intending to speak to her. Papa had pulled her with her face against the door. Then he had barred her there with his arm from her left shoulder to her waist. She could feel his tense muscle in his arm.

As a carpenter, Grey Cooper had arm strength enough to hold back twenty men, but in his home, he only used his strong arms to hold his Jewess wife, Linden, and their daughter, Gracie. Grey's

German lineage should have given passage to a life unmolested by the SS and those who believed themselves to be superior. Yet his black skin, his treasure from his own father, had set a curse in motion in the unrest of Germany in the early part of the century. His dark eyes were rimmed with deliberate lashes, but they could not compare to the beauty of the dark eyes that shone against the olive skin tones of the young Jewess he fell in love with and vowed to marry and protect until death would separate them. In his love for her, Grey spoke of Linden, his Lindy, with a tenderness of tone. Together, they had become pariahs in a society where dark skin and dark eyes were becoming mentally bleached from what was believed to be right. Together, they raised their beautiful daughter who grew with long softly curled locks that lay against her caramel skin. Together, they lived the lives of gypsies, traveling from town to town where his work as a carpenter could sustain and feed them. Together, they vowed to do what was best to protect their Gracie—at all costs.

Now at this juncture of life, Linden had agreed to flee Munich, trying to cross the Austrian border with another gypsy friend who also was running for her life. Linden had agreed to wait for Grey to come to the hills which would be their refuge. However, the danger of being caught in flight created two restrictions. They must travel separately from each other, and they must leave their daughter behind with the hope of her safety being outside of their home.

In the dark night, the young mother packed her bindle and kissed the sleeping Gracie goodbye. "Dream of me. Dream of freedom from this oppression," Lindy whispered into the moonbeam that had crept between window sill and curtain to lie peacefully across Gracie's sleeping face. "Kiss your Papa for me when he returns." Lindy inhaled deeply with the fortitude of a warrior as she held to her heart a picture of Grey before she tucked it into her coat and floated away into the night with her traveling companion who wept too loudly as she too pulled away from her family.

Two more fist raps and the wooden door slightly opened, with only enough space for Grey and Gracie to pass into the interior room lit only by a flickering candle.

"Please, Jahile, be my friend and protect my daughter." Grey's voice cracked as he pulled Gracie's face up to look him in the eye. "Gracie, I need to be elsewhere for now. Mind Herr Möeller and cause him no problems. I will return for you—not soon—but some day." With a quick kiss to the forehead, Grey spun and pulled the door shut behind him as he disappeared into the dispassionate darkness where street and sky were all one.

"PAPA!" Gracie yelled behind him as the stranger named Möeller pulled her screams and pleadings into his own chest and cradled her collapsing body into his own arms to allow her to cry for a life once known, once rugged, once full of love, now crashing into an abyss unknown.

For four days Gracie knew nothing of day or night and little of the bread and vegetables that Jahile Möeller diligently brought to the side of the bed where she lay hidden and sobbing until the tears no longer flowed and her head pounded with sights and sounds and memories that made her want to give up living. She had resisted the bright sunlight that seemed to waft with the fresh air rising through the windowpane below the loft where she comfortably lay on a small pallet. She had welcomed the darkness that surrounded her as she crept through darkness down the ladder and out to a common toilet in a small hut behind the house with the wooden door.

"Enough," Gracie said aloud, louder than she expected but with a voice of determination. "Get a grip on yourself, Gracie." She kicked back the quilt that smelled like lavender and rolled off the soft bed. She crawled and extended into a shape of a bent old woman as the rafter above her bed prevented her from standing to her full 5' 2" height in the loft. Then, she collapsed back down into a sitting position where she could pull her knees up to her body and support her aching head. "I have to find my family," she whispered as she listened for sounds from the open room below.

"*Guten Morgen, Frauline!*" chirped Jahile as Gracie's foot planted on solid floor at the base of the ladder. Expressionless, Gracie turned to look at the man who was holding her captive.

"Where's Papa?" Gracie asked without acknowledging the new morning and using the most authoritative voice she could muster.

"Your papa has made a trip for now. You are to stay here with me where I can help an old friend and keep you safe. Here, some food for you."

Gracie just stared through her dark eyes at the man who was setting a bowl of porridge on a wooden table. *Old friend.* Gracie tumbled the man's words in her mind. *I don't know how he can be old as he looks about the age of Papa. Neither have lived for even four decades, so how can they be old.* Gracie's thoughts were random and speechless as she stood frozen at the bottom of the ladder.

"I'm not hungry."

A broken half smile seemed to ruffle the rough whiskers on the man's face. "I know. But you must regain your strength and be strong for the sake of your papa and mama."

Reluctantly, Gracie shuffled to the bench beside the table where the hot porridge sat. Truly, her stomach was beginning to ache. She had survived times with small amounts of food before. This wouldn't kill her. Yet something the man had said seemed to ring true to her thoughts, "strong—for Papa and Mama." Gracie sidled along the bench until she was able to sit facing the table. Her head seemed to empty of thoughts and swirl with confusion of words all at once. She sat staring at the porridge—not talking, not thinking, not moving, just staring.

As if to understand, Jahile urged, "Eat. Later we'll talk." Then, he turned and walked out the door.

Long minutes passed before Gracie lifted the spoon to begin eating the sweet porridge that soothed her stomach as well as her soul.

Midmorning almost looked good to Gracie as she set her porridge bowl in the sink and drifted out the door to sit on the concrete step that threatened to pull away from the small cottage. *Funny,* Gracie thought as she buttoned her coat and pulled shut the wooden door. "That door looked more impressive when Papa first brought me here. I could probably kick it in if I tried." She eased down to sit on the step where she could watch Herr Möeller, feel the fresh air, and not have to talk to anyone. Herr Möeller glanced up and saw Gracie, but he seemed to understand the healing power of the time alone that Gracie would need.

By the time the sun had taken the chill off the morning, Gracie realized she had questions that she wanted answered. Why was she here? When could she leave? Why had her papa brought her to a stranger's house and left her? What would happen next? Hours passed before Gracie found herself sitting across a table from the stranger who did not make her talk. He opened his home. It would be weeks before Gracie would realize that he also opened his heart.

Herr Möeller's home had more solid walls than the home Gracie left, but the bread and broth were evidence that the food was the meager fare she knew too well. "Why am I here?" Gracie finally blurted out, a little more loudly than she planned and with a little too much food in her mouth. "I don't even know you."

"Ah, true, little dove, but I know your parents and love your papa like a brother. Sadly, though, our government is making him a step-brother to the nation, and the government has neither love nor inheritance for the step-child."

Gracie just stared at Herr Möeller trying to understand his tale that seemed to have no connection to the questions she asked.

"In another world, I would be your godfather. In this world, the government wants me to turn on my friends and have them arrested."

"Why? What has my papa or my mama done? They are not criminals!" Gracie could feel the heat rising in her face as her back stiffened. She accosted Herr Möeller as if he were the enemy.

Jahile raised his brows and tipped his head in understanding of her tone. "I guess you are not a child any longer. You have a right to know and understand the world you have entered." Jahile looked across the table, directly into the eyes that appeared to be floating in shallow pools of water as they stared back at him. "Right now there is danger for your parents—your father because he is a black man and your mother because she is a Jew. They are Romani, gypsies, but that doesn't really matter because due to their ethnicity, neither is welcomed in this Aryan society. We are the frog in the beaker."

Gracie furrowed her eyebrows. "What?" she scowled. She was getting tired of his strange way of talking.

"We sit and let the Reich gain more and more control over who can live in our country—our world. We do nothing, like a frog sitting in a beaker. When the beaker begins to be heated over a flame, the heat is so slight that the frog does not notice. The heat increases slowly until the frog is actually dead from being cooked in the heat he allowed. That is us—the German people. We are frogs accepting the heat of the Third Reich. We sit, content or afraid—I don't know which—and we will die in our ignorance."

Gracie sat with her head cocked as she noticed that Herr Möeller's voice had changed. He was speaking softer yet with a more terse tone. The muscles in his neck bulged in ruddy reaction with his words. Jahile exhaled as he realized he was gripping his spoon so tightly that his knuckles were pale and aching. "Sorry." He shook his head and stared at the broth in front of him.

"But, Herr Möeller, I don't understand," Gracie's voice softened. "What does that have to do with my papa and mama? Why does the Reich not like them? Does it like me?" Suddenly, questions were spinning in her mind. She was asking and not even sure if she was able to listen to any answers.

"We have distorted the Aryan race and narrowed it to be a small, select group of people until we have built walls of hatred."

"I'm German, so am I Aryan too? I don't hate anyone."

Jahile looked at the beautiful bronze complexion framed by long natural curls of soft hair. "Dear *Frauline*. You are equal parts of your papa and your mama. You bestow their beauty. You have their heart. So you need their knowledge and understanding. You are what is known as a *Mischling* because your parents have both Aryan and Jewish ancestry. You are considered a mongrel—a half-breed. People hate what they see, and they have no reason except fear—fear of being less, so they separate and identify by what they can see."

"But Papa is Aryan, so shouldn't we be accepted?" Gracie wanted to find a loophole, a way to have a family accepted by the Nazi Party.

"Gracie, the Aryan race is becoming a race of exclusion—a scientific racism is being born of evil hearts. Although German, your papa does not have the light skin, blonde hair, and blue eyes that define today's Aryan race. The Reich wants to purge the nation of all who are not Aryan."

Gracie stared at the man across the table with eyes, hair, and skin light in color that had not even been worth noting until now. "But you are light. Do you hate Papa?"

"Over twenty years ago, my family owned a bakery in town. Your papa and I met in *Grundschule* here in Munich when we were six years old. We became best friends who enjoyed playing together, running together, and even pulling pranks together. As we got older, we were careful not to be seen in public together as it was not good for a merchant's son and a gypsy to be friends. Even then the classes didn't get along. But by that time, our friendship had grown, and our brotherhood had bonded. Grey would stop by the back door of the bakery. My own parents knew I was sneaking him week-old food, but they knew he was my true friend. As adults, our love for each other hasn't quelled, and until now, our lives hadn't changed much. He is still a gypsy, and I have inherited the bakery. But friendships like ours didn't begin with color of skin or eyes or hair, and our friendship doesn't end with what the Reich decrees."

"So as the fire under the beaker is starting to heat up, you're trying to help the frogs jump?" Both Gracie and Jahile grinned at her use of the analogy. It was if they were speaking in secret code.

"That's right, Gracie. Life here in Munich is not safe for your parents right now, so they are leaving until they can safely reunite your family. For now, my job is to keep you safe."

"Me? I'm only fifteen! What does the Reich want with me?" Gracie sat up a little straighter, not in fear but in protest.

"Well, you do have your mama's spunk and your papa's brains! Even though you are young, you are a threat to the Reich. The Nuremberg Laws support anti-Semitism—this scientific racism—that has no concern for age. Anyone who is not what they deem as pure Aryan is in danger. Unfortunately, you have too many strikes against you. You have beautiful skin, but it is dark. You are a *Mischling*. Your mama is a Jew."

"That's not fair!" Gracie's voice rose with the words. "I won't sit here in this house and let my family be destroyed! You don't care because you look like … like … one of them!"

"Gracie! We can't fight what is or is not fair. However, regardless of how I look, I am not one of them!" Although they sat at a table behind closed doors, Jahile dropped his voice to a rough whisper. "Gracie, there are many of us who are not willing to sit in the beaker. We know, though, that our actions place us in as grave a danger as those whom the Reich is vowing to eliminate. I am a part of a group known as *The Watch*. I have also promised your papa that I will protect you."

"So what is *The Watch*?" Gracie narrowed her eyes and looked curious but suspicious.

"Don't worry about *The Watch*. I've said too much already. I want you to be aware but safe. For now, you'll stay with me."

"I can't hide in this house forever, if that's what you mean! I might be a girl, but I know what I'm doing!" Gracie quipped back.

Jahile said nothing but pursed his lips and refrained from lecturing as he looked across the table at Gracie. "I pray that you do, my dear girl. I pray that you do."

Night came slowly to Gracie as she lay on the pallet in the loft that was to be her home until her papa returned. Her stomach rolled with knotted pain. The dinner Herr Möeller fed her was good enough. Actually, it was quite good. She couldn't remember when she had last eaten bread made from wheat instead of the heavy barley and rye grains. She hadn't thanked Herr Möeller for the food. She hadn't spoken at all. What was she to say to someone who was her papa's friend but a stranger—an enemy as far as the government was concerned—to her. Gracie's mind seemed to tumble as much as her stomach. How nice it was to be in a warm loft, but this would not do. Herr Möeller was right. She was her papa and mama's child and as such, she must go to them and help them. They were family, and she would stand and fight with them, fight the Reich, fight the Aryans, fight whatever invisible force was threatening to separate them.

Gracie quietly rolled off the soft pallet and peered down through the railing of the loft. Herr Möeller was behind the closed door of another room, probably asleep as he thought she would be. Time was right for the little *Mischling* to stand as the young adult she was becoming. "Here's your Romani. I'm not afraid. I'll find you, Papa. I'll protect you, Mama," Gracie vowed under her breath as she moved stealthily down the ladder and out the wooden door that led to the quiet, dark Munich street.

The night air held a chill that seemed to touch Gracie's skin through her woolen mantle even though she pulled it tightly by crossing her arms across her body. She remembered the *Strickmütze* creating a bulge from the pocket of her mantle. She almost gave an audible chuckle as she recalled her foolishness from earlier in the week. Papa had commanded her to dress for the cool weather during their journey into the village. Gracie had refused to put on her knitted hat, thinking that Papa would not make her go if she were not dressed warmly as he had requested. Instead, Papa sighed a heavy breath, picked up the hat, and tucked it into the pocket of her mantle.

"So you're with me even now, Papa," Gracie said to the night air as she pulled the warm *Strickmütze* down over her ears.

She looked up at the sliver of moon that tore the night sky with its icy form and teased her by allowing glimpses of its cold light through breaks in the tall buildings of the town. She wandered deeper into the city of Munich, hoping the stone towers of civilization would provide more shelter from the cold of the night. She left behind the houses offering stifled light beams through curtained windows. She left behind the welcoming smell of wood burning in village chimneys. She left behind a tiny home that seemed to gather its warmth from a stranger named Jahile Möeller. Gracie denied herself the thoughts of what she had left. "I cannot be strong like my parents if I become like a child and begin whining for what I can't have!" Gracie scolded herself. Tired and cold, she entered a side alley where a stone building offered a recessed doorway. Gracie squatted in the doorway, pulling her knees close to her body. Wrapped in a woolen cover, the small frame of the youth lay curled like a motionless ball tossed onto the doorstep of the world, victim to the cold.

"*Frauline.*" Gracie's eyes opened and again softly closed against the dinginess of morning seeping into the dust of the alley. "*Frauline.*" Gracie didn't move except to wrinkle her brow in an attempt to sharpen her hearing. "*Frauline.*" A hand pressed against Gracie's shoulder prompting her to spring out of the doorway and away from the unknown. "Please, *Frauline.*"

Gracie scowled as she saw a dirty gloved hand extend toward her. "Please, *Frauline*, I will not hurt you."

The voice was scarcely more than a whisper that only offered good, but the sudden waking left Gracie puzzled and wary. "What do you want from me?" Gracie croaked through vocal cords that had become rough in the cool air.

From where it had stayed suspended in air, the dirty gloved hand turned to show fingers cupped around a biscuit. The fingers opened as the arm gestured. Gracie looked from the proffered bread to the face of a woman, a face full of wrinkles that appeared to have been made of a rough fabric that had been left to harden in the weather. Gracie relaxed the muscles of her brow as the eyes of the woman offered no malice through her direct stare. Slowly, Gracie moved her arm, allowing it to suspend less than a hand's breadth from her body. Again, the alley visitor moved her extended arm in gesture to accept the gift. Without breaking her contact with the woman's eyes, Gracie moved her hand into her peripheral sight until it hovered over the woman's open hand and the biscuit. In a mixed reaction of fright and flight, Gracie grabbed the biscuit and ran into the street, away from the gift giver. She ran hard, propelled by the strength of adrenaline until she was several blocks from the alley. Panting, Gracie dove into a grove of trees where she was covered from sight and was safe to eat biscuit and crumb.

Three days Gracie wandered without direction through the streets of Munich. She learned to find pubs and merchants who threw empty crates and boxes into the alleys. Such would become her night refuge as she would crawl until her body heat could be trapped between the rugged shelter and the hard ground where she would lie.

So often she had watched her papa stack rocks into a small cylindrical wall where she could deposit ash from coal hoppers at the back of buildings. A simple piece of shale or a discarded shard of pottery could carry enough hot ash to kindle a fire for warmth. The flat rock became her treasure as it could be used to carry ash, dig holes to cover her own body refuse, and even hack as a knife in case of need. Pockets of her mantle that once held the soft *Strickmütze* had become the reticule to carry her supplies—the bit of thread, the shard of pottery, the coin she found lodged in the cobblestone, the metal spike that had once been part of a nail, and the tin tobacco box to serve as cup or bowl. Gracie was not familiar with scouring the rubbish piles for needful tools, but she had grown up watching the resourcefulness of her Romani parents who recognized all facets of society's rejections as possible opportunities.

A week, then two, then a month of running, hiding, and scavenging passed with very few minutes of Gracie thinking about the warm cottage of Herr Möeller. Driven by desire to reunite her family and driven by a passion to stand against those who only knew hatred for her people, Gracie refused her mind any moments to regress into memory and weaken her own fortitude. Even at fifteen, Gracie applied her time to learning the streets of Munich and to survival. Words such as *Mischling*, Romani, Reich, and Aryan were allowed enough time in her thoughts to keep the flame of determination from being smothered by complacency. Too often hunger became her enemy using weapons of pain and weakness against her. She became adept in using stealth, hiding in the exposure of daylight, and having acute sense of sight and sound. She moved without sound and with confidence as if she controlled the streets of the city. Her passion and her protection were Munich's museums where she regularly whetted her imagination and sharpened her knowledge.

But the nights—the nights were the foreboding threats that smothered her courage. It was the terror of the night that tormented Gracie. Yet after each night came a day of determination to find her family, so Gracie persevered. Too often she would hold her breath out of fear of making a sound in the shadows. Structures and shapes of the day became dragons of hatred that loomed over her thoughts at night. Her mind begged for streetlights to expose the shadows, then cursed their beams for illuminating her shape against the covert darkness. Even stray dogs became loathe to her as they either frightened her with sudden appearance or teased her as they trotted through the night as if a destination of safety lay ahead of them. Twice she had encountered street people, uncouth and unclean, as they harassed her with their taunts until she had escaped out of earshot.

It was the terror of one particular night that threatened Gracie's existence. Weeks into her life as a street urchin, Gracie hollowed out a stack of lumber to provide her nightly shelter. She had learned that the dark alleys were the most foreboding but were also the least likely to expose her to scavengers in the night. On this night, however, the lurkers were not looking for food or shelter or other homeless companions. On this night, the lurkers of the dark were dark themselves, robed in long dusty coats that swung in folds and rubbed against the tops of military boots. They moved with heavy feet and odious bodies in search of anyone whose appearance countered the Reich who had programmed hatred into their beings.

Gracie's scavenging of the last two days had proven less than profitable for food, so the night under the lumber shelter had dropped her into a deep sleep. Thus, she did not hear the boots as they scuffled into the alley. She did not see the dark shadows that loomed over the lumber shelter. She did not smell the pungent warning of evil. It wasn't until the creatures of the dark lifted the wooden planks that Gracie turned her face upward just as a board was brought down across her face to break her nose. In weak reaction, Gracie tried to fight the attackers who used fists, boots, and wood in an attempt to decimate the young form. Gracie's struggle numbed into darkness.

Four days passed before Gracie felt a hand move under the nape of her neck. She flailed out with her arms, trying to kick in reaction and fear.

"Be still, my little angel. You are protected. No one will hurt you."

Gracie opened wild eyes that blurred from tears of pain and the blinding light of day. She wanted to run. She wanted to vomit.

Instinct prodded her into fighting whatever had taken hold of her, but her body ached and refused to listen to the commands of her brain. Her eyes fell shut against her efforts.

"Be still and drink."

Gracie flinched and jerked her head as she felt the hand still holding the back of her neck and a moist heat against her lips. For a second time, Gracie opened her eyes, but this time she slowly pulled her eyelids against the weight of sleep that held them down. Again shapes and colors were all one, a knotted confusion.

"Gracie, try to sip some broth."

Gracie allowed the heaviness of her head to lay cradled in the hand around her neck. Although her eyes hid her behind a blurry screen, she knew the voice. *Herr Möeller.* Gracie's mind spoke the name, yet her lips and voice made no sound. The broth was again brought to her lips. Without reasoning or wondering or fighting, Gracie let her swollen lips part enough to feel the warm broth pour into her mouth. Even a simple swallow brought pain and made her wince, but the warmth was good, and she realized she was very, very hungry. No sounds were made as Herr Möeller spooned a half cup of broth into the tiny body that lay bruised and battered.

"Rest for now. You are safe. You are home. Now, rest," Jahile quietly breathed aloud as he pulled away the hand that had cradled the delicate head that lay swollen from the terror of the night.

"How long have I slept?" Gracie spoke as she turned her head and saw Herr Möeller on the other side of the room where he stood with his back to her and washed his morning dishes.

"Ah, what a beautiful sound of morning!" Jahile turned and dried his hands on a kitchen linen as he walked toward the make-shift bed he had made by dragging a mattress to the common room of the small cottage where the wood stove provided the most heat. He smiled down at the young teen, pleased to see the bruised and swollen face beginning to return to its natural soft shape and color.

"I'm sorry," Gracie whispered. She didn't know what night-mare had brought her back into the home of her father's friend. She tried to remember anything that would explain why even breathing hurt, but her mind gave her no hints of what had happened. Yet she remembered rejecting the home Jahile Möeller had given her. She remembered days on the streets and days without food to fill the empty pain in her stomach. She remembered searching for anything to lead her to her parents. She remembered crying over parents who could not be found. She couldn't remember any reason to be back in Herr Möeller's home, but she was sure it was not because of any good she had done. "What happened? Why do I hurt all over?" Gracie searched Herr Möeller's kind expression for answers.

Jahile agreed to help Gracie understand what he knew about the night a week earlier when he rescued her. Gracie quietly listened as he detailed how he had searched—sometimes in daylight and sometimes in the dark of night—to find the runaway daughter of his friend. Jahile explained how he regularly stopped by *die Polizei* headquarters in Munich in hopes of hearing of a street urchin fitting Gracie's description. Gracie's fast learning, stealth on the streets, and days in the museums had kept her out of sight and away from suspicion of being a runaway. Then, the night a week earlier, Jahile had stopped to rest and check in diligence for a *Mischling* when he happened to witness a street woman run in from the streets, frantically waving her worn gloved hands, and demanding the *Polizei* converge on an alley where an innocent *Jugendlicher* was being beaten. Jahile overheard the woman's report of the teenager and reacted before the *Poliezei* had even begun taking the woman's report. Jahile grabbed the woman's shoulders and convinced her to lead him to the alley. Gracie had been hit and kicked unconscious by the time Jahile entered the alley yelling and swinging a metal billy club, a *Knuppel*, he had grabbed as he left the *Poliezei*. Jahile's rant took the creatures of the dark by surprise. He fought both creatures with an unleashed anger and adrenaline that strengthened the muscles of his military training. Even as they ran from the scene, Jahile fell over the *Jugendlicher* who was beaten and bleeding so badly that he could scarcely recognize her as the pretty *Mischling* welcomed into his home. Jahile hesitated and chose not to tell Gracie that he fell to his knees and retched from the sight of the bloodied child and the repulsive smell of the dark creatures—a smell his memory recalled—before he could steady himself enough to carry the child home to safety.

With a nearly imperceptible turn of his head, Jahile squeezed his eyes shut and put his forehead into his hands. The story was there, laid out before the *Mischling* like unfolding a tall-tale of fiction. But he couldn't tell the truth—not all of it, not the brutal facts of his own internal terror of coming face-to-face with the jaegers whose features were so horrid, Jahile couldn't find the words to describe what he saw and what he had to do to make these monsters flee. Throughout his time in the military and his time in *The Watch*, he was sure he had no fear of the devil himself, but the wounds he had seen these minions leave behind were sights no man should ever see or could ever shake from the nightmare that would haunt a man forever. Jahile shook his head to release the thought that his innocent godchild had lay on the edge of the hell that unleashed these beasts.

Gracie swallowed hard as she felt her broken nose and broken ribs wondering if they hurt more than Herr Möeller's broken heart. She spoke nothing as tears ran down the sides of her face while her godfather assured her that he would make good on his promise to her father to keep and to protect her until the government and the creatures of the dark were no longer a threat.

Days dragged past. Gracie's stomach felt tied in knots too often to enjoy eating the good bread from Jahile's bakery and the vegetables saved from his garden. After breakfast, Gracie passed the time by washing dishes and tidying the tiny kitchen. On one occasion, Jahile came into the house speaking in low tones to a man who was with him. Gracie felt that anyone who warranted hushed conversation was probably involved with *The Watch*, which meant she had a right to listen in even if it meant spying and eavesdropping. However, the men spoke in guarded tones. During one visit, Gracie feigned looking for a misplaced spoon from the morning's breakfast. She diverted her eyes from the two men but kept her ears turned to listen to their conversation. She frowned at not being able to comprehend complete sentences and hearing what seemed to be meaningless prattle with words such as *smell* and *jaeger*. At one point Jahile looked up and caught Gracie watching them. "Gracie, go to the loft. This is private business."

"I know what you are about. I have a right to know! I'm tired of being locked up like a prisoner just because you are afraid to speak your mind! I can't take this!" The silent thoughts that had been growing in Gracie's mind came out like an unstoppable whirlwind. Not wanting to lose her composure or appear weak, Gracie reached for the metal handle on the wooden door.

"Gracie! Stay here!" Jahile commanded.

"I'll be all right!" Gracie shouted, not looking back as she lunged out the door and into the street. Fighting tears, fighting anger, and fighting insecurity of doubt, she raced down the narrow street wondering if the pounding was the sound of her feet on the brick roadway or her heartbeat that threatened to pulse out of her chest. She ran in freedom from the house and in fear of the future until she had woven through streets and alleys like a mouse trapped in a maze.

By nightfall Gracie was back in Jahile's home, accepting the shelter and refuge.

Jahile didn't scold Gracie. He understood her angst, but more than that, he appreciated her stamina to fight back. The visitor came more regularly to Jahile's home. Although with less intent of spying, Gracie stayed alert in case the men's discussions would somehow involve her family. The visitor seemed to come at various hours of the day, but Jahile would always welcome him saying, "Thomas, so good of you to come!" as if he were doing a favor by walking through the door. On two separate occasions, the visitor stayed with them in the tiny home for three days. After cleaning up the breakfast porridge bowls one day, Gracie couldn't resist running her hand over the soft leather of the valise imprinted with the initials *TAR*.

Gracie was learning to enjoy her time running the streets. In the secrets of her mind, she promised herself to learn the passages of streets and alleys of Munich to be ready in time of need. She liked Jahile's home and conversation. Mealtimes had become enjoyable times for conversation, talk of her future, and even times for laughing. He was her papa's friend, her godfather, and he was becoming her confidant. Jahile trusted her in his home, and he trusted her in the streets. A couple times Gracie had returned home a little scuffed up. Jahile noticed she borrowed one of his caps and tucked her hair up under the band. She wore her clothes loosely so that at a glance, Jahile was amazed how the delicate young lady could pass for any boy living the life of a street urchin. He kept his thoughts to himself and sometimes muttered as she passed out the door, "Go ahead, dear Gracie. Learn the streets and the ways that may save your life some day."

Boys on the streets sometimes threatened, sometimes ignored, but always respected the kid with fire in her fists. She became known around the streets as Lil' Grey, the kid who would come out of nowhere and disappear into nowhere. For that, Lil' Grey was respected.

POLAND, JANUARY 1937

CHAPTER 5

Boxcar

"Ugh. Get your foot outta my back!"

"Sorry. I can't—I can't see you. [*Huff.*] It's hard to breathe in here."

"Hey! Where'd you come from? Look, Yari! There's a blue glow."

Theo snapped his head around to a shiny silver ball lying on the floor partially hidden by his backpack. "Quick," Theo puffed, "transform. I don't know where we are, but it looks like a better place for a dog than a robot ball."

"What's that?" a man stood over him roaring questions. "Say, who are you? What's in your satchel? Are you hiding food?"

A tiny form a short distance away in the darkness started to cry.

"Oh, really, Yari! You're scaring Sarai!"

Theo peered up through the dark trying to find detail in the dark form called Yari. Murphy lay still until his nose could no longer resist the urge to sniff outside the cover of the backpack.

"Agh! A rat!"

"No, no!" Theo yelled as he half rolled and tucked Murphy under his body.

"Get up!" Yari commanded. "You're taking up too much space."

"Sorry. Wh-where am I?"

"Honestly. How can you sit in this stinkin' boxcar for hours and not know ..."

"Be gentle, Yari," a nearby voice whispered. "Perhaps he took a rap on the head and was knocked unconscious from the rods the soldiers swung at us as we loaded."

Theo had not questioned the language of those crowded around him until he caught a glimpse of the blue flashing lights on Murphy's neck collar. The language transmitter was spanning the distance and converting the language of what Theo heard and what he spoke. He knew his safety would be threatened if he became separated from Murphy and the aid of the language transmitter.

"Uh, yeah. I must have had a blow to my head. Please don't hurt my dog. Where are we?"

The dark skinny figure shifted enough for the light from the uneven slits in the wall to fall half across his face. Theo could see better with the shaft of light; it wasn't a man at all. The dark figure was a tall, thin boy about his own age, but even with his limited sight, Theo could see the boy's fists were clenched. Shadows across the face of the boy revealed an expression that did not match the balled up fists. Yari's large eyes appeared as dark as the shadows and as mysterious as the unusual cap balanced on the back of his head. One fist relaxed as it reached down. Theo quickly cradled Murphy in one arm as he accepted Yari's hand that pulled him up to a sitting position. Yari folded into a kneeling squat beside the new kid.

"Sorry. Didn't mean to be rough on you. It's just that no one stuffed in this boxcar really understands. It's up to us grown ones to hold these kids together. It may be our only chance."

Theo stared through the dark trying to comprehend Yari's words. Grown ones? Since when has seventeen been grown? Chance? For what? He swallowed a gulp and spoke up, trying to act as if he understood. Murphy wriggled to get closer to a small hand stroking his back and to get away from the grip Theo was unknowingly tightening.

"That's all right, Yari. My name's Theo. I'll help, but I need to know …"

Just then an ear piercing screech came with a jolt as all the shadows in the dark wooden room tumbled into a heap. Silence. No one seemed to breathe as a panel of the wall opened with a metal grating sound that vibrated the floor. The light that jumped into the room hurt Theo's eyes as he squinted to see that he and Murphy had time jumped into a narrow boxcar crammed with more children than he could count with a glance. He noticed that all the dark-eyed boys shielding their eyes were wearing caps that seemed to adhere to the back of each head. Girls in simple brown cotton dresses were scattered among the boys.

What was this? A boxcar of a train overfilled with children where the grown ones were only 16 or 17. Why would …

Theo's thoughts were interrupted by the pressure of small bodies moving him forward as the mass flowed out of the boxcar like coagulated blood pouring down onto the hard, dusty ground. Puzzled, he looked for a way to escape the flow. He needed to contact IRIS and ask—

"Umph." Theo felt his face hit the snow on the ground. "Murph—" was all he could exhale as he saw Murphy roll into a ball and wriggle into the backpack.

"Go!" Yari yelled in his ear as Theo caught the backpack Yari flung at him while yanking him to his feet.

Theo knew that without IRIS's help, he only had seconds to look around and gather enough visual data to assess his time travel. Here in the sunlight, he had a better look at the children, all wearing a six-pointed yellow star on their left lapel and shoulder. He could see the boxcar that had transported him and the children. *When were boxcars made so narrow?* He noticed the olive-drab colored uniforms of the soldiers and the *Kepis* they wore on their heads. *Where have I seen a picture of these soldiers before? Think. Oh, there was something in history class about … children … soldiers … children with stars … Magen David …* Theo's thoughts were interrupted, and he jerked his head in the direction of a soldier just as a deep voice behind him jabbed him with the butt end of a rifle and shouted words he could not understand. Murphy must be balled around the language transmitter causing it to muffle the airwaves. Something about the language was similar to the language of the children. It wasn't the same language, but some words similar in tone …

"Think, Theo," he breathed to himself. "Yiddish!" Theo gasped from the soldier's gun forcing him forward and the recognition of the situation. The children were speaking Yiddish—a combination of a Jewish and German language. That meant the soldiers were—augh, he choked on the reality of his time jump to a concentration camp. His mind reeled in thinking how to react, how to keep his cover, how to survive whatever fate the German soldiers had for these Jewish children, how to contact IRIS.

Suddenly, Theo was grabbed by a husky soldier who half smoked, half chewed on the end of a cigarette. An arm circled with a red armband marked by a black swastika grabbed him by the collar, pulled the left side of his shirt toward a fellow soldier, and muttered a few snarly German words. The two soldiers laughed as if in on a joke as the soldier let loose of Theo's shirt by thrusting him aside. *Oh, good,* he thought. *They think I've only lost or removed my star. They don't realize I'm different from the other children. I need time to think. I can't blow my cover now.* The backpack began to quiver.

"No, Murphy," Theo growled in a harsh whisper. "Stay." A whirlwind of thoughts fought in slow motion through his brain as he tried to shake his thoughts into a progression of what to do next. He realized he was holding his backpack down at his side as he inched away from the laughing soldiers as they looked for a next victim of ridicule.

I can't risk their finding Murphy. If this is a Jewish internment camp, I can't bear to think what would happen if ... The grounds of snowy-mud looked as hopeless as the children who shuffled in a reluctant mob. Theo worked his way to the outside of the fluid mass of children. *Sorry for the rough ride, Murphy,* Theo spoke in his mind as if the dog could hear, *but I have to let you hang close to the ground so the backpack will be hidden in the movement of rustling dark-dressed bodies.*

Theo noticed that most of the buildings of this camp were either about to collapse from disrepair and chinks in the walls, or they were tightly domed canvass Quonset huts set in rows as a temporary fortress. The ball of moving children were being goaded past a long wooden structure that seemed to have better walls and even some smoke circling out of a pipe protruding from the side of the wall. This building even had a porch and three steps.

"That's it!" Theo's audible sound was covered by the shuffling feet on the icy gravel road.

Theo wriggled to the far right side of the mass and began to walk in a squat until he felt his quad muscles in his legs begin to rebel from the strain. Just as the human ball of children passed the porch, he flung his backpack and quickly dove unnoticed under where the steps joined the porch. Holding his breath so he wouldn't make a sound, Theo inched his body around to lie parallel under the hollow steps that were now his refuge. He knew that to be found would be a fate worse than death because even though Murphy looked like an ordinary dog, he carried too many secrets. It wouldn't take the ruthless soldiers long to misread his intents. For now, he and Murphy must lie still. He reached for the backpack and held his hand next to the zipper so Murphy would sense that his master and friend was nearby. Exhaustion overtook him as he couldn't fight the impulse to close his eyes.

A cold drop of ice fell into Theo's face. He grazed his head on a splintered piece of wood above him as he jerked and then froze in his covert location. Dirt mixed with snow continued to fall as the wooden steps, not six inches from his face creaked and gave way to the scraping weight of someone climbing onto the porch. He turned his face to the ground to prevent the bits of mud from falling into his eyes. Footfalls stopped as a dull sound suggested the person above was going through a doorway. *Sigh.* He must have dozed off until someone mounted the steps and woke him. Peering through the slits in the wooden steps, Theo saw no soldiers, no children, and no sign of any living being. He rubbed his neck to ease the tension from holding his breath and forcing his body to lie stiff and still. Poor Murphy. He must be ready for some position other than his form as a robotic ball. He deemed it was safe enough to pull Murphy from the backpack.

Murphy was ready for a good scratch behind the ears and was in a half pant when the hackles on the back of his neck stood up and a low sound seemed to seep out of Murphy's suddenly tense body. Before Theo could put a reassuring hand on his back, Murphy lunged under the porch and into a crawlspace beneath the building. Reacting to grab Murphy's collar, Theo dove through the two-foot square hole in the wall and found himself drowning in darkness under the floor of the building.

Control! Theo hissed in his mind as he tried to listen beyond the blood pulsing in his ears. Through the pitch darkness, he was sure he could still hear Murphy's gravelly growl. Digging his elbows and the toes of his shoes into the ground, he crawled forward promising himself that Murphy's sound was truly getting louder. He must get to Murphy to prevent capture. Besides, Theo needed the language transmitter within reception distance to understand the foreign language of the raspy voices he could hear from above. He was so intent in his crawl that he nearly buried his nose into Murphy's soft fur. He knew that Murphy could smell his master's presence, so Theo quietly nuzzled into Murphy and put his hand on Murphy's raised hackles.

"Sh-h-h-h!" Murphy allowed his master's petting to bring him down into a sitting position. The pressure of the darkness felt damp as they lay on the ground, listening to the voices above. Regardless of how Theo strained his eyes, the blue pulsing light of the language transmitter was the only thing visible in the crawl space.

"*Späh! Er ist der Regierung schuldig.*" Even though the voice above was gravelly and deep through the thick floorboards above the crawlspace where boy and dog lay, the transmitter around Murphy's neck made the heavy sound into words Theo could understand. *Späh, owes the government?* he turned the words over in his mind before he whispered to Murphy. "I don't know what Spah means. Is that a name, a place, or what?" Murphy looked at his owner through his glassy robotic eyes. "I must be letting my imagination run away with me. I'd swear I know that voice. Next thing you know, Murphy, I'll be going crazy." Theo lay still with his thoughts moving through the sludge of jumbled words in his brain. "I just feel I know that voice." The blinking lights on Murphy's transmitter collar let him know that the activity in the room above was continuing with intensity. "I wish

I knew what is going on," he looked at Murphy and whispered to the big eyes staring back at him.

Even in the dark, Murphy's low, constant growl was sensing something wrong, something evil. Just inches apart, boy and dog listened. "Murph, stay quiet so I can hear. That voice, Murph. I know it … but who?"

Theo tried to look into the eyes next to him. An image flashed in his mind. "Gun? Of course they have guns, Murph …" He didn't finish before he gasped from the sensation of being doused with water. "Murph, what's happening? Do you see anything? Why a gun? Water? What's the—" Again his thought was interrupted, but this time by the voice above coming through Murphy's translator collar. "I will kill Späh, but first, my plan. Do you forget that I have power that even the Reich doesn't understand? No one can understand my book!"

"Book? Why a … Brack! Murphy! It's him! He'll kill me! You know where we are, Murph? Remember the notes in the book—*back to the beginning, 1933!*" Theo swallowed hard and put his hand on Murphy's back. "We're there, Murphy—Brack's time jump. It must have been to Nazi Germany, and we're there!" He tightly squeezed his eyes and let his tight fists pound the hardened dirt at his sides.

Theo and Murphy lay silently with their heads resting on the cold winter ground. "We have to fight, Murphy. Nazi Germany, Murph. We have to fight until Dad gets us home. You and me, buddy. We have to fight." As if boyhood was washed away with the sprinklers in the explosion of Brack Towers, manhood came up from the dust of the ground under a cabin of Nazi Germany.

"I need to get outta here!" He turned and began to belly-crawl back to the edge of the building. Murphy did his best belly crawl like his master even though he barely needed to duck his head to walk under the building. As Theo reached the hole where he entered the crawl space, he turned to his companion. "Okay, Murphy, it's probably best if you stay in the backpack for now. I'm just going out to take a quick look around, and then I'll be back to get you. For now, I'll leave you in the backpack under these porch stairs. Now, stay quiet but keep your sensors on. Your sense of smell may come in handy getting out of this place!" He gently picked up Murphy as the dog rolled into a robotic ball that fit snuggly into the backpack. Theo pushed the backpack up under the stairs and inhaled, "Here I go," as he crawled back out into the dark night.

Theo sat in the shadow of the building as he scanned the grounds. *Yari and the others were taken to my left. Look, look!* he ordered his brain as he strained his eyes to look in the distance. *Where are the stars when I need them?* He fought exasperation in his mind. It wasn't that he couldn't see buildings in the dark. The mass of several buildings brought even more dark to the terrain. The puzzle for Theo to solve was determining which building looked like it could have a flicker of light surrounded by a boxcar load of children. *Sitting here is getting me nowhere.* He lurched out into the dark. *I have to find them!*

Theo was surprised how quietly he could move through the dark, and he almost laughed remembering how he used to play like a spy and sneak up on Murphy sleeping on his cozy dog pillow back home. The first building wasn't as large as the one he just left, so he wasted no time inching along the side to find a window. He found the window easily enough, but it was too high for Theo to see anything except a dim light hanging from a cord in the wooden ceiling. He moved along the side of the building where the ground sloped upward and the building seemed to angle down into the ground. The slope made the window at the back of the building low enough for him to peek in by standing on his tip-toes. The light on the cord was at the other end of the building where it outlined the shape of a man. Just inside the window he saw tables covered with rows of dark forms. They lay motionless like cold steel. *Guns!* Theo shivered a little from the night air and quite a bit from the realization of what he saw on the table. He didn't understand in a camp with only a dozen or so guards that he had seen, why so many guns? One thing he knew, Yari and the others weren't in this building.

He turned so quickly, he almost tumbled down the slope as he took a step to begin his stealth to the next building. As he rounded the first building, he could hear noises—not talking, but rustling sounds—coming from a building across the path. With a quick glance through the dark night, Theo plunged out into the open and squatted as he ran across the path toward the building of noises.

That was almost too easy, Theo thought to himself as he flattened himself panting against the wall of the building. He strained his ears to discern the noise. It was almost a scratchy sound with a background of little whimpers. He caught his breath as he inhaled. "Whispers!" he mouthed to himself. He listened to the mutters in the dark. "The kids!"

Keeping his body flattened against the side of the building, he turned his head. Again, above him was a window set too high for him to see in. Theo looked out across the shadowy grounds. He needed something to stand on. He needed to see in the window! Nothing seemed to appear in the darkness to help him. He mentally enumerated what he saw as he scanned the ground. "Rocks, piece of pipe or something long, dirt, wood pile, axe, wad of something ... Wait!" Theo flipped his eyes back to the woodpile. "That's it!" He dropped to a squat to crawl on hands and feet to the woodpile. "If I can find the right log ..."

He moved his hands over the stacked wood. "Figures," he sighed to himself as he found a log with a diameter larger than his palm. It was buried beneath five or six logs, but Theo lost little time moving the wood to uncover the larger piece. It wasn't until he pulled the larger log out of the pile that Theo realized his fingers were scratched and sticky from moving the rough logs. "Well, I've never heard of anyone bleeding to death by digging a log from a woodpile," he bolstered himself as he bent over the log he cradled in both arms and returned to the building of whispers.

This will be a trick, Theo thought as he stood the log on end under a window at the back of the building. He lifted one foot to the top of the log in an effort to hold the log and keep it from falling. *Where's a ladder when I need one?* He tried to humor himself as he gave a quick bounce with his right foot still on the ground. As he extended his left leg, he reached with both hands for the window sill. It wasn't much of a window frame, but he was able to get a pretty good grip with both scratched hands. He straightened his leg until he stood high enough on the wobbly log to lean his chest against the window frame. "Uhh!" a soft voice inhaled just as Theo's face appeared in the frame. The building had window frames with no glass and he found himself face-to-face with a small child.

"Sh-h-h!" Theo reacted to the boy inside the window. "It's me—the boy from the boxcar," he whispered. "Where's Yari? Do you speak English?" The young boy made no reply, but he heard a shuffling sound from inside as he half focused on not falling from his wobbly perch. After many long seconds, Yari's face appeared. "*Vas tustu?*" he hissed in his Yiddish tongue, asking what Theo was doing.

"I got separated from you, and I didn't know ..." Before Theo could finish, he felt a sharp pain across his back, and he lost his footing and fell to the ground. He winced as his head hit the ground. As he tried to raise up on an arm, he felt like a rocket hit his shoulder. "Ow," he instinctively reacted as he realized he was hearing voices he could not understand and feeling cold round metal on his face.

"*Steh auf!*" the gruff voice came with a kick to his back. "Okay, okay, I'll get up!" Theo reacted as he rolled up to his feet. Even in the dark, he could tell this was worse than being pulled from the boxcar. Uncomprehending, his body moved ahead of the nudges cold steel. "Guns." Theo caught the word in his throat as he remembered seeing through the window the rows of cold steel.

Shoved by the end of a gun, Theo tripped up the stairs at the front of the building. He half crawled, half squatted as he shuffled through the door thrown open in front of him. Silently, with his mouth hanging open, he fell into a heap on the floor, surrounded by the children of the boxcar. Yari stood in the middle of the half circle that closed in around him. *Willkommen kleiner Spion!* Two other soldiers laughed as the man with the gun called him a little spy. The door was slammed and fastened behind him.

Yari squatted beside Theo. Knowing the boy lying on the floor would not understand his Yiddish tongue, he put one hand on the stranger's shoulder and extended the other hand to help him to his feet. Yari reached into his pocket and took out a scrap of paper. He handed the paper and pointed to the new boy's side. Theo nodded and tucked the paper into the pocket of his jeans. The children moved into huddled groups. Theo followed their movements and waited as he wondered what was happening and why these children were captives.

Night continued silent except for a nightmarish whimper or moan from the boxcar children. Theo was trying to shake the cold night and the dark as a ray of light jostled with his eyelids. Pulling himself up to a sitting position, he tried to remember the events just hours ago and the faces of the dark. Boots were stomping on the porch of the building and the door was kicked open. The breaking dawn was a contradiction to the dark figures that stood in the doorway.

"*Steh auf!*" the guards shouted as they entered and used their guns to move the children who scattered into a tight circle. "*Verschieben!*" In the dusky light a soldier near Theo tripped over a woolen coat on the floor. With a surly guffaw, the soldier lifted the coat with the barrel of his gun and flung the coat toward Theo. Without taking his eyes off the soldier, Theo quickly put on the coat, causing a sinister laugh to come from the taunting man. The soldiers choked on their laughter as the mass of children were forced through the door and into the breaking daylight. Theo looked for a way to escape, but he could not escape the mass being moved inside a ring of a thirty or more guards holding guns and joining in the laughter as they poked at the children with the cold steel. He became aware that except for his own heavy breathing, the children were silent with sad eyes staring ahead as they were goaded along a path where the frozen snow had not been broken. About 30 meters past the last building, Theo wondered why they were in an open field, when the mass stopped moving.

"*Ihre Schuhe ausziehen!*" The children seemed hesitant with the foreign words until Yari dropped down and began to unlace his shoes. Children of the boxcar, including Theo, began to follow Yari's lead as they removed their shoes. Prodded by the guns, children were moved to stand in a circle. Each child was moved forward until his toes met the edge of a large hole that had been dug nearly four meters into the ground. Theo shivered and squeezed back tears that were burning around his eyes. The men chuckled and made menacing noises as they placed black rags around the eyes of each child. He stood and closed his eyes and tried to gain strength from Yari who stood tall with fists clenched. He felt his head jerked back as a cloth was tied around his head, pushing against his stinging eyes. Forcing his eyes to look down and see out the bottom of the blindfold, Theo could see the feet of Yari standing next to him on the rim of the pit. *"Yahweh. . .,"* Yari spoke aloud with a voice that barely quivered until a gunshot abruptly stopped his words. Theo collapsed in blackness.

By nightfall, the stars broke out across the sky. It was if a star was brightly shining for each of the boxcar children who were mercilessly executed and tumbled into the death pit. Not even the slight wind passing over the sad and silent mound of children made much more than a wisp of mourning.

Pain shot through Theo's leg. In a semi-conscious state, he lay unable to move. *Was this death? What has happened?* The thoughts in Theo's mind seemed as compressed as the air around him. *Think. Breathe. Think*, he willed himself. *If I am feeling pain, I must be alive.* Stifled in darkness and compression against his body, Theo realized his breaths were shallow and slow. Sight was not to come. Even an attempt to see through his half-masked eyelids was futile. Again, he realized pain was coming from his leg, but he could not reason why his body yielded to pressure and rejected his brain's commands to move. He lay, content to commit to thought before trying again to move. He remembered the men, the guns, the pit, Yari—Yari's words, the shots. Other than remembering that it had been daybreak, he could recall no more.

With sheer determination to stretch from his confines, Theo realized his left arm was extended above him. In the still darkness, he began to wiggle his fingers first for reassurance that he was able to feel his own hand and then to see what else he could recognize by touch. Movement was slow, and the reception of touch was sending little understanding to his brain. Yet there was something familiar under the palm of his hand. Bending fingers, opening fingers, moving his hand back and forth in small and what seemed insignificant progress,

Theo slowly began to discern what he touched. Although small, was it a hand? Or a foot? He gently squeezed, but the appendage gave no response by flinch or movement. Theo knew he had to move—even if the nerves in his leg coursed in pain. One hand had movement, so he set his mind to use every fiber of his being to writhe and move until he could press back against the pressures that encapsulated him. Finding his legs stronger than his arms, he rocked back and forth until his right leg was able to pull up, shifting pressures, and then press down against whatever lay below him. Mentally, Theo wanted to be an earthworm moving upward through the darkness, but his mind instead pictured that he was caught in a net. Again, he rocked and pressed out with his elbows as he raised his right leg against the pressures and again pressed back down against something using his toes to propel himself upward through the netting of woven bodies of children shot to death on the brink of the pit and on the brink of beginning their lives.

For the better part of an hour, Theo writhed and inched and pushed back against the pressures. He was exhausted but afraid that if he quit moving, he would be sucked back down into the abyss from which he had struggled. Just as he was taking in as large a breath as the pressures would allow, he let out an abrupt scream as fingers latched onto his extended arm. Fighting the urge to scream and to cry, Theo feared any more sound would bring his ruin, so he lay unflinching in the darkness. With a pulsing sensation of movement, he felt the fingers tighten and relax, tighten and relax, tighten and relax. Half through determination and half through reflex, his arm muscle bulged and tightened. The pulsing fingers lay still. Theo waited. Again, the fingers tightened and relaxed in a pulsating pattern until Theo intentionally flexed his arm muscle. The fingers stopped. Then, as if hungry for touch, the fingers extended as the hand writhed in an effort to touch more than the arm, to touch a shoulder. Shirking any fear, Theo wanted the touch, wanted to know the hand, and he too began to make movement to roll toward the searching hand. Theo struggled with more intensity to move upward as the hand grasped his arm and moved with him. *Move. Rest. Press back. Don't cry. Move. Rest. Press back. Fight harder.*

The silent pressures of the night and of the pit seemed unyielding. Yet two boys, unfamiliar to each other and determined to be indestructible, continued for two hours to press upward until one breathed the fresh night air. The air filled Theo's lungs compressed in his body and drove him to press harder to free his body and to bring the other struggling victim to the top. Another half hour passed before he was able to half sit, half stand, still caught in the pressures and reach both arms under the arms and around the shoulders of the other boy who shared his struggle. Together, the two fought harder to free themselves. With more strength than he knew he had, Theo gave a final tug as both boys were able to lie back at the top of the pit and pull their legs to freedom. In silence, the two boys lay looking at the stars that blanketed the sky, half-frightened to look at their surroundings.

A sharp pain shot through Theo's leg reminding him of what woke him from his unconscious state three hours earlier. He sat up and rubbed his leg. He didn't feel any conspicuous bumps to suggest a break, but movement was definitely painful. In rubbing the flow of blood back into his leg, Theo stopped to look where he was sitting. He glanced over at the empty stare of the boy next to him. It was then that he realized that they were sitting on bodies, bodies of the children of the boxcar, brutally shot and left in a pit destined to be their grave. Uncontrollably, his body shook from the trauma of the sight. No flood of tears and no silent gags as his stomach rejected the murders could calm the upheaval of his soul.

Nearly a quarter of an hour passed before Theo could convince himself to move. Lifting a hand in silence, he reached for the hand of the boy and urged him to follow. Together they crawled over the lifeless pile and reached the rim of the ground where they had stood in blindfolds the morning of that same day. The boy extended an arm and pointed away from the rows of buildings; Theo understood. Slowly, the two crawled close to the ground until they could stand against the mound of dirt that had been extracted from the ground. He knew they needed to give their bodies time to accept the flow of blood to reinstate mental and muscular strength that had been suppressed in the pit, but he also knew the night would not last and allow a covert escape. He looked at the boy who was smaller in size, probably even three or four years younger. He reached out and touched the arm of the boy who flinched as Theo broke the daze that had momentarily captured the youth. Both boys turned away from the buildings and began a staggered run across an open field to a hedgerow that would shield them from sight. The pounding of the boys' heavy feet and labored breaths seemed to beat the pace as a drum of war to encourage their escape.

Just as he stretched out his arm to touch the bark of a tree in the hedgerow, Theo realized the only sound of beating was his own heart and breath. He turned to see where the other young boy had fallen. Indifferent to the openness of the field, he turned and ran back until he too fell to land beside the boy. Facedown and still, the boy did not move. Theo rolled the youth to his back, exposing an expressionless and lifeless face. The yellow star on the boy's coat seemed as radiant as those in the sky, shining to pay homage to the boy, to Yari, and to the other young martyrs left behind. Theo turned to head for the protection of the tree line but stopped and turned back to the lifeless boy. Without knowing why, he reached down and ripped the star off the boy's coat. He closed his fingers around the star scrunched in his hand. With his head tipped back, the young time traveler vowed to the stars.

"I promise, Yari, I won't forget you, this boy, or any of the children." With wild instinct, Theo scurried to his feet where he stumbled and ran as the tears that had caught in his throat exploded under the cover of the woods.

CHAPTER 6

Dark's Passing

Another hour of night passed before Theo was able to recover from the struggles and the tears of mental and physical fatigue. The tears had been replaced with rage and anger; Brack was responsible for all this. He squeezed the yellow star in his hand one last time, then put it back in his pocket. Brack had manipulated his father and used his life's work to become a murderer of children. He had to do something. He heard his father's last words echo in his ears. But if his dad had known this would be the end result of his vision, he would never have attempted to build the TimeWorm or asked Theo to stay away from Brack. He sat in the silence, fuming but knowing he must escape but not before going back for Murphy. The brilliance of the starry night lent him sight but also threatened exposure in the death camp. He mentally traced a path of return to the first building. Crossing the open field was risky. He would need to use the covert of the woods, which arched at least a mile around the camp. Night would not last, and several hours had already been spent escaping from the pit. Theo rose with renewed strength and determination to return to Murphy.

Thoughts of the past day, past night, and plans for the night ahead swirled in continuous circles through Theo's brain as he trotted through the woods surrounding the camp. *Funny,* he thought as he jumped over a small stream and missed landing on the dry bank, *how I used to complain about getting my shoes messed up in puddles that splashed onto my driftboard, and now I don't even care if I splash mud up to my knees!* The terrain through the woods gave little resistance even as the snowy leaves and streams scarcely slowed his even pace. He felt secure in the woods as he could see the first building loom larger in the dark night as he approached from the back. Theo paused at the edge of the wood, allowing his eyes to canvass as much of the camp as he could see in the starlit night. He had come too far to risk being caught again. He knew he wouldn't be allowed to escape death a second time. He was still a long distance from the building where he and Murphy had listened from beneath the floor. *Oh, well. I'll just mark off the distance in my mind as I imagine I'm crawling the length of a football field.* Theo dropped to a squat for the first half of the distance and then down to his knees for a tedious crawl through the snowy field. He was sure he didn't breathe for the last several minutes until he reached the back corner of the building. He heard no sounds and even saw no vehicles as the camp now seemed abandoned. *Still,* he assured himself, *I will not take any risks.* He inched to the front of the building, staying as close to both building and ground as possible. He rounded the corner, rose enough to take one last look into the dark street through the camp, and dropped flat on his stomach to finish his trek to the open side of the porch steps. Theo almost cried when he saw his backpack, but he knew he had to grab it and get away from the camp in a matter of minutes. Tossing the backpack across his shoulder, Theo retraced his crawl along the side of the building and sprinted back into the woods.

Another football-field length of running into the woods, and Theo dropped into a hollow of bushes. He opened his backpack, allowing Murphy to unroll and cover his master with slobbery kisses of excitement. He fell back to the ground and lay exhausted beside his friend. A quick look at his watch reminded him that he was still out of satellite reach for communication with IRIS. He looked at the compass hanging from his backpack. He wished he had listened better when the instructor at summer camp had taught orienteering. Who needed a compass back home? He wouldn't have one now except that it came as part of the backpack. "Okay, Murph. Between what I can remember about using a compass and what you can do with your instincts, we need to find a way out of here until I can get where IRIS can direct me with a map. I don't know where I am, but north always seemed to work for the slaves Mr. Medi talked about in history class. Let's head for freedom!"

Theo dug down into his backpack and pulled out a box of nutrition bars that IRIS had insisted he put into his backpack before he left for his dad's lab. Downing a full bar and starting into a second one, he looked at Murphy and muttered through a mouthful of nutritional granola, "I really need to thank IRIS for this." Murphy just wagged his robotic tail. He zipped his backpack, and boy and dog started off on their journey. Finishing his second nutrition bar, Theo started to throw the wrapper on the ground, but in the back of his head, he could hear IRIS in her monotone computer voice reprimanding, "Now, Theodore, what if all people dropped trash, leaving their germs and filth for others to see?" He grinned to himself. "Okay, IRIS. I don't know how to contact you, but I can still hear you!" He crumpled the wrapper and shoved it into the pocket of his jeans.

As he did so, he felt the paper Yari had passed to him the previous night in the cabin of the boxcar children. "Hey, Murphy! Let's see how your transmitter does with Yiddish!" Theo squatted down as Murphy trotted over. The blue lights on the transmitter collar were pulsing with color. He passed the note under Murphy's collar and heard a translation through his earbud, "Maximilian Kolbe."

"Hmmm. I don't know that guy, but maybe he's related to Yari. At any rate, I'll ask about him when we reach a town."

Within half an hour, Theo and Murphy reached a road that passed beside the grove of trees where they walked. Following the road by staying in the cover of the trees, the two were able to walk and rest undetected even though only three cars had used the road while the two traveled beside it. By evening, Theo was getting tired. He had already tucked Murphy back into the backpack to prevent overusing energy and allowing Murphy time to recharge. "At least the road is paved," he sighed as he climbed out of the ditch and walked along the shoulder of the road. Dusk was beginning to settle when a car passed and slowed to a stop. Theo didn't know whether to run back into the woods or take his chances. "I'm too tired and hungry to run," he admitted in a murmur as he continued to walk up the road toward the stopped car. Intending to keep his head down as he walked past the stopped car, Theo glanced over when he heard the car door open. A lady who looked the age his mother should have been stood up and looked at him as he approached her car.

"*Guten Tag.*" Without being noticed, Theo slightly unzipped his backpack a little to better engage the language translator from Murphy's collar. He did not respond to the lady but, rather, stood with a knot in his throat as he wondered if a pretty lady in women's shoes could outrun him if need be.

"Do you need a ride?" the lady asked. Theo shook his head. The lady sat back down in her car, leaned across the seat, and pulled the handle on the passenger side to unlatch the door. Hesitantly, then resigned with no other plan, Theo turned to walk to the middle of the road where he could get into the passenger seat on the left side of the car. He pulled his backpack around to hold in his lap as the lady continued driving up the road.

"You seem rather young to be out here on a desolate road by yourself," the lady suggested. Theo was concentrating on simultaneously memorizing the land outside the car and searching the car for any weapons the woman could use to hurt him. "Do you talk?"

"Oh, I'm sorry," Theo responded when he realized she was talking to him. "Uh, no, um, I mean, well, I'm looking for my uncle, Maximilian Kolbe." He wondered if he sounded convincing.

The lady smiled and looked intently at Theo. "What's your name?" She studied the boy closely but didn't see any remnant of a yellow star. She was puzzled by his appearance on the road.

"Theo." He wondered if he should have made up a name but suddenly found quick thinking was not his forte.

"So, Theo, you're looking for your uncle?"

"Yes."

"Hmmm. I was unaware that Father Kolbe had any family in these parts. Everyone around here knows how to find him. I happen to be traveling to Warsaw tomorrow, anyway. This must be your lucky day." The woman ended and smiled kindly even though Theo's stomach was doing flip-flops. If only he had a way to talk with IRIS and find out what she meant with the name Father Maximilian Kolbe and whether he was good or bad.

Startled, Theo jerked awake as the car came to a stop many miles and several hours farther up the road. "Why don't we grab a bite to eat, Theo? This is my home. I live on the outskirts of Warsaw. I'll take you to 'your uncle' if he can wait for you to arrive tomorrow morning. It's getting late, and my husband and I don't mind a houseguest. My name is Emilie." Without allowing him a chance to accept or decline, the lady stepped from her car and started toward a quaint home. At first Theo sat frozen in the front seat of the car as he watched the woman walk away. *Did she punctuate the words* your uncle? *What if this is a trap? Why does she just walk away without seeing if I will follow? Am I reading too much into the lady giving me a ride?* The thoughts tumbled in his mind until he couldn't think what was right or wrong about anything since the lady stopped at the side of the road to give him a ride. Slowly and feeling numb, Theo emerged from the car and looked around. The neighborhood was simple and quiet. Nothing seemed threatening. This had to be right. Besides, a meal and a night's rest were long overdue.

"Come along," the lady urged via Murphy's language translator collar as she smiled and opened the front door. "Oskar. Come and meet a young man I found wandering the road!"

Theo walked toward the house, wondering why he wasn't frightened to meet Oskar.

Theo opened his eyes but lay very still in the small metal-frame bed. Murphy had snuggled down until he lay under the covers beside Theo's left ankle. The light penetrating the curtains of the room didn't hint of sunlight, but it seemed calming, nonetheless. Theo looked around the room, refusing to move the heavy quilt that was tucked under his chin. Nothing he saw was alarming. Nothing he saw was familiar. Yet the room with rugs that covered the cold boards beckoned him to stay tucked in the bed. Slowly, he pulled his left wrist from below the comforter.

"IRIS," he exhaled to the wrist that he had pulled beside his left cheek. "IRIS, please IRIS," Theo whispered, waiting in the quiet, receiving no response. He turned his wrist receiver until he could see the time. His thoughts still seemed scrambled, even though he felt more rested than he had felt for a long time. He stretched his legs, pumping his calf muscles both to rejuvenate his leg strength and to encourage the blood to waken his body. The movement against a dog down at his ankle made him smile as he remembered his little buddy who had come so far with him since the explosion at the lab. Before he could flex his muscles in his shoulders and move from where he lay, a wriggling beagle did its own stretching and shimmied along Theo's side until Murphy's friendly face popped out from under the quilt and plopped a friendly head between his master's chin and chest.

"Well, good morning to you too, little buddy!" Theo grinned for the first time in days as he rubbed Murphy's fur-covered metal head. Even Murphy's thumping tail wagging back and forth could scarcely move the heavy quilt. Boy and dog, friend and companion, adventurer and guardian—they were in this together, and neither felt threatened in the tiny bed of a stranger's home.

Together boy and dog crawled from the cocoon of warmth, dressed, and crossed the room to the door with a porcelain knob. Theo opened the door and was met with the warmth of a kitchen and kind expressions from the faces of the people he only knew as Oskar and Emilie.

"*Guten Morgen*," Emilie said as Oskar walked toward their visitor with an outstretched arm.

"*Setz dich,*" Oskar gestured as he swung his arm from the teen to a bench beside a table with a blue-and-yellow patterned tablecloth. "You must eat as you have a busy day ahead," he continued as Theo walked toward the table, keeping Murphy close so the language transmitter could keep the secret that he was a foreigner who did not know the German language. Oskar laughed as Murphy scampered onto the bench so close to his master that Theo sat on his tail. A half yap, half growl emitted from Murphy so quickly that the teenager jumped, and all laughed as Murphy swung his backside to prevent any more mishaps.

Even though Theo would not be able to understand Oskar or Emilie without Murphy's language transmitter collar, he felt safe in the kitchen as he sat eating a warm breakfast of porridge, eggs, toast, and a roasted tomato.

By midmorning Theo and Murphy were sitting in the front seat of the car with Emilie sitting in the driver's seat wearing a trim blue dress, blue hat with slight veil and feather, navy-blue Mary Jane shoes, and a tender smile on lips of ruby red. Theo tried not to stare at Emilie, but he thought she probably looked a lot like his mom would look. He missed his mom, and he felt no shame in pretending he was riding beside his mom on this particular morning. He squeezed his eyes shut and leaned his head back against the seat until the warm sun shining through the window gave him a reason to look out the window and watch the countryside pass until he could turn his thoughts back to the challenges that lay ahead of him.

"Emilie," Theo finally bolstered himself enough to see if the kind lady could help with the puzzle of the mysterious name. "Do you know Herr Kolbe?" He asked the question while looking out the window as he had learned to wait for the lag time needed for Murphy's transmitter to convey the question in German. Within seconds, he turned to look at Emilie who continued to face the road but allowed her eyes to smile.

"*Herr* Kolbe? Of course, I know *Father* Kolbe. He has always helped me when I find youth walking alone on the road," she added as if she wanted to give a hint to Theo. He looked at the road ahead, trying to understand but having more questions instead. The lady named Emilie seemed to read his mind.

"He will help with whatever need you have. You will be in good hands."

This time Theo returned her smile, content to ask no more questions and finish the ride to Warsaw in the quiet warmth of the sunshine and of the compassion of strangers named Oskar and Emilie.

Theo was excited to see the change of scenery as the city of Warsaw brought a busyness of activity. He realized he had almost pressed his face against the side window of Emilie's car. Even Murphy was vying for window space to look out on the busy world. "Wow," he said aloud, not in conversation to anyone but himself, "this city could be my home. The buildings look a lot like the old ones in Dad's complex ..."

The sudden memory of his dad made a lump suddenly swell in his throat. His thoughts continued, but his voice was only in his head. He couldn't risk even this nice Emilie woman knowing about the TimeWorm fiasco.

Don't worry, Dad. I'm not sure where you are or how you're doing, but I won't let you down! I'll find Brack and get back that book with the sketch of the TimeWorm. I'll do it, Dad. I'll get back to you!

His thoughts became overpowering and almost a whirlwind of the explosion, Brack's face, Yari, words overheard at the concentration camp, Emilie, and Father Kolbe—whoever that might be. Theo gave his eyes a quick and hard squeeze shut, one: to refuse any tears making his eyes swell in their sockets and two: to clear his vision for a good look around in case he needed to plan an escape from this foreign place. *Huh! Who would have guessed I'd be living in a HoloGame! Maybe playing all those "brain-drain games," as IRIS called them, will help me with some street smarts.* He found himself grinning to the world outside the window. He almost breathed out loud, "Bring it on!"

As the car slowed to a stop, Theo turned to look out of Emilie's side window. She had driven up to a narrow but tall stucco building that had two big wooden doors. He liked the look of the doors and thought it was cool that each door was rimmed in metal. Where the doors met, the twisted iron handles were horizontal and big. The handles extended outward and made the doors look like they suspended a big iron cross. He hadn't been to church since his dad started working so many hours on the TimeWorm, but he knew a good sign when he saw one. He moved swiftly with an accelerated heartbeat. "Murphy, it's time for you to take a nap." In an instant, Murphy took his cue and rolled into a ball to be placed in the backpack.

"Nun, Jakob, sollen wir deinen Onkel kennenlernen?" Emilie was speaking, but her words were difficult to understand.

Oh no! I forgot to leave my backpack unzipped enough to allow Murphy's transmitter collar to pick up the language! Theo inhaled his unspoken thoughts and unzipped about two inches of his pack all in one quick move. *I guess no one would have understood me, either!* The thought of confusion for all made him grin. He didn't speak but turned, nodded to the nice lady, and reached for the door handle. *I wonder if IRIS would call this a classic car.* He pushed open the heavy door on the 1935 Opel Olympia.

The inside of the little church had a heavy smell of aged and musty wood, but Theo intentionally drew in his breath as if to pull in the comfort of the dark. This building wasn't like his church back home, and he had never been in such an old building that was still in use. Yet there seemed to be a calm heaviness that beckoned to his soul. He stood in the quiet and let his eyes survey the dark oak surroundings, high ceiling, and colored glass windows. The smell—yes, that was it—the smell pulled from his memory the strong and almost floral aroma of the church during his mother's funeral. *I thought my science teacher said I couldn't recall smell.* Theo smirked to himself. *Wait, no, I can't recall smell but smell can recall memory. Gee, no wonder I got so confused on tests!* He was content to wait in the silence to allow himself time to think of his past life with his mother, but the heavy whooshing sigh of a door and the nearly muted sound of someone walking across the wooden floor caused him to turn his head in curiosity.

"Willkommen, Theo!" Flipping the backpack half under his arm to allow the unzipped side to pick up what sounds were able to convey in the dense air, the young man turned to the voice. Father Kolbe was not at all what Theo expected. Just the moniker of *Father* made him suppose he would be meeting a corpulent, older man whose sage face was marked with wrinkles. Instead, Father Kolbe was a slender man. His square jaw and cleft chin seemed to compete with the round glasses he wore. Although Father Kolbe scarcely had an abundance of hair, the fair stubble didn't seem to age him. In fact, Father Kolbe looked much younger even than his new friend Emilie, even younger than his own father. The robes Father Kolbe wore hid but did not disguise the physique of a muscular frame. Theo took such mental

note because although he had not known this man longer than his presence in the room, Father Kolbe's arm extended for a hand on his shoulder and warm smile expressed that they had known each other for years as dear friends. A fleeting thought in Theo's mind suggested that perhaps instead of meeting a kind priest he had met a guardian angel—a prophecy that later held true.

Emilie reached out to the youth from the roadway and cupped the side of his head in her delicate hand as she looked him in the eye. "Theo, you are in good hands here. Although he doesn't know you or your family, Father Kolbe will see that you get where you need to go. You and Murphy are safe." In a gentle movement, Emilie's hand dropped to his shoulder, gave a quick pat, and swung down to her side as she pivoted and left the church. With the past few days of extreme tempest followed by calm, Theo had learned to have no expectations. So he did not understand the sudden tightness in his heart as he turned to watch Emilie walk out of the church and out of his life.

"Thank you," he rushed, too late for Emilie to hear as the oak door and cross closed behind her.

"Well, let me gather a snack for the road and a few belongings before we begin the next leg of your journey." Father Kolbe broke into the silence.

"Are we going somewhere?" Theo wasn't averse to leaving. He didn't know what he would do if he stayed. In truth, he didn't know what to think or even what to plan to do.

"I want to know how best to help you, Theo," Father Kolbe continued. "But I have an appointment in another town, and I think it will be better for you too, where you can get 'lost in the crowd,' so to speak. You don't seem to have the fair hair or light blue eyes that could ensure your safety wandering the highways of the countryside where Emilie found you."

Hmph. Theo knitted his eyebrows but tried to hide his confusion. *Even with Murphy's language translator, I can't understand what in the world this man means!* He shrugged his shoulders and readjusted his pack.

"Emilie said you are not alone. Does your friend need anything?"

Theo tilted his head just as he had seen Murphy do so many times when his owner had perplexed him. "Oh! Murphy!" Theo realized almost shouting as his voice raised in quick response to Father Kolbe. "No, he's fine. I mean, he doesn't need to eat, but he really might like being out of the backpack if that's okay with you. Can I just let him down—right here in the church?"

Father Kolbe laughed a robust laugh that put Theo quite at ease and left a smile on his face. "Well, you know, God does understand animals. He made them, you know, so I doubt if he minds having one wander through His house! Besides, when I was a boy, I wanted a pet very badly, so I won't mind at all having your little friend roam around."

Theo joined the laughter and unzipped the backpack nearly too slowly for the beagle who was already unrolling and ready to stretch his legs.

By early afternoon the young Father Kolbe, Theo, and Murphy were off on a road trip down the same highway Emilie had driven that morning. Although Father Kolbe didn't ask any prying questions, Theo found himself comfortably talking with his new friend about America, his driftboard—which Father Kolbe saw as part fantasy—and skating skills and spills, his dad, and even a little about his mom. He felt his heart skip a beat when Father Kolbe explained the pain of losing his two little brothers. The two found the pain of loss as a secret tie of brotherhood and even as a part of life. Theo found himself glancing sideways at the good priest, a new friend—a very, very good and trusted friend. Laughs were as free flowing as the brisk air coming in through the car windows. Murphy was joyfully perched between the two on the front bench seat of the sedan.

Eventually, Father Kolbe hit a serious note when he confessed, "I have a passion for the Lord's work, and that includes helping children like you."

"Like me?" Theo didn't mask the question in his voice.

"You seem to have a pretty happy outlook on life and a pretty carefree attitude, Theo, but surely you understand that you don't fit the profile of the Aryan this regime wants to keep around. As the government might see you as an *Untermensch*, a subhuman creature, it's best to find a way to protect you."

"I thought the Germans only hated the Jews!" Theo quipped back, wondering what else he had missed in old Medi's lectures.

"Perhaps it began that way, Theo," Father Kolbe explained. "Unfortunately, even the innocence of a child is of no worth these days." The young man watched Father Kolbe's bright eyes seem to dull and sadden.

For the most part, conversation was light, but moments of seriousness encroached as the highway signs made promise of approaching the town of Munich, Germany toward the end of their day of travel which began in the morning and ended well past midnight.

"There aren't many street lights in this city," Theo sighed as he was looking for adventure out the side window of the car.

"No, Theo. It's best we arrive in the dark of night for better cover," Father Kolbe said in a soft voice. "We can rest in the car for the remaining hours until daylight.

For the umpteenth time in one day Theo turned to look at Father Kolbe in an effort to understand his cryptic comments of stealth and secrecy. He had not felt alarm since he and Murphy had found a road to put distance between themselves and the camp of death where he lost his new friend Yari. But even a seventeen-year-old knew when to sit quietly and stop asking questions. The silhouette of Father Kolbe seemed to show nothing but calm and determination in this quest into Theo's unknown future.

The young traveler opened his eyes. "Uh, I ... uh," Theo sighed as he blinked his eyes and looked out the window trying to waken his thoughts. The road trip from Warsaw to Munich had taken the entirety of a day and started into a second. He had tried to stay awake the entire trip and had found their brief stops refreshing, but by daybreak the sunlight whispered that his eyes had closed.

"Nice nap?" Father Kolbe took a sideways glance at the boy and dog who were simultaneously beginning to stretch their legs as much as the confined passenger seat would allow. "We'll walk to a café that has a warm breakfast and a sweet-smelling aroma. It is one of my favorites and often one of my first stops in Munich."

Although Father Kolbe's snacks of bread, cheese, and warm milk throughout the journey had been good—actually, better than Theo would have guessed—his stomach was beginning to rumble after the long ride. He finished his stretch and reached for Murphy just as a thought gave him a moment of panic. "Oh, I don't have any money ... um, I don't have any German Marks!" Theo said a little too loudly. This was one time he had listened to Mr. Medi's lesson and knew the name of German currency. He had tried to bargain with Mr. Medi to raise his *grade mark* if he could find a *German mark*. Mr. Medi had retorted, "Whatever, Theo." The brief memory of home was ended by a kind offer from Father Kolbe.

"You and Murphy are my guests. There will be no cost for your meal."

"Oh. Murphy doesn't eat, I mean, Murphy will just eat from my scraps. I'll bring some from my plate if that's okay." Theo was learning to think fast on his feet. Keeping a robotic dog a secret was difficult when he looked and acted like a cuddly canine.

"You know best. Now let's not keep good cooks at the café waiting for customers. Here we go. It's just around the corner."

Murphy dropped to the seat and put his head between his front paws, doing his best to give a big-eyed look to Theo, but his promise to look cute and just stay in the car didn't work. Murphy relented and rolled into a ball as his master ignored his performance and unzipped the backpack.

Father Kolbe had parked his small Audi on a side-street where more bicycles than cars were parked until the owners could return. Theo tossed his backpack across his back and enjoyed the chance to stretch his legs as he kept a fast pace with Father Kolbe on their trek up the quaint street to the café. The combination of car ride, good company, and fresh air lightened the young man's spirits. He tried to mimic the lively step of his newest friend. He noticed how Father Kolbe walked with his head tilted a little back as if he were expecting a sign from heaven to drop a message or a miracle. Perhaps it was the calm demeanor or even the slight smile that formed across his face, but Theo was drawn to the man Yari chose as his protector.

Half out of courtesy and half out of ignorance of the language, Theo deferred to Father Kolbe and ordered the same meal. From the warmth of the café, a small table with two chairs by a window gave him a chance to enjoy the sight of the narrow street bordered with tall stone buildings. He noticed the alleyways were narrow like the buildings, a contrast to the city spread across wide blocks and thoroughfares where he called home. He found the food delicious and would have eaten it all had Father Kolbe not reminded him to "put away a bite for Murphy." Theo grinned and agreed as he rolled the last of a bratwurst with half of his *Bienenstich* in the wax paper wrapper that held the sweet yeast pastry. Secretly, he was glad to have the food tucked away for a later snack.

Father Kolbe excused himself to go inside the café to settle the cost of the meal. Theo relished the opportunity to move his backpack to his lap as he sat back to enjoy watching the people move along the streets. He scarcely seemed to be thinking any thoughts at all when he scrunched up his nose in reaction to a horrid smell that had overtaken the sweet smell of the café. He started to turn in his chair when the smell became so strong, he thought his stomach would give up the breakfast he just ate. A black-gloved hand landed across his shoulder just as he caught a glimpse of a shadow of a man covered in a coat that hung to the tops of black boots that laced up the front. With the balance he used to turn his driftboard, Theo stood and careened out from under the grip of the gloved hand. He scarcely glanced at the coated figure of stench, for his eyes first landed on a face he knew too well.

"*Guten Tag*, Theodore," Viktor Brack grinned with the good day greeting. "I see that you have made some interesting new friends."

In an instant, Theo knew he needed to run—run away from the horror of Viktor Brack which meant running away from his dear protector, Maximilian Kolbe.

CHAPTER 7

Unknown

Youth and driftboarding skills were Theo's strengths as he ran without looking behind him and without hesitation. He could feel the weight of Murphy as the backpack jostled against him as he ran an uneven and winding course. He didn't know who or what could smell that bad, it was almost inhuman, but he knew the danger of Viktor Brack. Only later would he know the driving force behind his father's former friend.

Viktor Brack, scientist of the 21st Century, had inherited the journal of his namesake and was determined to live the life of his great-grandfather, a scientist and an officer of the Third Reich in 20th Century Nazi Germany. Theo remembered his dad's warning to avoid Brack, but never did he dream that jumping to the same country would put him back in the path of the madman.

The streets were beginning to darken. The height of the buildings and the narrow streets and alleys did little to allow the winter sun to offer light to the dusky Schlachthof borough. He ran from the area where the cafés and pubs provided a means of hiding among the patrons enjoying their meals. People brought too many unknown faces, and he couldn't risk being seen by evil men. The slaughterhouses of the same borough, however, provided dark corners and cattle pens to cover him from sight. He ran through two pens before he squatted in a fenced corner to regain his breath and to think of a plan to find the book and to escape a city where he could not hide until his dad could time jump him back home.

While he squatted in the corner of the fences forming the stock-yard corral, Theo slid off his pack and pulled it around where he could curl around it and tuck the pack and Murphy inside his arms. He waited for what seemed an eternity. The smells of the stockyards were strong, but they were not as unpleasant as the odious smell of the man—or beast—that lay hand upon him at the restaurant. He smiled as he realized his pack was moving and a snout could be heard inching along the inside of the zipper. He unzipped just enough of the backpack to reassure Murphy that the two of them were still together in the foreign city.

"If only I could contact IRIS to let Dad know we're okay but ready to get back home as soon as we get our hands on that book! I don't understand why my connections aren't working. We have all the modern technology ... oh, duh, modern technology. Ugh. Let me think. I know Brack's jump had something to do with 1933. What did IRIS tell Dad and me?" Murphy just peeked out of the pack with his big eyes scarcely exposed and his muzzle resting where it poked out of the zipper track. "I think she said I would jump the same location as Brack, but it would be a later year. So I'm pretty sure it's later than 1933. I remember from my studies with Dad that radio communication via satellite didn't start until around 1945. Whew. Do you think we're stuck somewhere between '33 and '45, Murphy?" The big eyes in the backpack just gave a couple blinks in response. "So if we are, it's no wonder I can't hear from IRIS. Our commu-nication form hasn't even been invented! What rotten luck, huh, Murphy." A wiggling backpack suggested that the robotic dog—even further out of sync with time than his master—was doing his best to show friendship in a dark and unpredictable country.

Murphy did his best to unroll and stretch in the canvas back-pack, but the weight of his master's napping head made any move-ment difficult. He didn't want to rush his master's quiet, but a thump with a back paw was Murphy's attempt to create space after a long nap. Theo shot up to his feet and was standing wide-eyed in a mat-ter of seconds. With a cramp in his neck and a headache behind his eyes, he stood half dazed for a moment, trying to remember where he fell asleep and why he was there. As slowly as he could gather his thoughts, he looked around the stockyard corrals. "We can't stay here all day, Murphy. I just wish I knew where we are and where we're supposed to go." Theo never had been able to wake up very fast, and even in a foreign location and an unfamiliar time, he struggled to shake his sleep from the night.

"You know, boy, it's best that you stay in the pack for now. The last thing I need is to be chasing you around streets with signs I can't read. Trust me. I'll wake up and get us out of here." Murphy seemed to understand as he curled back down into the pack as Theo pulled the zipper closed over the pup and the blue collar language transmitter.

Theo allowed himself to stroll back into the café quarter of the Schlachthof borough. Although he had no money, he figured a way to walk close enough to abandoned café tables where scraps of food had not been taken away. He could brush against a table, or reach and have a pastry in his grasp without breaking his stride and without being noticed. After a couple blocks of grazing, he was pleasantly filled with fine German food and had even stashed a few pieces of *Brot* for a snack later in the day. Theo knew the sweet breads would sustain him if he had to miss a meal.

The day was cool, but the sun could not bring warmth due to the high rise of the buildings along the streets. Theo found museums to help him pass the time of the day and to slacken the chill. He had learned to appreciate art from the oil paintings his mom would create. He remembered how he would watch her paint and wonder if the images were already hidden in the canvas or if they flowed through the oils streaked by the brushstrokes. He loved watching a portrait come to life as his mother's delicate hand brought the image born in her mind into life on the canvas. With such pleasant memories, he entered first one, then another museum that seemed to beckon warmth and memory, thus lightening his load.

As day passed into early evening, Theo looked for another district of pubs and cafés where he could sample some of the scraps and build a supper for himself. He wanted the familiarity of the Schlachthof borough, but the horrors of Brack and the odious creature from the previous day was a danger he did not want to meet again. As he walked from one borough into another through the streets of Munich, he studied the eyes of the people around him. He cautioned himself to watch for evil eyes, and he prayed for the compassionate eyes of his friend, Father Kolbe. Neither evil nor good fell within his vision as he passed from one district and borough into the next.

Theo knew he needed to focus less on people and more on a place of safety to spend the oncoming night. As dusk settled, doorways seemed deeper than the shadows. Alleys were narrow and dark, but most were filled with crates and boxes that had been discarded. He decided to find a quiet alley to rest for the night and even to spend some time holding his backpack companion so the dark would not swallow all his memories of home.

A wooden boardwalk edged a millinery store at the end of a string of businesses. Theo sat on the steps leading down from the boardwalk where the path crossed a narrow alley. "You know, Murphy, I think we just found our home for the night." He sat with his back against the storefront and enjoyed the crisp air as the daylight became colored with pinks and oranges of a setting sun. He saw four boys walking toward him. As they approached, he could see they were close to him in age, but there was something different about them. He grew wary as they closed the distance. He hated being alone and wanted friends, so he disregarded his own intuition. Perhaps they would stop and talk. He thought of Yari, a boy he had scarcely known but whose life had ended so bravely and so young.

The quiver of the ball in his backpack should have been a warning. The teens were part of an organization based in Munich where the young were trained and recruited in the ways of the Führer to serve Germany. They were known as the *Hitlerjugend,* or Hitler Youth, and their ways were not welcoming to someone like Theo who had dark hair, dark eyes, and who did not hail the Führer as the ultimate power.

The confident swagger of the teens was product of indoctrination by a Reich and a madman. "Hush!" Theo softly commanded the growl that could be heard through the partially opened zipper of the backpack. He looked intently at the boys approaching. They walked as if boards had been placed between their jackets and shirts, preventing their spines from bending. They looked back at him with eyes that seemed intent and cold. They approached with an air of dominance, remembering the words of their leader, Adolf Hitler, when he introduced the *Hitlerjugend* in 1933.

> My program for educating youth is hard. Weakness must be hammered away. ... I want a brutal, domineering, fearless, cruel youth. Youth must be all that. It must bear pain. There must be nothing weak and gentle about it. The free, splendid beast of prey must once again flash from its eyes ...

"Du beschmutzt unsere Straßen."

Theo heard the words that had no meaning to him, but he could tell by their tone that the words were laced with evil. How could he know he was being accused of defiling their streets when his translator was tucked away in the backpack? He made no move and clamped his jaw to make no expression as he only inched the fingers of one hand around the zipper pull on the backpack resting on his lap. He grasped the pull and shifted his weight to distract from being seen as he pulled the zipper open a few inches to allow the reception of Murphy's language transmitter.

One of the boys reached down and tousled Theo's hair before pulling away with a yank on a handful of hair. "What is this? Dirt in our city? On the head of a coward?" The boys laughed and tightened their circle. He sat up straighter in defiance to the abuse, pulling the backpack closer to him.

"What's this? Does the baby have a toy?" A second boy from the group grabbed the backpack from Theo's lap before he had a chance to realize and tighten his grip. He stood in reflex and anger.

"Give me that backpack. It's not yours, and you have no right to take it!"

"Ah, what's in it for me?" A youth yanked open the zipper and tossed the contents to the ground. "A little food, a cap, and a ball? Are you really ready to die for such toys?"

Theo stared at the silver ball. *Don't unroll, Murphy! Don't unroll!* He pushed his thoughts as he wished Murphy could read them.

One of the group stomped on the cap and kicked the ball into the alley where the robot dog in his sphere hit the stone side of the millinery store. Theo jumped in reaction as the group of antagonists closed in around him.

"You have no right!" Theo yelled as the four began punching, kicking, and tossing him like a rag doll until he fell to the ground. The biggest of the four grabbed him by the ankles and began dragging him farther back into the alley. Theo knew his strength would be nothing against the abusive powers of the youths, but he fueled his ability to fight by letting anger that had been hidden in his heart explode—anger for losing his mother, anger toward Viktor Brack who destroyed his dad's dream, anger for the loss of Yari, and anger for the abuse of his dedicated dog. He swung and kicked as he spat and yelled words of hatred until his lungs felt they would burst from the heaving, the hits, and the force of air behind his words. The hatred was returned blow for blow until he could no longer stand or even defend himself. He was knocked to the ground where a foot stomped his face against the stone pavement of the alleyway.

Dazed and curled up for protection when he could no longer fight, it seemed to Theo that he heard new shouts in the alleyway where he lay. The kicks and hits that buffeted his body relented and eventually gave way. His eyes seemed swollen in their sockets. He was scarcely aware of the quiet that surrounded him—quiet except the sound of someone beside him, gasping and breathing in quick heavy breaths.

"*Steh auf!*" the voice beside him panted.

Theo's body screamed in pain with each breath he took. His hand lying across his body touched his bloody side where his shirt had been torn by kicking and his ribs had been broken.

"*Steh auf!*" the voice commanded between its own panting breaths.

"I won't ... let me ..." Theo tried to argue back but found each breath sucked in to form a word only intensified the pain in his side. "Leave me ..." He wanted to die alone and be beat no longer, but a vision passed through his memory. "Murphy!" He tried to yell, but his battered body emitted only a faint cry. He raised his head and tried to focus on the wall where Murphy had been kicked by the youth. Unsure whether the ball lay in one piece or many, he saw only darkness against the wall. "Murphy!" He tried to crawl. His vision was too blurred from the beating to focus on detail, but he knew in his heart he was moving toward his friend.

Suddenly, a form stood beside the ball and two hands reached down to scoop it out of Theo's sight. "No!" he yelled with all the power he could force through his lungs until the pain left him in blackness.

Murphy's tongue swiped across his master's face. Theo half opened one eye, trying to see through the blur. "Murphy. Good dog. Oww." Murphy responded with his muzzle against his master's cheek. "Oww. Murph." *Murphy? What happened?* He chose to think with his eyes shut to make sense of why he felt pain coursing through his body. Murphy sighed and laid his head between his master's chin and chest. Theo moved a hand to touch his companion. "Ugh." Without opening his eyes, he tried to roll toward Murphy. A spasm of coughing made him cry out and reach for his side. "What happened?"

"You were jumped by boys of Hitler's Youth."

Theo forced open his eyes and made a futile attempt to push himself away from the voice next to him. "What ... Leave me alone!" He reached to pull Murphy toward him.

"Lie still. I'm not the one who beat you. I dragged you under this pile of boxes and boards because I thought you should be hidden. Otherwise, they would have killed you."

"Who? Why do they ..." Theo had questions, but another painful coughing fit collapsed him back to the ground.

"Look. You need to lie down. I'll get you help once I think the streets are clear, but for now, you need to be still."

Theo wanted to argue with the voice, but he had no strength. He moved his hand to the furry head that had plopped back down on his chest. *Murphy is here*, he assured himself silently as he slipped back into darkness.

"Stay here," the voice in the dark commanded.

Theo turned his head in the direction of the voice. Murphy's even breathing seemed to be the only comfort he could feel. Slowly, he opened his eyes. Darkness and blurry vision did little to expose the person next to him. He stared silently, blinking away the fog covering his eyes until he could see what appeared to be a small person sitting just inches away from Murphy's tail. The boy was sitting on the ground with arms folded and resting on bent knees.

"Who are you?" Theo's voice cracked just above a whisper.

"I should be asking you that question," the boy turned his head to face Theo.

Theo could make out strands of hair dropping below the cap resting just above the boy's eyes. He looked different from other kids. Even under the makeshift shelter of boxes and boards, He could see the boy had darker skin than anyone else he had met. "Please, just tell me who you are. I can't fight any more."

"You don't have to tell me you can't fight. I saved you! You should learn how to defend yourself if you're going to tangle with Hitler's Youth. They easily could have killed you!"

"You saved me?" Theo had a hint of doubt in his voice. He was glad to be alive, but the slight frame sitting next to him hardly seemed to be the warrior he would have called to battle the four youths in the alley.

"Yeah, well, kind of. I dragged you here and covered you so no one could find you and do you in."

"Dragged me? What about the guys who jumped me?"

"I don't know what happened to them. I heard a lot of yelling, and I could tell the *Hitlerjugend* were attacking someone. So I ran to help you."

"Huh, you don't look big enough to take on four angry boys."

"I'm not. I just ran knowing I would think of some way to distract them and get them away from you."

The boy's story seemed a little too far-fetched, but something or someone stopped the boys from beating him to death. Theo ended a coughing spasm, wrapping his arms tighter around his painful ribs. He knew he should rest, but the small boy's rescue didn't make sense. "So how'd you do it?"

"I didn't. I ran at the boys, screaming and throwing rocks at them. I guess my noise brought someone else. Some man came running up and pushed past me to get into the alley. It was really strange. He didn't look real big. Actually, he had on a long flowing jacket, you know, like a priest wears. But under that jacket he must have had some pretty big muscles. He started yelling and grabbing the boys and pulling them away from you. He got his glasses knocked off. I ran and picked them up so they wouldn't get stepped on in the scuffle. The boys tried to fight him, but he had unbelievable strength. The boys were getting thrown to the ground. I kicked when I got a chance, and I know how to hurt a boy. One of the boys yelled, *"Los weg!"* and they ran back out of the alley. The man in the long jacket ran after them. I was afraid the boys would return and finish you, so I dragged you back here, away from where they beat you, and covered you with this trash."

Theo lay quietly but he could feel his pulse and breathing increase as he heard the story unfold. "Glasses? Do you still have them?"

"No. I snuck back to the opening of the alley and laid them on the edge of the porch step. On my way back to check on you, I thought I saw a ball moving by itself over by the wall. When I went over to pick it up, I saw it wasn't a ball but a dog instead. I brought the dog to your cover, and it seemed to know you. So I waited here until I could safely get away. When you woke up, I tried to talk to you, but you didn't stay awake for long. I went back and looked for the glasses after you passed out a second time, but they were gone. Why do you ask?"

"I think I know the man," Theo whispered, not caring if the boy heard him or not.

"The way he appeared and disappeared from nowhere, he must have been an angel."

140

Theo knew it was difficult to see under the pile of boxes and boards, but he was unashamed of his tears.

"Stay here," the boy commanded again.

"Wait," Theo tried to sound forceful but exhaustion and pain had left him powerless. "What's your name?"

"Gracie."

"What?"

"Gracie."

"Isn't that a girl's name?" Theo gulped. "Are you a girl?"

"Welcome to the obvious. Just rest. I'm going for help. I'm staying with a man who knows how to help kids who make dumb decisions and get into trouble on the street." Had he been able to see better, Theo would have seen a slight grin break across Gracie's face.

CHAPTER 8

Revelation

Jahile's heavy sigh turned Gracie's head. She had tried to be as little of a burden to him as possible since he saved her from the dangers of the street months ago. His bakery brought in enough to provide both with sufficient and good food. She helped with what little upkeep the tiny home required. His visitors were few and mostly late at night, when the streets and skies were dark. Most of his visits were from *ein guter Freund*—actually, a very good friend whom Jahile called TAR. The visits would last anywhere from a few moments to a couple days. TAR seemed to like Gracie and called her the girl with the dreams, but their interaction was only a welcome at the door or light conversation when they fellowshipped at the table over a good meal. Life seemed to be what a quiet village would expect, but today Gracie looked at Jahile as he treated Theo's wounds and noticed her guardian's skin a little more wrinkled, a little older, a little more strained. Although she didn't ask to be dumped on his doorstep, the past year under his care and gentle smile had drawn him into her heart. She was beginning to understand how this Aryan could be Papa's dear friend. She didn't feel she loved him as she should love a godfather, but she cared enough that she didn't want to add to the weight of the world that was piled onto his shoulders—whatever that weight might be.

For nearly a fortnight Theo did little besides moan, sip broth that was ladled to him, and sometimes shriek out in restless sleep. Most of his words were unintelligible, but Jahile took note of names—Dad,

Iris, Viktor Brack, and Yari—that floated in the air during the boy's fitful stirrings. Some fits were stilled by soft pats, but others required a firm grip of Jahile's hands on each shoulder until Theo could still and fall back into the depths of his sleep. These were the times when the names hung in the air and seemed to also penetrate Jahile's soul. Gracie watched so often that she wondered if Herr Möeller and the young man had some connection other than their chance meeting through her.

By the third week of rest and healing, Theo was alert and able to sit and even move about the small home. Also by this time, Murphy had been so sufficiently pampered by both Gracie and Jahile that he was quite pleased with his new home. Murphy seemed to perform silly antics and make great effort to find ways to elicit a rolling laugh from Jahile. For that, Gracie loved Murphy even more as he had a way of lightening the mood in the cottage. Since the first night Theo was brought into Herr Möeller's home for healing, Gracie had carried Murphy to the loft to snuggle beside her and pass each night. Secretly, Gracie did not look forward to the day when the young man would be well enough to expect to have his dog beside him again.

Gracie didn't seem to mind the extra work of helping Herr Möeller prepare meals and clean up after one more person. Jahile seemed to enjoy the cottage filled with the two teens who were beginning to speak more about Murphy and ask questions about Munich. He waited for Theo's strength to return and was ready for the first meal that opened their lives to each other. That same meal was followed by days of talking, listening, guarding words, praying, and eventually by planning for a tomorrow that would forever change the lives of all three.

Just as Murphy had been the lifter of heaviness in the cottage, the little dog with the blue light collar became the catalyst for exposing and embracing three worlds brought together for one plan. One evening as Gracie cleared plates from the table, Jahile started conversation.

"Tell me about your dog, Theo. He seems most special."

"Oh, Murphy's just a silly dog that likes to ride in my backpack and go on adventures with me."

"Theo," Herr Möeller cleared his throat, "my intent is not to pry, but these are times when people are guarded out of fear. I opened my home to you because I want to help. I believe there's more to Murphy, to you, than what I know. Gracie tells me she thought she saw a ball, and when she went to pick it up, she found Murphy. Since we brought you here, once—only once that we have seen— Murphy rolled into a ball again. How he keeps lights on his collar is a mystery."

Jahile paused for a moment. He leaned back and turned his head to look directly at Theo before he continued.

"Now, what lead to your being attacked in the alley?" Jahile glanced at Gracie who joined them at the table. "Gracie can, for the most part, handle herself on the streets. However, the night of your beating, the attackers were four *Hitlerjugend*, boys being trained as Hitler's Youth. My little *Mischling* is brave, even to times of getting herself in over her head, but she could not have deterred the attackers. She admitted to me that a man dressed in a flowing black coat—like a priest's vestment—came to your rescue. He ran in full speed from the streets without hesitation as if he knew you. During your illness, you would struggle against terrors of your sleep and yell names—some of those I am assuming are dear to you. But one of the names I recognize as more than terrors of sleep." Jahile smiled and clasped his hands on the table in front of him. "Now, I have told you what I know. It's your turn. You return the favor and tell me about yourself. Gracie has enough secrets of her own. She poses no more threat to you than I do. Let me help. Tell me."

While Herr Möeller was talking, Theo was watching his face and slowly petting Murphy who had crawled onto the bench where his master sat at the table. Gracie also had been watching Herr Möeller talk, hesitant to breathe for fear of missing any of his soft words. Slowly, now, she turned to look at the teen who had dropped his head and was staring at the oak table. Jahile did not rush the silence.

"It's not that I don't want to tell you ... to tell you about ... to tell you anything. It's just that it would seem impossible and you would think that I'm lying." Theo raised his head but kept his voice low.

No one broke the silence. Theo and Gracie shared the oak bench at the table across from Herr Möeller, and Murphy filled the common area between the teens. Feeling a need to move yet stay still, Gracie too began petting Murphy. Caught up in the two-sided back-scratch-lovin' he was getting, Murphy let out a big puppy sigh, rolled to his side, and would have landed on the floor had both Theo and Gracie not realized Murphy had overextended his roll beyond the bench. The teens cracked heads as they reacted to catch Murphy. Everyone laughed, thankful for Murphy's distraction, as the dog settled back into his spot on the bench.

"I guess I should start with Murphy," Theo began. "I was alone and struggling after my mom died a few years ago—in 20 ... well, never mind. My dad thought a dog would be a good companion for me. He brought Murphy home from his lab. Oh, I guess I should mention, my dad's a scientist. He, um, he builds things. Anyway, Murphy is programed to help me."

"Programed?" The words Theo had chosen were not clear to Jahile, and he needed honesty.

"Yeah, well, okay," Theo stumbled over his words then continued after a sigh. "Murphy can roll into a shiny silver ball because he's not really a dog." Gracie's expression was almost comical as she looked crossed between anger of disbelief and confusion.

"I mean, he's a dog, but he's a robot."

"A robot?" Jahile repeated but kept a calm tone. "So you mean he's actually mechanical?"

"Yeah."

"Well, that explains why he doesn't eat, and I never see him poop when I let him out for exercise!" Gracie huffed.

"Anyway, the blue lights on his collar are actually a voice transmitter and translator." Theo looked a little sheepish but felt he should confess as much as would help explain without going into any detail he wasn't ready to reveal. Besides, he wasn't sure that even he knew all of Murphy's programmed abilities. "I don't speak German. I don't even understand it! You hear me speaking German because the collar translates the words on the airwaves. I understand your words because his transmitter translates the words and send them into my earbud."

"Your ear butt?" Gracie gave a look that showed she didn't believe Theo's tale.

"No!" Theo laughed at the silly girl who was not trying to be funny. "My *earbud*! Look!" He pulled the earbud from the cuff fit to his ear. "This is like a tiny radio that sends words straight into my ear."

Both Jahile and Gracie looked with interest until the teen replaced the earbud.

"Without the translator, I can't understand anything!"

"Gracie, why don't you pour some buttermilk for all of us? I think I'll close up the house for the night and turn down the light. I can light the kerosene lantern and turn up the stove. We may be in for a long evening." Jahile spoke kindly, but his wisdom perceived the conversation of the evening would not be one to be heard beyond the walls of the tiny home.

Murphy trotted around following first Gracie then Jahile until all were settled back around the table. Murphy settled back between the teens.

Jahile took a big swallow of buttermilk before he continued. "Theo, if you don't speak German, why are you in Munich?"

"I was hoping to find, Vik … um, someone my dad knew—a fellow scientist from America. He came back to Germany." Theo tried to sound calm and convincing without any excitement in his voice.

"Viktor Brack?" Herr Möeller looked directly into Theo's eyes without flinching though his words were terse.

"Uh, yeah. How did you know?" Theo couldn't hide his surprise. "Do *you* know him?" His stomach started turning flips. He wondered if the secure home was actually a den for the enemy. How else would Herr Möeller know Dr. Brack?

"Brack was one of the names you wrestled with in your sleep. Why are you looking for Viktor? Is he here in Munich?"

The questions stuck in Theo's mind, but he struggled to sort out what to say. "I need ... he has ..." He looked back into the eyes of Herr Möeller.

Although at first Jahile seemed tense, he tried to express his concern to Theo. He couldn't risk being this close to someone who knew Brack without guarding his speech and his intents. "Theo, why do you need Brack?"

"He has a book—my father's book. It's just science. I don't even know what all the science stuff is about. I just know it is personal property of my dad's, and I came to get it back." The words rolled off Theo's tongue.

"Is your father in Germany?"

"No, he was hurt in an explosion. Brack is responsible. I just want the book back." The questions and answers had excited his mind. Theo was ready to fight for his dad—even if it meant standing up to what seemed to be a good man.

Gracie stared first at one than the other. She didn't know the man and hadn't even heard the name of whom they spoke. Still, their voices, though both controlled, gave warnings of agitation in their souls.

"Is he here in Munich?" Jahile repeated slowly and deliberately.

"Yes, I think so. But Herr Möeller, in all fairness, you tell me. Is he a friend of yours?"

Jahile's eyes deepened and he didn't even seem to open his teeth to spit out the words. "I know him, and I despise him."

Theo's shoulders relaxed to know he did not really know Herr Möeller, but he knew he was his friend. "He tried to kill my dad." He fought the emotions of the bitter memory.

"Is he wounded? Your dad?"

"He's paralyzed!" Theo dropped his eyes back to the table. He didn't even care what the girl next to him thought as a tear landed on the oak table.

"Okay." Jahile's hand reached across the table and gave a firm but soft squeeze to Theo's shoulder. "Did you see Brack?"

Theo looked up and released a sigh. "I was at a café with Father Kolbe. He went inside to pay. Someone, something that smelled very bad, put his hand on my shoulder. I turned and saw a man in dark clothing and Brack. I ran and hid until I thought it was safe to move in the dark of the night."

"So Brack didn't find you?" Jahile seemed surprised.

"No, I was safe hiding in the stockyards. It wasn't until I went to sit on the sidewalk where an alley passed a store that I was in danger. The rest seems sketchy," Theo admitted.

"The *Hitlerjugend* wouldn't need any reason to beat up on someone," Gracie added. "I've seen them kill a kid by beating on him. They scare me, but they know my name, Lil' Grey, from the street and know I'm a girl, so they just spit on me and harass me. I know to stay away from their fists. They were giving you a pretty good pounding that night when I heard you yelling."

"Yeah. Thanks for the reminder." Theo smirked and rubbed his ribs. Then, he widened his lips into a smile.

"Theo," Jahile returned to the night of the beating. "You said you were with Father Kolbe."

"Yeah. Do you know him?" Theo's pitch raised in hopeful anticipation.

"We have similar interests," was all that Jahile would admit. "Gracie, the man with the long flowing coat, you said he got his glasses knocked off. Were they round glasses?"

"Yes. I grabbed them so they wouldn't get broken. I set them to the side, intending to give them back. Then, I pulled Theo under some boxes in the alley and hid under the boxes with him in case the *Hitlerjugend* came back. When I finally crawled out to come get you to help, the glasses were gone. I guess the man came back and got them." Gracie enumerated the events.

"Ah, Maximillian Kolbe," Jahile exhaled with a grin.

"Father Kolbe? He came to help me? He must wonder where I am!" Theo had never questioned what kept the *Hitlerjugend* from killing him.

"He's a good man, a man of God, but he's more. There's no doubt he saved your life, Theo—maybe more times than you realize. What brought you to be with Father Kolbe?" Jahile's questions turned back the teen's memory.

"Herr Möeller, I would tell you all I know, but I'm not sure I remember everything right now. A nice lady named Emilie found me on a road and took me to Father Kolbe. He was coming to Munich, so I came along with him. The rest you know from when we stopped to get dinner." Theo spoke matter-of-factly. He didn't try to keep anything from his new friends, but he was tired and didn't see any need for further detail.

Jahile continued, looking around the table as he knew his wisdom would be words that Gracie too would need to understand. "Maximilian Kolbe is a priest from Warsaw who has a calling to help people who are sent to concentration camps. Beginning in March of '33, those who opposed the government were the first to be sent. Since then, more and more the government considers to be socially and racially undesirable—Jews, gypsies, *Mischlinges*—are being sent to camps. Father Kolbe especially has a heart to help children who are left without parents and who are sent to camps."

"Yari," Theo whispered.

"I don't know the name, but I heard you cry out for this person while you were healing. It was always a sad and soft cry—the same voice as you used for your father—so I assume this Jew, by name, is a friend," Jahile said softly.

"Yes. Was a friend."

"Well, whatever his plan, I know Father Kolbe's purpose for you was good. I'll take over for my friend," Jahile vowed.

"How do you know him?" Theo looked at Herr Möeller.

"Let's just say we have common course. That's where Brack comes in. He is evil, Theo. Stay away from him. You too, Gracie! Stay away!" Jahile's voice rose.

"That's the same thing my dad told me just before I jumped … uh, I mean, before I jumped on the plane to come over." Theo silently scolded himself for his near-mistake.

"Plane? You came to Germany on a plane? How? You're not a soldier or anyone special!" Gracie reacted, ready to call him a liar, while Jahile just looked silently across the table.

Theo caught his breath. "Uh, I didn't finish. I *meant* to say on a plain old boat," he recovered.

"Translator or not, you need to learn to talk better," Gracie huffed at the other teen for his confusing words.

The word confusion gave Jahile a chance to get his emotions and anger under control. "Again, stay away from Brack. He has built concentration camps and works on the punishments within."

"Like what punishments?" Gracie asked feeling disconnected from the conversation.

"It's not for you to know or worry about. We've said enough. The name Brack will not be mentioned again in this house unless I mention it!" Jahile again struggled with control. He momentarily closed his eyes then opened them to see two innocent young people looking directly at him, wondering what caused his fury. "We have visited enough for tonight." Jahile pushed back his bench and carried the buttermilk mugs to the sink. "We rest for now." He tried to add a lilt to his voice as he crossed the room and closed his bedroom door behind him.

"I knew that was his voice!" Theo whispered into the air.

"What voice?" Gracie scowled at him.

"Nothing," Theo left the table, carrying Murphy with him to the bed at the side of the room. Now he knew. Until Herr Möeller mentioned Brack and concentration camps in the same sentence, he had forgotten hearing the voice of Viktor Brack at the concentration camp. His memory returned to his first night in Germany as he lay hidden under the building in the camp where he met Yari and the other boxcar children. He had heard a voice he thought he knew. Herr Möeller's words verified the connection. Now he knew for sure that it was Viktor Brack who spoke in the building at the camp! He squeezed his eyes shut and rubbed Murphy's head as if doing so would help his memory. "Murphy, what did Brack say that night? Oh, if only IRIS could communicate with me. She has the memory to help me." He closed his eyes again. *Think, think!* He tried to see the buildings at the camp and feel the damp and dark crawl space under the building. "He said something about the government, paying the government, no, giving, no, owing! Yeah, owing the government! Murphy! Why can't I think? I think that's right, but there was something else, something I didn't understand—a word ... augh! I give up." Murphy just looked at his master who was staring at the ceiling, missing the blue flashing lights that formed a message, *Späh owes the government.*

Gracie lay facing out of the loft, watching Theo's restlessness below. She wasn't surprised when she saw the young man roll Murphy into a ball and put him into his backpack at the foot of his sleeping pallet. She quietly pulled on her clothes and her shoes, ready to follow quietly into the night as she watched him pull his coat from the peg and silently lift the door latch to sneak out into the night.

CHAPTER 9

Search

Theo didn't know where to find Viktor Brack, but he knew where he would start looking. He now knew that Herr Möeller hated Brack for building government concentration camps and something even more heinous that was unspoken at their evening talk. There were times he had heard his dad complaining about the government budget or decisions or actions overseas, but he had never experienced a government working against its own people. Even in history class, some of the stories that Mr. Medi would tell seemed surreal and impossible to believe, but his short time in Germany, his own experience in the camp with Yari and the other Jewish children made Medi's stories a sickening reality.

Theo's thoughts began to connect. *Brack must have wanted to jump to 1933 to be part of the National Socialists who took power. He probably worked on the concentration camp at Dachau that Medi told us about. What did old Medi call the government and court buildings? Something about a Palace. Palace of Court, no, Government, no, Justice? Augh! I wish I could remember his lectures! Brack ... government ... hmmm. Maybe the courts are in the center of town like in America.*

Viktor Brack's calloused attitude of selfishness left a dark cloud in Theo's memory. Strangely, from the little that he had learned of Nazi Germany, he was beginning to see how Brack could not only turn on his scientist colleague but also heartlessly injure, try to kill, and walk away from his old friend. The thoughts played and replayed in his mind giving him a burning heat in the cool night as he made his way to the town's square.

Gracie had spent enough time on the streets in both daylight and darkness to know how to navigate the streets and alleys without being seen, especially by someone like Theo who had no street sense and no clue of danger. Twice she was hailed by other street urchins who called out to Lil' Grey and welcomed her to stand by their fire barrel. Both times she stopped just long enough to ask about the trail of a boy walking in the night and to threaten any who considered roughing him up for sport. Always, she left the urchins with a wave and a promise to join them on another day.

Besides staying alert to dangers of the night, Gracie thought about the conversation at the table. She tried to remember exact words. She tried to mentally picture Herr Möeller's expressions and reactions to what the young man said—especially the names. "What was the name Theo said that upset Herr Möeller?" Gracie asked only loud enough to shake her memory. "I remember it sounded like something common like brick or brot." As she remembered how Herr Möeller tried to hide his anger, she remembered he said something about the government. *Ah, I know just where he's headed!* She had a new passion of pursuit and started a slow jog toward the River Isar and the *Marienplatz*, the center of town where the Palace of Justice stood.

Whether it was the full moon or the anxious thoughts that swirled in his mind, Jahile Möeller could not sleep. Giving in to his restlessness, he dressed and quietly walked through the common room of the small cottage. He knew Theo may be lying half awake at the side of the room, so he moved with quiet stealth as he lifted his coat from the peg by the door. The night air was refreshing against the anger that still burned inside of him. Jahile lit a cigarette as he stepped away from the wooden door. He hoped to clear his mind and wait for daylight to resume his thoughts. Sliding his hand down the woolen jacket to put his matches back into his pocket, a thought flashed through Jahile's mind. Jackets! How many jackets were on the pegs by the door? Without care for quiet, Jahile spun and opened the wooden door and felt along the wall for the empty pegs in the darkness. The realization that the jackets were gone sent his heart into a rapid beat.

"Theo!" At first, Jahile called out in a hoarse whisper, then louder as he approached the bed by the wall that sat empty except for a backpack at the foot of the bed. "Gracie?" Jahile tilted his head back, trying to see into the loft. Skipping ladder rungs, Jahile found the loft empty and knew that for whatever reason, both teens were gone—gone from his home, gone from his protection. Jahile moved quickly back down the ladder and ran out the door and into the night.

Theo moved recklessly as he ran through the streets until he reached the river. Night had fallen dark as the skies held promise of an upcoming storm. From the bank of the river, he could see the center of government located on the square. The view of the *Justizpalast* gave his feet a reason to stop for a minute and take in the beauty. Lights at the top of the tall edifice seemed as high as stars in the dark sky, towering so high above the city trees that it reflected on the water of River Isar sending a million sparkling diamonds across the gently washing water. In a slow jog that gave his leg muscles a gentle workout, Theo never took his eyes off the regal building as he ran from river to city center. Not knowing the tall structure's name was *Justizpalast,* the Palace of Justice, Theo was sure the words *castle* and *beauty* were somewhere in the name. Taking a deep breath, the young American promised himself to return when the animosity of mankind had settled and see the Munich capital in the daylight. *At least*, he thought, *the lights give me direction for getting there. Now, if I can have such luck finding Brack!* Again, he ran until he could see his goal—the *Justizpalast*. He paused at the bottom of the steps looking up at the word carved into stone. It had been too long since Theo had given his legs a workout on the driftboard, and so he found the run up the capitol steps taxing on his recently healed ribs and yet a welcome exercise. The large wooden doors opened into an empty vestibule. Pulling open the doors gave his mind a quick memory of the wooden doors with the handles of a cross that he had opened when he met his friend Father Maximilian Kolbe. For a moment, he wished Father Kolbe was with him.

"Well, God, I guess I'll just have to say my own quick prayer that I can move in ways to help and honor my own father," Theo whispered while stepping inside and backing to a wall for a better look around. Before him lay a grand, hanging staircase made of marble steps and edged with dark wooden banisters. His eyes followed the stairs to a second level that lay exposed as it rimmed the rotunda that had begun on the first floor. Although the grand staircase ended at the second floor, he could see another narrower staircase off to the left on the open second floor. This second set of stairs moved along a wall and disappeared from the open sight from where he stood. The three-story rotunda and grand staircase were capped by a glass domed ceiling that appeared to be made of clear ice that cooled the openness of the room.

The walls formed around the floor and offered doorways of great height and heavy frame though the doors themselves were narrow. "What's with all the doors? This is too open for anything I need. Whatever dirty dealing Brack is doing will be in a dark hole somewhere." Theo hurried up the stairs, wrapping one arm around his side to put pressure against the pounding on his ribs. He didn't stop on the second level, but he reminded himself to return someday and gaze down over the banisters around the open rotunda. The steps to the third floor were heavily carpeted, so he was not detected even though all matters of stealth were far from his intent. The stairway to the third level emptied into a narrower walkway around the rotunda but offered four hallways with doors to hidden rooms.

"Yikes," Theo muttered. Which hall would hold a no-good, rot ..."

"Ugh." Theo felt a sharp pain shoot up his shin as he landed face first on the woolen carpet.

"Shut up!" a voice hissed as a hand grabbed and pulled Theo's T-shirt. "Get in here!"

Theo swung his arms in defense as he grabbed his shin, tried to stand, and fell again as he was yanked into the recess of a doorway.

"What's the matter with you!" Gracie scolded in a harsh whisper. "Geez! You scared the cr—"

"When will you learn? You have a head on your shoulders, but I'm pretty sure it's empty because you certainly don't use it to think!"

"What do you know? What do you even care? You think just because you can speak English you can boss me around! You don't know what I'm doing!" Theo yelled back at her as he reacted out of embarrassment and anger.

"I don't have to understand what you're doing to know that it looks like you're trying to get yourself killed. This is the Palace of Justice you're using for your little game. Either you need to tell me what you're doing, or I'll start screaming and let everyone behind these doors know you're here." Gracie pursed her lips and squinted her eyes to let Theo know that Lil' Grey needed to choose sides.

"No, no, no, no," Theo whispered waving a hand in front of Gracie's mouth and putting the other hand on her shoulder to urge her to calm down. "Okay. I'll tell you what I'm doing, but I don't want you to stop me. I don't care if you leave, but don't—stop—me!" He threateningly punctuated the last three words. Then he dropped his hand from where it rested against Gracie's soft mouth.

"Brack, Viktor Brack, the man you heard me mention with Herr Möeller—he is a horrible man. I know enough about what he plans for the future and what the government will do that would make your skin crawl to know it."

"Oh, so they've let you in on their secrets, have they? You, the kid who can't even take care of himself, *you* know what the government plans to do?" Gracie knew the young man's talk seemed inconceivable, and she was offended that he would think she was so credulous.

"Look, Gracie," Theo's whisper became softer yet filled with more passion. "I don't expect you to understand. There's so much I haven't told you. Please, though, believe me when I say that Brack is bad. He has a book that I need. My father needs it, and I will do anything for my father. More than that, it will be dangerous if the government gets it."

"A book? You're risking your life for a book?" Gracie let her voice show that she was not taken in by his antics.

"It's more than just a book. It's a journal. It has dates and diagrams and plans for a future of destruction. Brack is a scientist gone mad. He is dangerous." Theo paused and looked directly into Gracie's eyes. Deliberately, he placed both hands on her shoulders and gave them a soft squeeze. "I don't ask you to get involved. I just ask you to let me go find Brack and find the book."

There was something about Theo's voice and behavior that Gracie knew expressed truth. She sat staring into his eyes remembering his words about doing anything for his father. She let her thoughts drift back to her own father. She hadn't seen Papa for over a year. Maybe God put this stranger in her path to give her a reason to help her own papa too—her papa whom the new government hated. She looked directly into Theo's eyes and let her shoulders relax in his hands. "I'll help you."

An impulse that he didn't understand made Theo pull back his arms without releasing his grip on Gracie's shoulders. For a brief moment in time, they were in an awkward but heartfelt embrace.

"Okay," Theo dropped his hands as he half-coughed, half-whispered. "Where do we look first?" Both teens looked around at the halls that seemed to spin off of the open flooring of the rotunda.

"I think better on my feet." Gracie rose and started inching her way around the top floor with her back almost touching the wall that held up the glass dome. The teens paused at each opening to a hall to stand and listen and peer into the darkness before continuing around the room.

Paused in the arched entrance to the third hallway that spun off of the rotunda like a spoke of a wheel, Gracie saw Theo tilt his head as if Murphy had taught him to cock his head to better listen. She held her breath to hear what he had perceived. They both dropped their eyes to the thick woolen carpet and noticed two doors away a light made a defined line at the bottom of the tall door. Theo pointed to the door. Gracie nodded. Both moved in the direction of the door.

Even without a clock, Jahile knew that close to half an hour had passed since he realized the teens were gone. *Enough running like a chicken with my head cut off!* Jahile scolded himself as he sat down on a fountain in the city square to capture and organize his thoughts. He reached into the pocket of his coat for a second cigarette and a match. The flame flickered in the windy rain that was beginning to pound against the stone street. He drew in the taste of the cigarette as his eyes slowly scanned the *Marienplatz* and drew in the quiet of the night that was trapped inside the buildings and river that bordered the square. His mind reflected on the past several months. As always, the bakery had kept him busy, but his work with *The Watch* had consumed growing amounts of time. His work in secret was tedious but it was necessary—not just for himself, scarcely for himself—more for the country he loved and believed in. Surely, he had tried to convince himself, one dictator can't convince an entire country that any part of mankind is to be annihilated. Jahile's thoughts drifted.

With a slight puff of air exhaled in a near chuckle, Jahile thought of how his life had changed over the past year, not just from work but from promise—the promise to a friend to guard and protect Gracie. There had been times when Jahile felt Gracie was in the way and prohibited his work with *The Watch*. There had been times when Jahile felt he was too old to raise a self-willed teenager who hated him. But more than the times of doubt and discouragement, there were times when Jahile had found himself laughing, singing silly songs, and believing that the lives of his two dear friends would continue through their daughter. There were times, more often than not, when Jahile admitted to himself that he loved the ray of spunky sunshine that filled his cottage in the form of a godchild.

His cigarette burned down to a nub, and Jahile remembered his need to find Gracie and the boy of secrets and shared hatred for the enemy—Brack. "Brack! Of course!" Jahile swiftly turned and looked at the *Justizpalast* standing in grandeur at the side of the square. Not only did a lighted window on the third floor of the Palace of Justice beckon the man in the dark of night, but the suspicion of finding both boy and enemy prodded him across the *Marienplatz* and into the capital's vestibule at the top of the stairs.

The soft carpet on the third floor of the *Justizpalast* muffled any sound of the teens' footsteps. Nonetheless, they moved in stealth and allowed only shallow, soundless breaths as they crept closer to the tall door with the line of light that separated door and carpeting. The language was hard for Theo to understand. Gracie knew the Deutsch tongue, but she dare not translate and risk any sound in the hallway. Theo realized how dependent he had become on Murphy's translator collar now that Murphy was curled up, probably sleeping comfortably on his pallet back in Herr Möeller's safe cottage. He reached for the cold metal doorknob and looked at Gracie. Even in the dark, she could perceive his warning that he intended to open the door and to be on alert to run if necessary. In place of sound, Gracie reached up and touched his arm to convey her consent to his action. Slowly, he turned the knob until a click froze the motion of his hand.

The conversation inside the room intensified in volume, and again Gracie reached up and touched his arm to encourage him to continue with the door. Each teen inhaled, exhaled, and inhaled again before Gracie put her hand against the door to help pressure its opening. The light in the room poured into the dark hall, undetected by the men in the room. Theo pressed the side of his face against the door jamb as he peered into the room. Conversation that at times seemed loud and heated poured out with the light—conversation in a foreign tongue that meant nothing to him. Only a few men from the far side of the room were sitting in a position to see the slightly opened door. He willed his eyes to make sense of the congregated men as his eyes moved across the room. Gracie stood with her ear close to the door in an effort to hear and to understand the politics being voiced in the courtroom. Minutes passed without any more movement of the door until Theo sucked in a breath and pulled his head away from the open door and back into the hallway where they stood. Gracie turned her face up to the young man's, even though he could scarcely make out her expression of curiosity. Before moving, indeed almost before breathing another breath, he pulled the door closed and slowly unwound the doorknob that he had held turned since he first lay hand upon it. As if any movement could be detected in the room behind the now-closed door, Theo pulled Gracie's face up as he bent with his lips close to her ear.

"Brack, inside," Gracie heard him whisper with a soft breath that defied the danger of the situation.

Without further words, both teens began a soft and deliberate move toward the entrance that connected the spoke of a hall to the hub of the third floor of the rotunda.

"If Brack is in that room, that means he's not in his office."

"Meaning?" Gracie was still unfamiliar with the connection the young man had to Germany's Third Reich Socialist.

"Meaning, if I can find his office, I can find a book that needs to be returned to America and to my dad!" Theo huffed in a whisper.

Gracie sighed. She was exasperated that she could not know the secrets of Herr Möeller, his friend TAR, the government that hated her parents, and the secrets of a foreign boy just over a year older. Gracie knew, however, this was no time to demand explanations. "Most offices are on the second floor. I've wandered around in here a few times when I was trying to stay warm. I don't remember the name Brack on any door. Can you give me an idea of who he is? Maybe then I can narrow the search because the halls are divided by activity of the Reich."

"How am I supposed to know what he does?" Theo snapped back in a hoarse voice that threatened to explode from a whisper.

"Sorry!" Gracie quipped with mock apology. "I just thought you would want to go straight to his office instead of wandering from room to room in the dark!"

She listened to his exhale and knew she had convinced Theo that he was letting his anxiety and emotions attack the person who, at this moment, could help him most.

"Okay. All I know is that when I first arrived in Germany, I ended up in a place where the kids were all killed. That was where I first heard Brack's voice."

"A concentration camp?"

"How am I supposed to know? I was just dumped there! I didn't pay that much attention to Mr. Medi's lessons to know what camp kids were shipped to just to be killed!" Theo's quavering voice expressed his agitation both at his lack of knowledge and the stress of his time in Germany that seemed to be compounding.

"Mr. who?" Gracie asked, not wanting to know that another person was involved. "Oh, never mind!" she huffed and walked away from the confusing boy as she peered down over the rail in the middle of the rotunda. "Okay. Fighting will get us nowhere. Let me think," she strained her eyes to see down to the second floor in an attempt to recall her memory of the halls. "Let's go down to the second floor. I'm pretty sure I know which hall had offices of military for the Reich." Gracie walked to the stairs with Theo following in silence.

On the second floor of the *Justizpalast* administration building, Gracie circled the hub of halls one and a half times, pausing to look down each dark hallway. After her first rotation around the rotunda, Theo crossed his arms and stood with his back against the wall and one foot propped up on the wall behind him to wait for Gracie to make a decision.

"Go ahead," Gracie spoke in a voice louder than they had used in the building to this point. "Run up and down the halls until you find what you want! I'm trying my best to remember. I know you're tired of waiting on me, but you're starting to annoy me with your huffy body lang—wait! This is it!" Gracie's voice changed in tone.

"The hall?"

"I'm pretty sure the military offices were in this hallway. Maybe Brack is a military leader and has his name on a door." Gracie had a hopeful lilt in her voice.

Theo rushed to the other side of the round room, forgetting his pout of having to wait for a girl to decide his next move. Again in silence, the teens flanked the hall and began a trek from door to door where they pressed their faces to see the names written in raised paint on cold granite plaques fastened into the wall beside each doorway. Although the teens moved carefully and swiftly, the end of the hall seemed to be too near to reward their search.

What if I can't read Brack's name written in German? What if he's a nobody? What if we're in a wrong building? Theo's thoughts began to war against his determination to find Brack's office.

"Viktor?"

"What?" Theo stopped and turned toward Gracie.

"Is his name Viktor Brack?" Gracie stood with her back to a door and had there been light in the hallway, Theo would have seen a grin beaming across her face.

"Yeah! That's the guy!" He nearly stumbled on the woolen carpet in his lunge to cross the hallway and reach the door where Gracie stood.

"Viktor Brack," Theo traced the name with his finger.

"Okay, so when we get in the office, what exactly are we looking for?" Gracie was ready to move to the next step.

"I told you—a book."

"Seriously? Just a book?" Gracie retorted without disguising the incredulity in her voice.

"Look, trust me. This is a very important book—not just for me, but for you and your country. I can't explain it now. You'll just have to believe me. I can tell you more when we return to Herr Möeller's *after* we find the book."

In a sigh, Gracie nodded. "Okay, so what can you tell me now so I know what to look for?"

"The book is leather—only it may be in a plastic case that protected it when the lab was flooded." Theo began the description.

"Flood? What flood?" Gracie interrupted.

"Never mind! Just look for a leather book, maybe in a plastic case. The title of the book is *Societatis.*"

"That's Latin."

"Who cares what language it is! I just need the book!"

"Yell at me one more time, and I'll walk out of here and let you see how much you can do without me." Gracie's eyes narrowed as she spoke.

Theo realized his shoulders raised as well as his voice. He shook his head. "Sorry. It's just that I need that book."

Gracie saw him take a deep breath and drop his shoulders. "Don't worry. I'll stay and help, but a few kind words would go a long way." Gracie reached up and patted him on one of his tense shoulders in an effort to show support. Then, she dropped her hand and turned to open the door.

"It's locked," Gracie wiggled the knob that refused to release the bolt from the striker plate.

"Ugh. Just once I'd like to do something that doesn't cause more problems!"

"Do you have a pocketknife?"

"Oh, sure I do—back at Möeller's—in my backpack!"

"Hmmm." Gracie turned and began to look up and down at Theo.

"Give me your necklace," Gracie commanded as she reached toward his chest.

"What?"

"Your necklace. I need it."

"For what? I don't see what a piece of leather strap is going to do for you," Theo argued.

"Just give it to me." Gracie held out her hand with her open palm right below his chin. "I don't care about the leather. I want that metal thing hanging off of it."

"That's a silver driftboard. It's kind of my reminder of some of the things back home that I have lost since I've been in this German nightmare." Theo's words expressed frustration as he reached up to unclasp the necklace.

"Whatever. I just hope it's not real silver because that might be too soft for what I need." Gracie removed the tiny driftboard charm from the leather strap and turned to the door. Theo was sure both the door striker plate and the charm would be ruined as Gracie slid the charm between the metal plates and pressed until the once curved end of the driftboard was flattened. "Now maybe I can use this ..." Gracie spoke mostly to herself as he watched the girl from the streets use the driftboard as a tool to move the bolt that held shut the office door.

Again, Theo found himself standing with his back against the wall while he waited to be rescued by a girl. It wasn't just that a girl was helping him. He admitted to himself that he wanted to do something to help Gracie, even possibly to save Gracie. He admitted to himself that she was becoming not only his companion and friend, but someone he was beginning to ...

"Click." The dull sound of the bolt was scarcely heard before Gracie pushed the door inward.

"Let's find it!" Gracie sang out as the sound of the bolt made Theo turn so quickly that he bumped into Gracie in the doorway. "Okay. Let's find a bookshelf, or a desk ..." Gracie let her voice fade as she reached back and took his hand in hers and walked into the office.

Tall windows lined one wall of the office, but the storm brewing in the night air added another layer of blackness to the room. Even though their time in the halls had helped their eyes adjust, the dark office was an enemy to the kids, keeping hidden the etched title of the leather book.

"We need to see better." Gracie found a desk and began touching everything until her hand stopped on something round and glass. "Ashtray."

"So. Maybe he smokes."

"Feel around for some matches. We need light!"

Quickly four hands moved over the surface of the desk near the ashtray. Theo was unfamiliar with matches. Every light source used by smokers in his world was produced by a spark on a lighter. He wished for Gracie's wisdom and searched for anything odd to his touch.

"Found it!" Gracie said as she tore a match from inside the cover of a small book of matches. She struck the match that burned too quickly to see more than a stack of papers and a newspaper on the desk. "Ouch!" The match extinguished as Gracie dropped it to the desktop.

"Careful! With all these papers, you'll start a fire before we— hey! Wait!" It was Theo's turn to find a resource. "Give me a minute to find that newspaper here on the desk." He searched with his hands until Gracie could hear a crumpling sound. Tightly, he rolled and twisted the newspaper. "Okay, make another spark of fire."

Gracie tore and struck another match from the tiny booklet. This time, as soon as Theo saw the flare, he held the tube of newspaper beside the tiny flame. The light spread to the paper, and Gracie dropped the match into the ashtray.

Gracie reached up and moved his hand to position the flame above his hand allowing the flame to move slower down the paper torch. In a slow wave, he moved the paper torch to expose the contents of the office.

"There's a bookshelf." Gracie pointed to a wall behind the desk.

"No. This is not a book that Brack would put away on a shelf." Theo continued to use the torch to scan the room. "If I were Brack, I would probably put the book where I could quickly put my hands on it." He paused.

"A drawer?" Gracie questioned as she moved behind the desk and sat in a leather chair that looked more comfortable than it felt. She opened the drawer centered under the desktop and began feeling with her hands, too impatient to wait for the light. She opened another drawer to the right.

"Left!" Theo moved the paper torch to Gracie's left side. "Brack is left handed. He would keep a left handed drawer for his quick-reach items."

Gracie turned to the left and pulled open the drawer. The light exposed only a shallow drawer with a few pens that rolled across the wood bottom. Without closing the drawer, Gracie turned her attention back to the drawer on the right and began to dig through the profusion of papers, pens, and notes. "There's so much junk in here that I can't see that he'd hide an important book in ... hey!" Gracie spun back to the drawer on the left. "Why is this drawer so empty?"

"It looks like it's too small to hold anything," Theo reasoned.

"Yeah, looks like, but the front of the drawer looks the same as the others. I think it has a fake bottom!" Gracie plunged her hands under the desk where the chair would have cubbies. "Maybe there's a button to ..." Gracie didn't even finish speaking her quest until she pressed a round knot under the desk. The wooden bottom of the left drawer popped up, exposing a book.

Theo was behind the desk and standing beside Gracie before she had time to read *Societatis* as she rubbed her hand across the cover. Gracie sprang out of the chair as the young man wrapped his arms around her encasing the book in her arms locked between them.

"Oh," Gracie exhaled.

"Sorry. I didn't mean to hug you so tight …"

"No. That smell. What is that sm—?"

Gracie had not even finished when Theo caught a whiff of an odious and strong smell. Driving the paper torch into the ashtray to extinguish the fire, he recognized the smell of danger, of something bad, of someone or something connected to Viktor Brack. Before he could turn back to the doorway, he felt the icy grip of a hand between his collarbone and his neck as if a lightning bolt from outside had pulsed through the window. He tried to hold tightly to Gracie, but the lock of the hand was both choking him and pulling him backward to the floor. Gracie fell with him and screamed as her hair was yanked. The book remained clutched in Gracie's hand tucked between their two bodies. Theo tried to keep his wits as he knew he had to fight back. It was his turn to be the protector, and though the smell prompted him to relent and vomit, he didn't want to let go of Gracie. He would get her through this attack of man or beast. Gracie pressed her head into his chest as she felt his left arm tighten around her. She kept the book between them and ran her other hand under his arm, where she could clench his waist.

The vice-grip of a hand was causing Theo to gurgle and gasp. If only he could get his muscular legs into a position to kick the ogre, but he could do little under the weight of Gracie and with his feet nearly under the desk. He could hear Gracie screaming until a sickening thud pounded her back with a force that he could feel beneath her. Gracie coughed as her body fell limp. Theo could hear his own voice yelling as if wanting to attack, scream, and give up all at once. His head began to pound in the dark room until a dizziness passed across his forehead. Then air.

The hand released its grip. Theo could hear noises in the room—Gracie sobbing and shaking in his arm, the voice of a man, a scuffle, a grunt from a flying fist, furniture knocked over. But the fight was no longer against him or Gracie. Shafts of light from the storm outside were creating momentary flickers of vision.

What's going on? Theo tried to pull together thoughts. *Who's fighting?* He kept his arm wrapped tightly around Gracie as he pulled his legs under him and lifted both of them to their knees behind the desk. Grunts, pops, swishing against the woolen carpet, glass breaking—the sounds of a fight continued. He frantically searched for the ashtray and the book of matches on the desk. Releasing Gracie, he tore a match from the book as he had seen Gracie do. With the other hand, he crumpled papers from the desk and pulled them under a match that he struck. Just as he lit the papers, Gracie reached for a book from the shelf and laid it beside the papers on the desk. The pages of the book at first hesitated against the flame, but eventually, the leather of the cover held a ball of flame large enough to cast a faint light in the room. Theo and Gracie squatted on their knees behind the fireball and desk, looking up to see the scuffle between a creature in a long black coat and Herr Möeller. As if propelled by the thunder of the sky, their guardian's swift arm was a piston of punches until the dark figure slammed him against the wall.

The light of the burning book was enough to see an odious beast back away as both men and the teens saw Jahile pull back his shirt sleeve just as a lightning bolt exposed a triquetra inked into the flesh on his arm.

"Run!" Jahile commanded, and the two teens were out the door and down the steps that rimmed the rotunda without looking back. Gracie grabbed Theo's arm as he headed toward the double doors on the first floor.

"No," her voice could scarcely be heard over his panting. "We've made enough noise to alert the third floor or to be followed by that goon. Follow me."

Gracie pulled Theo back into the shadows of the vestibule. He looked at her with a confusion of question and curiosity. He could see that her left arm clutched the book across her chest and her right hand held a finger across her lips to signal silence. Gracie willed her eyes to refocus in the dark, but it seemed flares of light obstructed her vision with the memory of the symbol on Herr Möeller's arm. She wanted to think. She wanted to look down at the book. She knew, however, this was a time of danger which allowed little time to do either.

Theo stared at Gracie, waiting for a cue. This was no time to challenge her decision making. For whatever reason Gracie didn't want to lunge through the front doors and into the black night, he knew he had to trust her instincts. Together the two teens slid with their backs against the curved wall until they could be sucked into the abyss of a nearby spoke-like hallway. It wasn't until they had backed possibly five meters into the empty hall that Gracie hissed, "run—quietly, but run!" Neither stopped until the wall at the end loomed in front of them.

"Now what?" Theo half asked, half accused as if Gracie had trapped them.

"The last room on the right of every hall has a wall panel that's actually a secret door to a hidden staircase. The stairs lead to a short tunnel that comes up in a garden arbor."

"How did you find this rabbit hole?" Theo shook his head as he looked at Gracie.

"I told you. I spent a lot of days in here when I was trying to stay warm on the streets. Sometimes I'd curl up in the shadows. No one noticed me. I could stay warm for hours. I'm just curious, and I noticed that sometimes men with the SS arm bands would go into rooms and not come out. So I'd follow them, but then I'd find the room empty. It was always the last room on the right of the first floor halls. Once I followed closely enough to hear the panel scraping shut. Pretty fun, huh?"

"Okay, but being strangled by that monster wasn't so fun. Let's get outta here."

"Umm, sorry, but I'll need to borrow your dirtboard so I can move the bolt on this locked door."

Theo sighed as he reached around his neck to unlace the leather lanyard holding the charm. "Uh, it's a driftboard."

"Whatever. Here, hold the book."

While Gracie pried at the door with the driftboard charm, Theo turned the book in his hands. No longer did a plastic case hide the leather cover. He rubbed an index finger over the etched title. "What does *Societatis* mean, Gracie?"

Gracie stopped her prying with the charm. "What?" She looked up at him.

"What does *Societatis* mean? I don't know Latin, but I know this book has a lot of stuff that deals with people and the German government—good and bad from the looks of the drawings."

"It means a society or fellowship or community."

"Could it be like a faction inside a government? Like a secret group?"

"Sure, if you believe governments have secret groups," Gracie returned to picking the lock.

"Don't you?"

"Don't I believe the government has secret groups?" Gracie paused in speaking just as the bolt clicked out of the striker plate. She turned the doorknob as she turned to Theo. "Why else would there be secret doors and tunnels?"

Theo tucked the book inside his coat. He had a large inside pocket, but he didn't trust the obvious. He moved the book to the back of his jeans and tucked it inside both T-shirt and waistband as he had seen concealed guns tucked by characters in the HoloGames. He moved inside the room where Gracie was already running her hands along the paneling.

Theo pulled the hall door closed behind him. "Where's the trigger to open the secret door?"

"If I knew that, I wouldn't be wiping my hands all over the walls, now would I?"

"Sorry, Miss Know-it-all! I just thought you knew!"

Ignoring the other teen's rude quip, Gracie commanded, "Feel the edges of each panel. I have seen the SS officers move a piece of the molding on the panel to op—"

"Mold?"

"No! Molding! The raised wood at the sides of the panel! Good grief!" Gracie didn't hide her exasperation at having to explain what to her had become common knowledge.

"How am I supposed to know your German words?" he defended himself.

"Uh, since you don't have Murphy with you, I have spoken nothing but the English language so you don't get confused. Is there another language you've learned in school that I should use?"

"No, thanks, Miss Smarty-pants." Theo had already begun the search for the hidden trigger and felt a piece of the molding give to his touch. "Sorry. I'm just not as educated as you are—at least in languages. But for now, I have a surprise for you!" He pressed the panel as he moved the piece of molding. The panel pivoted open. "After you, my dear." He waved a sweeping arm for Gracie to enter the hidden stairwell first.

Gracie gave Theo's arm a quick squeeze as she bolted past him. Both kids moved into the stairwell, down the five steps, and into the short tunnel in a half trot. He was glad the tunnel was dark so he could imagine he was in a large room instead of a narrow tunnel with a low ceiling. He reached one hand forward to rest on Gracie's shoulder to reassure her that he was with her and to reassure himself that his fear of close spaces would not kick in.

"Umph." Gracie fell onto a set of steps rising up from the floor of the tunnel just as her lanky friend also hit the bottom step and tumbled on top of her.

"Sorry, ouch," Theo rolled off of Gracie and rubbed his forehead where he hit it against a step.

"Found the way out," Gracie chuckled, "at the expense of my shin! I bet I'll have a bruise tomorrow." She sat on a step and rubbed her leg. Theo sat beside her in the dark stairwell.

"Okay. So you said this opens into an arbor in a garden. Where exactly are we? We need to get home."

"The gardens are behind the *Justizpalast*. Actually, the *Marienplatz*, this market square, is rimmed with beautiful gardens. But the tunnels from all the halls empty into a section of the back gardens. Once we come out, we'll be near the river, but it may be safer if we take some back streets to get home," Gracie explained and made a plan all at once.

"Well, since this is one game I've never played, I'll follow your lead."

"Okay, but even though we'll be outside, I think it's best if we don't talk."

"You're the boss." Theo stood and began his climb up the short set of cement stairs.

At the top of the stairs, both teens leaned on a wooden panel that easily gave way to fresh air and a snowy little den tucked inside bushes. An opening in the bushes created a niche for a cement fountain of a little girl holding her hand out to feed a cement duck.

A glance at the fountain made Theo stop in his tracks. He blinked his eyes. *Man, the moonlight must be glancing off the snow. I'd swear I just saw a spark.* Again, he saw a flash at the fountain, but this time the flashes of light were colorful and snapping like fireworks. "Did you see anything?" He didn't move his eyes from the fountain.

"Like what?" Gracie was running a hand over a branch laced with icy snow.

"Like, um, sparks, you know, fireworks, there in the fountain." Theo pointed at the fountain but turned to look at Gracie.

"No. The breeze is probably causing the ice in the fountain to melt just enough to look shimmery." Gracie turned from the bush. The two walked past the fountain and turned to look at what looked like nothing but ice crystal arbor and snowcapped bushes.

"Amazing," Theo whistled and looked at Gracie who was holding an index finger across her lips. He nodded as he tucked his hands into his pockets only after looping one arm through Gracie's arm. Without staring, he was pretty sure he saw Gracie grinning in the frosted moonlight.

CHAPTER 10

Diversion

Murphy exercised his little mechanical legs after wiggling his nose in the zipper of the backpack and worming his way out. Several jaunts around the quiet house gave Murphy a chance to nose around, more out of curiosity than of needing anything. He wandered into Jahile's sleeping quarters where his eyes saw a picture of three people. Murphy trotted to the picture thinking he would see Gracie in miniature form. However, the robot eyes did not determine a likeness to anyone in the picture except the form of a younger Jahile. The other two subjects, a beautiful woman and a smiling little girl, were unfamiliar in any of Murphy's data recollection. He blinked at the picture as the camera lens in his eye remembered the picture. Besides a nap on the comforter on Jahile's bed, all other sites around the tiny house were familiar and of little interest to the little robot. Thus, the excitement of his friends returning home gave reason for his tail to wag until he was cuddled up on Gracie's lap.

Gracie and Theo spoke little and kept questions and thoughts private until all could be discussed when Herr Möeller returned.

"Theo, I'm worried. We've been home at least an hour. Where's Herr Möeller?" Both had wrestled with anxious thoughts kept silent in their minds. "Do you think something happened? I mean, do you think that smelly ogre maybe hurt Herr—"

"No! He's fine. I'm sure he is. Herr Möeller's smarter than the two of us together. He's probably just meeting with some friends or stopping somewhere to warm up with some coffee." Even to Theo his excuses sounded lame, but both teens were willing to believe them.

By one in the morning, Gracie had fallen asleep in a chair across the room from where Theo lay restless on his bed, unable to sleep due to worry for Herr Möeller and unable to relax the muscles in his neck that had been hurt by Brack's goon. Murphy had welcomed both teens home by lying across Gracie's lap and letting her pet him while she and his master talked in soft tones.

A thud against the front door startled both kids awake. Murphy sat up in Gracie's lap and stared at the door, but he showed no signs of alarm. Again a thud on the door as the latch scraped open letting the door swing inward. Jahile staggered through the door. Murphy tumbled to the floor as Gracie lunged for Herr Möeller and hugged him as Theo rolled off the pallet and rose to meet him.

"You're wet!" Gracie exclaimed.

"I'm okay. Give me a minute to dry off, then we'll talk. No lights." Jahile went to his room.

"He doesn't seem to be walking very well," Gracie whispered as Theo wrapped an arm around her shoulders.

"It's just good to have him home."

By the time Jahile returned to the oak table, Gracie had heated some cider, and the teens and Murphy had taken their places on the bench across from where Jahile would sit. Theo had pulled back a small portion of curtain where the cold moon allowed faint beams of light to fall across the table. Slowly, Jahile made his way to the bench. He sipped a few drinks of the cider before he returned the expectant gazes.

Theo spoke first, "Herr Möeller, I'm sorry for going out without letting you know wh—"

"Enough. We'll talk about what needs to be said, but we will share all that is necessary. Theo, I understand your passion. No one understands the evil contained in Viktor Brack like I do. He will do anything to serve *The Society* and help the Third Reich reach ultimate power—even if it means the cost of innocent lives to make a point." Jahile rubbed his forehead as his head suspended over the table. *Control, Jahile,* he promised himself. *Control.* "I don't blame you for going after Brack after what he did to your father.

"We got the book, Herr Möeller!"

Jahile looked up at the boy. "What?"

"We got the book!"

"How?"

"I found Brack, and Gracie found his office. We found it in a secret compartment in his desk drawer."

"You could've been killed."

"I know, but Gracie knew a secret way out! We—"

"No, you don't know, Theo! This man has power and he has jaegers who will kill for sport at his command."

"I didn't mean for anyone to get hurt, but I came here to help my dad. This is the only way to keep Germany from rewriting history to an end that annihilates the world!" Theo's voice rose with excitement of trying to state his case.

"Look, Theo, I don't know what you're saying, but I do know you're driven by a power I don't know. We must work together, and that will start with honesty and complete truth."

Theo nodded and looked directly into Herr Möeller's eyes. Murphy moved from the bench to Gracie's lap as her gentle petting had become intense back rubs as she was not sure how to react to the voices rising in the room and the words she did and did not understand.

"What's a jaeger?" Gracie's soft voice drew the faces of both men to turn and to look at her.

"I don't really know. It's a feeling of sheer ugliness—worse than an old woman with a wart on her nose," Theo added trying to lighten his own thoughts. Both teens giggled. He sucked in a deep breath. "Seriously, it's something dark," he glanced up and paused, "and repulsive."

"Have you ever seen one before tonight?"

"No, I don't think so—at least not face-to-face," Theo admitted.

"Then how do you know it's repulsive?" Gracie pushed further.

"The smell—that smell in Brack's office, a smell of … well, a smell of evil," Theo half closed his eyes trying to recall enough to put a jaeger into words. "You'll know when you see the next one," he warned. "This is one evil even a street rat should run from."

Gracie wanted to ask more, but the convincing tone of his voice as it fell to a gravelly whisper caused a shiver to run down her spine. Theo turned to look at Herr Möeller and wait for his response.

"I'm not sure I know exactly, but a jaeger is an awful smelling beast that works for Brack. Jaegers are the epitome of evil. They do as they're told. The strength in one hand can kill a man. The only defense against them is intelligence. They can't think their way out of a paper bag. They're dumb brutes. They're dangerous. Avoid them at all costs. You're right, Theo. You'll always know one is around by the foul smell."

"That explains the guy who attacked us in Brack's office," Gracie grunted.

"Now it's my turn for a question." Jahile looked across the table. "Where's the book?"

"I have it." Theo reached back inside his waistband to retrieve the book. He set it on the table in front of Jahile.

Jahile took a moment to look at the title etched in the leather cover. The limited light from the hazy moon scarcely allowed more than the shape of the book to be exposed. Nonetheless, Jahile fanned the pages of the book, stopping a few times as if reading the pages in the dark. He handed the book back to Theo. "Keep this somewhere safe. You may not get a second chance to get it back if it's taken from you again," Jahile warned.

Theo nodded and replaced the book under his belt.

Gracie broke the pause as worry that had welled up inside caused questions to roll out without waiting for an answer between. "What took you so long to get home? Why were you wet? Did you get hurt? Did the jaeger follow you? Did he hurt—?"

"Gracie." Jahile reached across the table and put both hands on either side of her face. Even with hands rough from working, he could feel the moisture on her face and knew she was crying. "Gracie, dear girl, I'm okay. I'm okay," he repeated as he hugged her face with his hands. She let her face drop into his palms as sobs came from the depths of her soul. Theo scooted into what had been Murphy's spot on the bench and wrapped his arm around Gracie's shoulders.

Lil' Grey cried and felt no shame.

The men waited in silence. Murphy put his muzzle against her neck so she would wrap her arms around his little body. The few silent moments of crying felt good for Gracie as she realized the heart she had tried to turn to stone actually still loved and still cared.

"Okay, sorry guys." Gracie rubbed the tears from her face and looked around the table. "I'm ready to go on."

"What happened to you, Herr Möeller?" Theo wanted to know.

"Oh, I got roughed up a bit in Brack's office. Just the smell of that jaeger was enough to take me down, but he threw some pretty good punches too. Once I was able to get to the doorway, I was able to outsmart the smelly creature." He paused and patted Gracie's hand. "Next time, maybe I need my Lil' Grey to help me know all the secrets of the building so I can make a quick escape." They all grinned. "Once I got down to the street, I stayed in the shrubs and in the shadows for what seemed like hours. Eventually, I made the mistake of going out into the open. Those jaegers can multiply like rabbits, and they seemed to be every direction I turned. I'd just get shook of one and another would show his smelly face."

"So how'd you lose them?"

"Well, Gracie, here's some street wisdom that may come in handy for you some day—I hope you never need to know this, but it's good to remember. Jaegers are afraid of water. They can't swim. So as I was trying to get away from two that were giving me a work-over, I ended up flat on my back on the walkway beside the River Isar. I rolled to miss a punch and dove for the water. It was freezing cold, but I swam to keep my circulation going. I knew that as soon as I got out of the water, ice would start to form and my body temperature would continue to drop. I tried to swim far away from the *Justizpalast,* but I stayed in the shadows under the walkway. In one spot, the land under the walkway had eroded, so I crawled out of the water and under the walkway where I could wring water out of my clothes and be sheltered from the air. It was like I had my own little cave. It was enough to prevent further freezing, but I needed heat to prevent frostbite." Jahile looked over at Gracie. "What would you have done, Lil' Grey?"

"Well, I have plenty of friends with their street fire barrels where I would … Hey! Did you find a group of people at a fire barrel?" Gracie's excitement in her voice was proof that she felt camaraderie with the street urchins.

"That's exactly what I did. But I only stayed long enough to get enough heat in my body and in my clothes to make it home. So here I am."

"I've never been so glad to see someone walk through a door," Theo admitted.

"Herr Möeller," Gracie's voice came out as a whisper. "What's that mark on your arm?"

Jahile covered his forearm with his hand even though the flesh was already covered with his sleeve. "It's a symbol."

"Meaning?" Gracie prompted. "We saw that horrible man, or whatever he was, back away when you showed your arm."

"I suppose you've gotten yourselves into more than simple child's play." He hesitated. "Understand that what we discuss here at this table in the dark of our home is not for further discussion. Agreed?" Both teens shook their heads without speaking.

"It's a triquetra, a symbol for *The Watch*. It's a symbol for good, but it's recognized by the evil of the Reich."

"I've never heard of a tri … whatever you called it." Theo spoke through the knot in his throat.

With a heavy sigh and a hesitation, Jahile looked at his arm lying on the table before slowly unbuttoning his cuff and methodically rolling up his sleeve to expose the ink stain on the inside of his forearm. "Triquetra." Jahile used an index finger to outline the symbol as he explained. "Tri, of course, means three. In *The Watch* we make three vows—to protect, to honor, and to love our homeland and the good people of Germany." Jahile's voice slowed and stressed as he spoke the word *good*. "Here in the center," his finger tapped a circle with an eye drawn in the center, "to hold the three vows is an all-seeing eye. We will watch, for good, for eternity." Jahile punctuated each phrase, paused, and looked at each teen as he unrolled his sleeve and covered the vow inked into his arm.

"Does everyone in *The Watch* have a tattoo? Can we be part of *The Watch*? Do you have meetings?" Theo's curiosity rolled out with questions and an excited voice.

"Well, we need to do some serious talking, but I think we all could use a little sleep right now." About that time Murphy rolled and stretched on Gracie's lap, giving a little snort as he did so. Everyone around the table laughed, and Theo reached over and scratched Murphy's floppy ear.

Jahile got up from the table first. "Thanks for the hot cider, Gracie." He stood behind the teens and gave Gracie a hug around her shoulders and a firm pat to Theo's back before the three retired for the night.

Jahile tossed and turned half from terrors of the evening he couldn't wipe from his mind and half from wondering about the past and the mission of a young man named Theo. *I can't be too hard on these kids. Only twenty some years ago I first felt enough passion for my own beliefs to take a stand against the government. I remember my quixotic actions driven by my heart more than by my mind. By the grace of God I was not killed, though the eight months I was sent to the country to heal from an SS attack only intensified my desire to stand for my beliefs.* If the moon had been shining enough to give light to Jahile's room, it would be evident that the wrinkles of stress on his face had softened to lines of reflection. *I'm actually glad to know today's youth still hold beliefs strong enough to stand against wrong—even if the wrong is our government. I just wish I knew ...* Jahile's inability to sleep prompted resolve. *That's it. Theo must talk!* He rose from his bed and headed to the main room where a young man lay in restlessness with his own thoughts.

Theo bolted upright and sucked in the night air in reaction to the hand that touched his shoulder. Jahile quickly shushed him and pointed to the oaken table. He had not lit the candle he so often used for night-time meetings at the table. The light would have been nice, but Jahile did not want to waken Gracie. She had grown strong and determined. She would be a true force of good, but for now, he only wanted answers from the boy. Instead, he walked to the window across from the oaken table and pulled back just enough curtain to allow in a few yellow streaks from the street light a block away. Out of more curiosity than understanding, Theo waited until he saw his older friend take his usual place on the bench before he rolled from the pallet, tucked Murphy under his arm, and took his place at the table. Murphy's translation collar would be necessary. Neither knew where the conversation would lead, but both were ready to talk when Jahile began.

"I have brought both of you into my home and have treated you as I would my own children. Unfortunately, there are circumstances that leave you in danger if you stay in Munich."

"What danger is here? I'm not afraid of Viktor Brack, if that's what you mean," Theo defended himself thinking Herr Möeller saw him as a boy and not a man.

"Young man, it's time you listen more than you speak, but first I have questions for you. What is so important about the book you took from Viktor Brack's office that we risked our lives?"

Theo knew he could trust Herr Möeller, but the book was his connection to his dad, and he couldn't risk losing that connection again. "Oh, it's just a book that belongs to my dad. I think the goons were just excited about us being in Brack's office."

The boy's tone of voice was too light for Jahile to accept that the book held no deeper meaning. "There is truth to what you say, Theo, but I fear you are not telling me all that I want to hear, all that I need to hear. Now, how about you let me look at the book that nearly cost my life?"

Reluctantly, Theo's eyes looked where his backpack was slid between his sleeping pallet and the wall. "I don't want to give up the book."

"Perhaps you can begin by explaining to me about your past, your father, and your connection to Viktor Brack. Then we can discuss the importance of the book. Hmmm? You must trust me, Theo. By breaking into Brack's office to steal the book, you have become involved with a rolling ball that will crush and destroy. I suspicion your involvement is more than a book and a man named Brack. You don't know the enormity of power that lies behind that man. For your safety, and for Gracie's safety, I must know the truth—all of the truth." Jahile never raised his voice or even used a threatening tone. His whispers across the oaken table wouldn't have even lifted into the loft to waken the sleeping *Mischling* loved by both.

"There's a lot to say that you won't believe and so little to say since I came to Germany that you don't already know. I'll start with the easy part. I came to Germany just days before Gracie found me beat up in the alley. My first stop was actually an extermination camp in Poland where I escaped after falling into a pit. I was probably supposed to be shot like the rest of the kids who stood around the pit, but I think I passed out and fell before any bullet hit me. After I crawled out of the pit, I walked until I found a road. On that road a nice lady named Emilie stopped and gave me a ride. She and her husband Oskar let me stay overnight in their home. The next day Emilie took me to Warsaw to a church where I met a priest named Maximillian Kolbe. He said I needed a safer place and brought me with him to Munich. We ate in a small café, and I stayed at the table while he paid. I smelled the stench that I now know is connected to Brack's goons. When one of them grabbed my shoulder, I saw Brack with the goon and knew I was in trouble. I ran, hid, and later went to the alley. That's where Gracie found me. I lost the people who had helped me, but I gained you and Gracie. That's it. That's my story of Germany in a nutshell."

Jahile's soft breathing was almost audible as it formed a sigh combined with enough of a grin to form wrinkles at the sides of his mouth. "Oskar and Emilie Schindler. May God bless them."

Silence fell between the two until Jahile crossed his arms on the oaken table and looked at Theo to let him know the rest of the story needed to be told.

Herr Möeller's right. So far, he's only shown kindness and helped me. Besides, even after he knows the truth, will he believe such an incredible story? He'll probably think I'm crazy. Theo looked up from the table after collecting his thoughts. "What year is it?"

Without blinking, the older man just folded his hands on the oaken table and looked him in the eye as if to read any hidden thoughts. "1937."

"I had seen a year 1933 in the book, so I figured I was close." He looked down and shook his head as he continued. "Sorry. This is confusing for me, and I even know how I got here. I actually don't live in 1937 or anywhere in the 1930s." Theo stopped and looked to see what response Herr Möeller would have for his incredulous story. Surprisingly, the blue eyes across the table didn't change expression. If anything, he felt his German friend had a more intent look of curiosity on his face.

"My dad's a scientist. So is, or at least, so was Viktor Brack. They were friends—good friends. Dr. Brack even came to the funeral when my mom was killed in a car wreck." He dropped his eyes to the table and swallowed to dissolve the knot that popped into his throat and threatened to close his airway.

Jahile said nothing but chose to let the silence hang in the air between them. He needed to know—even if he couldn't understand the youth and his past—or else the future could hold danger and even death.

"They worked together on a project—a time machine. I know that probably sounds crazy, but—"

"No," Jahile interrupted. "It doesn't sound crazy—impossible maybe, but not crazy. Brack isn't the only person with books. I have a friend you shall meet who has shared some books with me that suggest a possibility of time travel, but it's only suggested, not reality by some machine."

"Well, the machine created by my dad and Dr. Brack wasn't from the 1930s. I'm actually from the future." Theo stopped and chuckled. "Wow, that sounds really weird. But it's true. I live over a hundred years from now. Geez, this doesn't even seem to make sense to me!"

"So Brack helped your dad create a machine that somehow sent you and Brack back a century? Where's your dad?" Jahile didn't know if he was playing out the boy's fairy tale or if he verged on unbelievable reality.

"My dad is still in the future. He was hurt in an explosion. Ugh!" Theo tensed his fists in wanting to tell the facts and make them sound believable. Jahile sat silent with his hands folded on the table. "Okay. Dad wasn't happy about using their invention because he wasn't sure all the bugs had been worked out. He wanted to test the machine using an object. The day of the trial run, Dr. Brack was acting weird. They were having problems getting power to the TimeWorm—uh, that's the name of the machine. Dad didn't know, but Brack had cut off all access to the outside world so that once the time transfer began, no one could interfere. Brack knew Dad wouldn't allow a person to time-travel just yet. As power was concentrated on the machine, Brack intended to travel back to now—actually, 1933. He blew up the lab and nearly killed my dad in the process. The last I saw of my dad, he was paralyzed from an injury during the explosion. I was locked in the room with the TimeWorm. My only way out was time travel. Dad knew he could get me back to the future, and I was willing to do anything for my dad."

Once Theo started the explanation, the details seemed to dog-pile, and he spoke quickly to keep from leaving out any detail.

"So what does all this have to do with the book?" Jahile tried to sort out what might or might not be believable.

"I'm really not sure, but—"

"We are almost killed for a book, and you're not sure?" Jahile was caught between wanting to be angry for the rash actions of the youth and wanting to know more about the book. He closed his eyes and inhaled as he realized that he too had balled his hands into fists. He slowly exhaled. "Sorry. What do you know about the book?"

"After the explosion, Murphy found the book in the lab. Dr. Brack held a gun on me and forced me to give him the book. But before he came and took the book, I looked inside. I don't understand what was in the book, but I saw symbols, drawings, and a language I didn't know. I'm now guessing it is written in German."

"Did you see anything in the book that you understood?"

"Well, I saw some symbols, you know, like a swastika, and a sickle and hammer like on a Russian flag. Actually, I even saw one that looked like your tattoo!" Theo pointed an index finger toward

Jahile's sleeved arm. "I know I saw a drawing with *Time Worm* and *1933* written beside it."

Theo relaxed his tense shoulders. "I didn't understand the book then, and I'm not sure I understand anything even now, but I know it's a driving force behind a good scientist turning evil. I'm going back to my dad, and I'm taking the book with me." He straightened up as the courage built inside of him. He had come a long way from a kid with a driftboard who liked to spend days in the imaginary world of HoloGames.

"Theo, I won't take your book." Jahile spoke without a promise in case his words would not ring true. "I ask that you let me look into the book. You've entered a world you don't understand. The information in the book may be something I should know for safety—the safety of the German people—the safety of Gracie." Jahile looked across the table at the young man. He hoped his last few words persuaded the young traveler to share the book.

Patting Murphy's head as it lay on his lap, Theo rose and crossed to the pallet where the backpack was wedged between the mattress and the wall. With his back to the guardian friend, he ran his hand across the cover before he returned to the table. "Herr Möeller, will you give it back to me?"

"For now, Theo, I need time to look into the book. Sleep for now. We'll talk more in the daylight." Jahile rose from the table and walked past the window where he dropped the curtain before crossing to his room behind a closed door.

Murphy stretched legs and neck in three directions as Theo lifted him from the bench. "Thanks for the light," he patted Murphy as he carried the sleeping robot to the pallet. Sleep came easy as the burden of the time jump seemed lighter now that Jahile had heard the truth.

The sound and smell of bacon sizzling on the fire made Theo roll over to face the kitchen even though his eyes remained shut. He had slept soundly out of exhaustion of mind and body from the night before.

"Hey! 'Bout time you rolled out of bed." Gracie's voice was as crisp as the cool air. "Herr Möeller's in a mood to fix a Sunday breakfast, and it's only Wednesday! If you sleep through breakfast, I'm eating your share." Gracie teased Theo as she plopped down on his legs to force him to squirm in the bed.

"Now, Gracie," the gentle voice at the fire chided and joined in with the teasing. "Theo needs his beauty rest."

"Comedians! You're all so funny. Besides, how can I get up when there's an elephant sitting on my legs?"

Gracie squealed and punched as she fell across her friend. Laughter rang out in the tiny home, and three hearts felt blessed to have such good friends. Even Murphy popped up and started yapping and pulling at the pillow under Theo's head.

"Father, we thank you for blessings. We ask for protection. Amen." Jahile's prayer seemed to punctuate the word *protection*. Talk was light as they ate. Gracie carried empty plates to the sink and began her daily routine of cleaning up when Jahile called her to join them again.

"Gracie, let the dishes sit for a while. Come to the table. We need to have a serious talk."

Jahile's voice was soft yet frank in tone, so Gracie didn't question or rebel as she sat at her place on the bench beside Theo with Murphy between the two. Her eyes flashed from Theo to Herr Möeller. She noticed they were staring into each other's eyes as if they shared a secret.

Jahile turned his face toward Gracie, but his eyes stayed on the boy. "Gracie, Theo and I had a little talk last night, and I've done quite a bit of thinking. Theo, you'll get the book back, but it will come with a price."

"You mean you're going to make me pay for my own book?" Theo blurted out.

"No, no," Jahile chuckled at the misunderstanding before his demeanor became serious again. "No, I just mean that I'm asking you and Gracie to do something, and the book will be involved."

"Okay." Gracie quipped to show she was ready for any adventure. "What'll we do?"

Jahile began. "First, understand that right now your safety is my priority. Theo, I do understand quite a bit in the book. I also understand why Brack will stop at nothing to get the book back. Because of that, there is not an alley, street, or building in Munich where you two will be safe from Brack and, as you call the jaegers, his goons." All three faces softened with a grin at Herr Möeller's use of the term. "I need to get you out of town, and I'm going to ask a favor."

"Cool!"

"Sure!"

Theo and Gracie both responded in eager tones.

"I hope you believe the danger because we must use stealth. However, both of you seem to be driven by a courage of soul. It's this courage I will ask you to use to both guide you to safety and to help stand against the evil of the Reich."

The two teens listened intently, eager to show their maturity and help their guardian.

"Just after dark tonight, I'll get you out of Munich by taking you up the Main River until we reach Frankfurt. It's a distance, but Theo, your muscles will help me row."

"Hey, just because I'm a girl doesn't mean I can't row a boat!"

"Oh, believe me, little princess," Jahile chuckled, "I'm confident you can do anything either of us can do. I just need you to help navigate and carry supplies. We'll need to make this look as innocent as a picnic, and so you'll at least have to play the role of the helpless *Frauline* for now."

"Augh!" Gracie's grunt was less than she wanted to say, but she knew not to cause problems at this point. "Okay, but that means I get to hold Murphy!"

"Agreed."

"So what do we do after we reach Frankfurt?" Theo was ready to hear the plan.

"I'll take you up the river to a road that leads to the city's center. It will guide you straight to the Alte Oper. From there, you will cross the city in a most unpredictable way."

Jahile outlined a plan as the teens listened. "We'll rest until tonight. I'll pack some food."

The challenge lay great before them, but driven by the hope of one day seeing their parents again, their hearts pulsed with eagerness to begin.

PART III

FRANKFURT, GERMANY; MARCH 1937

CHAPTER 11

Frankfurt

"Gracie, watch your step. With all this fog the dock will be slippery."

"I will," she replied with fake disgust. It was nice to have someone worrying about her. She looked at Herr Möeller. She could see concern in his eyes, and she was grateful for this moment. Gracie knew his worry was warranted. The road ahead was going to be a tumultuous one. She reluctantly reached up and grabbed Theo's outstretched hand.

Theo quickly pulled her up and handed up her own backpack as she got her footing. After making sure Gracie was safely on the dock, he reached down grabbed the extended hand. "Thanks, Herr Möeller. I'll tell Erich hello for you," he assured the older man.

"Thank you, Theo." Herr Möeller looked at the lanky young man and then past him to see Gracie putting on her pack and tightening the straps. "Take good care of her. She is a special young lady."

"I will." Theo shook his own backpack into place. "Are you sure you can't come with us?"

"As much as I would love to see my sister's boy, I am greatly needed back at *The Watch* headquarters in Paris. I've been gone for far too long. Those jaegers are heading somewhere, and we need to find out where and be ready to respond once you find out."

"I'll do my best to find out. Herr Möeller, I'm still not sold on this plan to get back to the States." Theo confessed his doubt with intense concern in his voice. "These airships don't sound like the fastest or safest means of transportation to me. I'm also pretty sure one of them crashes or something like that," he added, straining his memory to recall another one of Mr. Medi's lectures. He made a mental note that if he ever made it home to really start paying attention in history class. He laughed to himself as he remembered questioning Mr. Medi about the purpose of learning history, and how he said he would never need "this old history stuff." A smile crossed Theo's face at the thought of Mr. Medi discovering where he had transported and to what year!

An endearing expression crossed Herr Möeller's face as he reassured in a soft voice, "Do not fear, Theo. These vessels have been tested and are reported to be very safe."

"We'll see," Theo replied with a hint of doubt in his words. He gave his friend a firm, final handshake and turned, walking away to allow Gracie a moment with Herr Möeller.

"Take care, Herr Möeller," Gracie paused and stared one last time at her friend then down to her feet. "Thank you," she whispered.

"Take care, *Fraulein*," he whispered back as he pushed off the dock and slipped silently into the night, using the fog to cover his escape and sadness.

Gracie stood motionless for a minute, trying to visually hold the diminishing outline of her friend, then wiped her eye and turned to rejoin her two traveling companions.

"You okay?" Theo asked as she caught up with him.

Gracie brushed her long curls back across her shoulder. "Yes, now let's get to the church," she said clearly irritated at her lack of emotional control. "Remember what Möeller told us."

Theo paused and took a deep breath forcing the cool air to enter his lungs before he exhaled slowly, scanning the night for anything out of the ordinary. Unable to see any movement in the dark and thick fog, he closed his eyes and let his ears do the work. He could have sworn he heard Gracie mumble "idiot" under her breath, but as he was about to question her, she got his attention.

"Uh-huh," Gracie loudly cleared her throat. Theo opened his eyes, to see her outstretched hands holding a metallic sphere. "Why don't you just use Murphy?"

"How did you get him out of my pack without my noticing?" he quipped, letting her know he was annoyed.

"Street rat," was all she said as she tossed the sphere into the night air and headed north up the road that lead to the city's center. Theo shook his head and jogged to catch up to her and Murphy as they quietly and carefully made their way toward their destination. They were making good time with Murphy leading the charge. His hyper-sensitive hearing and night vision made the threat of running into an SS patrol—or worse a jaeger patrol—event less probable.

As they made their way from the Main River, Theo noticed how the open space was quickly becoming crowded with houses and buildings that seemed to be practically built on top of each other. The streets were so small between some buildings that he was not sure if even a small car could drive down them. He could also see a spire poking above all the trees and rooftops. "Is that the Kaiserdom?" he asked?

"Yeah, why?" Gracie never took her eyes off the streets ahead of her, all the time looking for possible danger. Her life on the streets had taught her to be observant, and this was one of many times she was thankful she had learned day-to-day survival.

"Just seems silly to go all this way around when our destination is literally just few blocks away. Isn't that large building ahead the town hall? What's it called?

"The Römer?" Gracie replied with a half-irritated tone. She was beginning to wonder if someone so ignorant of Germany's language and culture should be on such an important mission.

Oblivious to Gracie's irritation, Theo continued speaking a little louder than Gracie liked. "Yeah. Why not go around the Römer the other direction and come up the backside of the church? We would still avoid any patrols." He stared up at the church spire.

Gracie stopped and spun around before Theo was aware. He slammed into her, knocking them both to the ground into a pile of entangled arms and legs. "What's your problem?" Gracie huffed angrily as she tried to get herself out from underneath him. "Get off of me!"

"Nothing! I am trying to move, so if you'll just stop thrashing for two seconds, I can stand up!"

"I swear to—"

"Shhhh." Theo cut off Gracie's retort and put his hand over her mouth to stop her from saying anything else. Gracie instinctively readied to bite his hand but caught the look in his eyes. A look of sheer terror had replaced his schoolboy good looks. She followed his gaze to where Murphy stood with his ears and tail sticking straight up. Even his short, robotic hackles were in a tight ridge along his back.

Gracie was still on her back from their fall, so everything she was seeing was upside down making it difficult to see beyond Murphy. Theo quietly rolled out of their tangle and helped her up to a squat while he motioned for her to look again. He mouthed the word *jaeger*. She tried to make herself as small as possible and turned around fearing the worst.

Both teens could see a dark figure in the near distance, perhaps only a few meters away. He looked like a bulky mass under a street lamp at the side of the brick roadway. Neither spoke but backed into a wall of shrubbery that lined the same roadway. Minutes passed without communication as each youth studied the creature in the night, trying to isolate detail and so remember the nemesis. Although he stood in the rays of the streetlamp, the dark figure seemed to absorb the light. His long coat brushed the tops of his laced boots. His arms swung without exposing his hands, and with his back to Theo and Gracie, no face was evident in the large head covered by a Schiffchen, where the light seemed to glance off the metal SS pinned on the black wool cap. Surely, the light played tricks in the darkness. The guard looked hunched but his height seemed to loom taller than an average man. Theo wrapped his arms around Gracie's shoulders in a sideways hug to silence her as she gasped aloud. Almost as if the night was on the jaeger's side, the man-beast turned and became one with the shadows. The teens strained their eyes and slowly backed farther into the shrubs. In an instant they lost sight of the jaeger.

A quarter of an hour passed without sight of anyone, man or beast, on the roadway before Theo relaxed his grip on Gracie's shoulders keeping his face close to hers. "Only one, which makes me really nervous. Möeller warned us that they always hunt in packs of two or three. So where are the other ones?" he whispered scarcely louder than an exhale. He looked up the street and saw the jaeger had emerged from the shadows and was standing with its back to them. Theo scanned their surroundings to see if he could catch a glimpse of any other jaegers.

Quietly, he moved around Gracie and motioned for her to follow. Stepping behind the shrubs, he flattened himself against a fence that edged the lawns and opened ahead of him into a garden. He slipped up behind Murphy and ran his hand down his back, which calmed the robot canine and relaxed his protector mode. Murphy's tail fell toward the ground as he turned to see Theo's face so near to him. In anticipated excitement, Murphy's tail began to wag back and forth. "This way, boy." He gestured for Murphy to take the lead into the large garden.

Murphy looked up to his master. With the instincts of a guard dog wanting to attack, he obeyed Theo's point in the opposite direction. Murphy gave another quick snarl and snort in the general direction of the unsuspecting jaeger then made his way toward the garden gate. Theo watched Murphy slip under the fence then turned and grinned at Gracie's confused expression until they heard Murphy jump and the latch give a "pop." Gracie and Theo grinned as their beagle robot companion unlocked the gate from the inside.

Theo and Gracie crept into the garden and locked the door in the fence wall behind them. They both knew that the large wood and cast iron door would stop a normal human, but it wouldn't stop a jaeger from getting through if it wanted them. "Whaddaya think we should do? If that thing comes down here, it'll probably not end well for us." He looked into the garden and softly whistled Murphy back to his side.

Lost in his own thought, Theo murmured, "I know by the smell that jaegers are real. I wish they were just holograms, but I know they're dangerous—fatally dangerous."

"Holo-what?" Gracie wrinkled her forehead and looked at Theo hoping he wasn't just talking nonsense.

"Oh, never mind," Theo sighed. "Just know, they're evil!"

After her past year of living on the streets Gracie felt she wouldn't fear the devil himself, but his voice sounded convincing; yet more frightening than the sound of his voice was the way his skin seemed to pale.

Gracie watched as Murphy anxiously paced back and forth in front of the gate like a sentry on watch with his olfactory radars on heightened alert. "If we can take that path north a few more blocks, then we should be able to get to the Alte Oper, and from there we can get to the tunnel that should lead us to the old Kaiserdom."

Theo looked at the crushed stone path that started at his feet and ran north, eventually disappearing into a jungle of thick linden trees and brush. He took one unsure step and cringed as the rock underneath his feet made a noise that shook him as if a gunshot exploded into the still night air. "This is going to be tricky," he said aloud but more to himself as he took another cautious step, setting his heel in the ground first then rolling his foot flat to muffle each step. "Keep your eyes and ears open. There has to be a jaeger or two around here." He painstakingly made his way into the edge of the tree grove where the light could not penetrate the thick, heavy branches.

Slowly and stealthily they inched through the darkness, cringing at every noise that broke the eerie silence of the night. Theo could feel his heart pounding in his chest. The blood pumping in his ears was deafening. He worried that he would reveal their position to the hunters who were somewhere out there—just on the edge of the darkness, just beyond where he could see. He began to sweat in the cool night air. With each snap or crack of the night, he prepared for a jaeger to burst from the darkness and end their quest and possibly their lives.

After what seemed an eternity of creeping and catching their breaths, light from the moon poked through the ceiling of trees. The trio's slow pace became a crawl at a spot where the path ended as they were wary of stepping into the light and out of the cover of darkness.

"There it is. Isn't it beautiful!" Gracie exhaled in a whisper, too overcome by the beauty of the opera house to worry about being heard. "Look at that," she murmured.

"*Dem Wahren, Schönen, Guten.* What does that mean?" Theo read the inscription on the front of the opera house.

"To the true, the beautiful, the good." Gracie stood and began walking out of the tree line. Murphy was the first to react as he jumped behind Gracie and clamped down on the cuff of her pants. He was a small robot dog, but when he dug his feet in, he was very difficult to budge. "Murphy, what are you doing?"

"He's keeping you alive." Theo answered for his canine companion. "Get back here before they see you!"

"Before who sees me?" Gracie was puzzled, thinking the jaegers were left on the other side of the gate.

Theo pointed at the roof of the opera house. "Look on the balcony, past the gargoyle at the center of the roof." He and Murphy pulled Gracie back into the protective shadow of the crushed stone path and wooded hedgerow.

"That might be a member of *The Watch*." Gracie snapped back defensively but mentally chided herself for making a dangerous mistake.

"It might also be a jaeger or SS officer waiting for us," he countered. "What I don't understand is why they're all spread out. This city should be crawling with Nazis. It just doesn't make any sense. Herr Möeller told me that this is one of the first cities that fell under Hitler's hate regime."

"We need to take a minute to think!" Theo reasoned aloud. Inwardly, he was surprised how his heart had raced when he realized Gracie had walked out of the cover of the trees. He hadn't planned on having anyone tag along—especially not a know-it-all girl. He sighed as he glanced over at Gracie who had crawled back into a cover of trees. Theo noticed that she actually looked delicate sitting with her arms wrapped around her legs pulled up to her chest. He dropped down to the soft, cool ground and half crawled over to Gracie and sat beside her. Neither moved nor said anything. Murphy took the cue of getting some good belly rub and cuddle time and snuggled between the two teens.

"We're lucky to have these trees for cover." Theo finally broke the silence.

"They're linden trees."

"What?" Theo thought this was a strange time to be thinking about a biology lesson.

"Linden trees. They make me think about my mother." Gracie spoke in a whisper as if she didn't care if anyone else was even listening. Her thoughts were her own comfort.

"Uh, if you don't mind my asking, why would a tree remind you of your mother?" Theo gave in to his urge to turn his head and look at Gracie. Even though Murphy was between the two, rolling around and enjoying having ears, back, and belly rubbed, Theo could smell a faint, almost powdery scent from Gracie's skin. What little light filtered through the trees outlined her profile with a thin blue line making her seem, well, more of a tender girl than a street rat.

"My mama was named after the linden trees because my grandmother thought the tree was beautiful and strong."

"So was your mom's name Linden?" Theo asked wondering why girls always talk around issues instead of giving direct answers.

"Well, her birth name was Linden, but Papa called her Lindy." Gracie turned to Theo and gave a slight grin.

Theo caught a small glimmer of light that seemed to come from a slight dampness under Gracie's eye. "There's nothing around here to remind me of my mom," he admitted, "but you somehow made her seem very close." He dropped his eyes to the ground and was content to let the silence cover them for a few moments.

"Well, we're not making any progress by just sitting here." Theo slipped back under the canopy of shadows and began taking stock of the situation. He slowly scanned the *Marktplatz* before him. Their destination sat in the middle of the square. Getting into the Alte Oper was going to be more difficult than he previously imagined. The huge stone building sat in the middle of a wide-open area, bordered by a large parking lot on the west side. The east side was just as large and open but had picnic tables and benches sprinkled throughout with an occasional fountain. The biggest problem was the elaborate walkway that stretched out from where the front lawn began and extended to the front steps. The openness of the *Marktplatz* was marked only by a huge fountain in the center. Theo saw nothing they could use to mask their approach.

"I don't see any way that we can get across that courtyard without putting ourselves in a lot of danger. That guard on the balcony and all the ones we can't see will spot us after about five seconds if we go strolling out into the open." Theo's voice couldn't hide disappointment in facing further complications.

Gracie put her hand on his shoulder and moved closer to him to get a good look. "You're right." She paused for a moment. "We need a distraction if we're going to make it inside the Alte Oper."

Theo twisted around to look at Gracie. "Say we actually make it. Do you think you can find the tunnel door?"

"We need to make our way to the basement storage area. How hard can it be to find a door to a concrete tunnel? Herr Möeller said the tunnel will be narrow and changing but we'll be able to reach the Kaiserdom by the underground passage."

Satisfied with her answer, Theo turned back to take another look at the open terrain and to devise a plan. He attentively glared at the rooftop trying to see exactly how many possible threats were up there. His eyes searched the long parking lot and searched the windows, rooftops, and darkened doorways for more predators. Each time his eyes focused on a spot, he hoped to catch even the slightest movement or hint of a presence. Meanwhile, Murphy was content to lie on the grass, keeping his radar eyes fixed in the direction of the opera house. His only movement was the continual scan of lights across his transmitter collar.

Theo repeated the same slow, methodical process of examining the rooftop a second time and then took his attention to the east side of the building where benches and tables were arranged in a pattern. After a few minutes of deliberation, he knew what they needed for a distraction.

"Murphy, come here." The order fell reluctantly from Theo's heart.

Obediently, Murphy slowly backed to his master, never taking his eyes off the open space in front of him. Most of his attention was given to the signatures his heat sensor detected on the balcony of the opera house. Theo knelt down beside his canine companion and whispered in his ear. Murphy looked up with a set stare at his master then licked his face. "Gracie, get ready to move when I say."

"What's he gonna do?" Theo did not respond to Gracie's curiosity.

"Go, Murphy!" Without hesitation Murphy transformed into a silver sphere and rolled silently into the open courtyard. "Don't take any chances, Murphy," he quickly added as the dog rolled toward the largest fountain located in the exact center of the opera house yard.

"Theo, what's he going to do?" she asked again with a little more forcefulness.

"Are you ready to move?"

"I'm not going anywhere without Murphy."

"Trust me and get ready. Stay close to me. Don't stop for anything." Theo reached back and squeezed her hand. "He'll be all right. I promise."

"He better be," Gracie murmured and gave his hand a squeeze back.

Hearts were pounding as both teens watched Murphy roll toward the fountain. He rolled so quickly Theo was not sure if he would be able to spot him if he had not watched from the moment he left. The sphere streaked across the courtyard and leapt up over the base of the fountain disappearing into the water with a splash.

Gracie let out a quiet, shocked gasp as she watched the sphere vanish into the fountain.

Theo looked back at Gracie and gave her his sly smirk of a smile. "Ready?"

She shook her head with worry for the dog and worry for Theo and herself. Suddenly, she felt she was going to throw up as the realization of the situation hit her like a punch to the stomach. She took in a huge deep breath and let the cold night air rush into her lungs before she exhaled, trying to rid her body of the worry crushing down on her.

"It'll be all right, Gracie," Theo assured her. He could see the worry and fatigue were not only his to bear. "I'm worried too," he said with a nervous smile and turned back around waiting for his plan to unfold.

The silence of the night was abruptly shattered as strange noises and weird lights lit up the spraying water of the beautiful fountain. "How in the world"—Gracie paused watching the light show—"is he doing that?"

Theo smiled at the spectacle. "I'd explain it to you, but since you don't know what a computer or microchips are, it wouldn't make any sense at all."

"All I need to understand is that your dog is amazing." The momentary distraction made her stomach feel a little better as she marveled at the lights and crazy noises coming from the fountain.

"Where are they?" Theo whispered anxiously. "This should be getting their attention."

Both teens' muscles began to ache as they squatted, ready to spring into action at the exact right moment. Seconds turned into minutes as nothing happened. Theo strained his eyes and ears trying to pick up the slight hint of movement letting him know that his plan was going to work and he had not needlessly put his best friend in danger.

After what seemed an eternity, the noise and lights died without warning. The silence was unnerving after all the commotion Murphy had created. Theo held his breath, worried that something unnoticed may have happened to Murphy and that his plan had failed.

He dropped Gracie's hand and started to creep out from the cover of trees and darkness. Gracie reached out intuitively and grabbed his arm. "Look," she whispered as she pointed to the front steps of the Alte Oper.

Lights that had been off had come to life inside the opera house. Men began shouting and the stillness of the night was once again broken with noise and chaos. Theo looked up on the balcony as three guards appeared out of darkness, guns pointing toward the fountain.

"We have to go now." Theo grabbed Gracie's hand and moved to the outside of the tree line, sidestepping and hugging the edge of the trees.

Theo scanned back and forth between what was in front of him and the fountain in the courtyard hoping to see movement from Murphy. As he guided Gracie, he glanced back and thought he saw a pair of metallic ears pop up for a brief moment then disappear behind the brick base of the fountain.

Theo led Gracie toward the buildings that ran along the street west of the opera house. As they approached the end of the linden tree grove and were about to step into exposure, he looked back to search the fountain and rooftop for any threatening signs. "Once we cross the street, we need to stay as close to the buildings as possible and keep an eye out for trouble. We can do this!" Fortunately for them, the armed guards' attention seemed to be the now lifeless water fountain.

"Those guards are almost to the fountain. Do you think Murphy made it out of there yet?" Gracie tried to sound factual and not worried.

"Let's hope so, but we have to make it inside or all this is for nothing." Theo yanked on Gracie's hand once more as they made a dash for the cover and safety of the buildings across the street.

They slipped into the recessed doorway of the first building they reached. From the new vantage point, they watched nervously as the men with machine guns surrounded the water fountain. As the men got closer to where they had last seen Murphy, both teens fought the urge to sprint into the courtyard to distract the armed guards. Just as rational thought was about to leave them, once more the light and noise sprang up from the water gushing out of the fountain.

Theo almost let out a yelp as the spectacle caught him completely off guard. "Go!" he shouted. His dog was giving him and Gracie the distraction they needed if they had any hope of getting inside the Alte Oper and into the tunnel system beneath the city of Frankfurt. "Move it!"

Gracie and Theo broke into dead sprints as they crossed the courtyard undetected by the guards. They could see a side door to the opera house just a short distance away. Both ran as hard as they could, trying to keep an eye on both the building and the fountain. Their lungs and leg muscles were on fire from the intense pace. Again, the lights and noise stopped without warning.

The night seemed to be darker now that the light show had thrown off everyone's perception.

"Was ist das?" came a voice from a guard at the fountain. Unexpectedly, a scream of pain broke the silence. The next sound was what the teens feared most: gunfire filled the night with sparks of flame as bullets leapt from the rifles' barrels and began ricocheting off the stones intricately laid around the fountain.

The sound of barking and gunfire filled the courtyard and filled the night in all directions. Theo stopped just short of the side door and began walking mindlessly toward the barrage of bullets aimed at his dog.

"What are you doing?"

"I have to help him! If Murphy gets hurt, it's all my fault!" he shouted with guilt heavy in his panicked voice.

Gracie sprinted in front of Theo and pushed him back with both arms. He looked at her with disbelief. "Stop! We don't have time for this!" She pushed against him with all her might. "Turn around and get in there." She pointed with a shaking hand.

Theo dropped his head and started to turn until a shot rang through the air, followed by a yelp. "Murphy!" Theo screamed without concern of giving away his position and making them both the new target of the night watch.

"Da sind sie!" yelled a thick German voice.

"Oh no! They're coming for us!" Gracie cried as she quickly translated the words and the meaning behind them. "We have to go. Now!"

Theo made one last halfhearted attempt to push past Gracie, but she stood her ground and kept both outstretched arms firmly in front of him, pushing him back one more time. He nodded in despair and understanding. He knew his robotic best friend had sacrificed himself for them, and he did not want to waste that gift.

CHAPTER 12

Alte Oper

Both teens turned and lunged for the side door of the Alte Oper. Gracie reached the door first and leaned with her weight to lower the handle and press against the door with her shoulder. Theo took her cue and slammed the door with the back of his shoulder hitting both Gracie and the door as the latch gave way and dumped them on the dark floor just inside. Adjusting to the darkness, Gracie felt more secure having her strong friend close beside her. Holding his breath as if breathing would make noise, Theo moved Gracie's hand from the handle as he returned the door to its snug fit in the doorframe. Neither moved away from each other or the wall just inside the door. Both fought thoughts of fear of the unknown and thoughts of extreme sadness in losing Murphy.

Again, Theo was first to run from silent thoughts and to take action. "We've got to move. Since it doesn't seem to be a performance night, there's little chance anyone is in here. At least we have that on our side!" Glancing back at Gracie, he reached back intending to grab her arm and pull her along. Instinctively, Gracie reached up when she saw his hand and put her own hand into his. He turned back to react, caught himself, and told himself to keep his focus. With Theo leading, the two followed the wall as the floor slanted upward until a velvet curtain opened into a marble vestibule.

"Whoa, this place is huge." Theo's voice filled with awe. The sheer size of the building caught him off guard.

"And beautiful! Boys always miss the obvious." Gracie gave a sarcastic eye roll. "We need to find the basement stairs before those guards realize we made it in here. This place is big but not a great place to hide from men with machine guns." It was Gracie's turn to pull the other back into the curtains along the hall.

"Good point, but where should we go?" Theo looked up at the second and third level balconies that stretched from both sides of the stage and wrapped all the way around the open auditorium. He slowly scanned the main seating area all the way to the other side. He could see more beautiful curtains draped across entranceways.

He couldn't help but be impressed by the intricate interior features. Beautiful, massive sconces extended up to the ceiling with light that filled the vastness of the vaulted structure. He also noticed delicate and sophisticated woodwork carved into the massive beams that stretched from floor to ceiling and ran from one end of the roof to the other. Gracie followed Theo's gaze and thought how the dreamy, small twinkle lights in the dark ceiling gave the impression of an open sky. The expanse of the open ceiling seemed to momentarily free them from fear. Then, as if a cold wind swirled in the openness, the large room threatened exposure.

"Come on," Theo snapped back to the need to hide. "Let's see if we can find a door or a hall that's not out in the open." They continued up the slanted hall to a staircase. Gracie couldn't help but pull away from her friend long enough to run her hand along the cold marble of the steps and the firm oak banister.

"Hey!" Theo hissed. "Do you want to stay here petting the steps or do you want to get a perspective of this place?"

"Sorry." Gracie whispered without moving her eyes from the staircase. "This Swedish marble is so beautiful even in the dark, and the ban—"

"Seriously? Our lives are in danger. I just lost my best friend, and you want to caress a stairway?" Theo snapped.

Gracie dropped her hand to her side and quipped back, this time making direct eye contact and allowing only a dispassionate, "Sorry."

Theo felt just a little ashamed to have been so harsh and tried to bring Gracie back. "So how do you know anything about marble or stairways?"

"Story's too long—let's just say when I first hit the streets, I spent a lot of time in museums. They were warm and cheap and a good place to hang out without anyone bugging me to leave." Gracie turned her eyes from the staircase to look directly at the boy who understood so little.

A quick wink from Theo as both turned and with a little less aggression began climbing the staircase. Gracie mentally ticked off the steps as she climbed, " … eighteen, nineteen, twenty." The marble ended in padded flooring that felt like velvet compared to the firm marble steps. In silence, the youths slowly turned and scanned the mezzanine level.

"The balcony should be to the right." Theo checked himself and gave a quick glance toward Gracie. She stood still with her head tilted as if listening. She too had heard a noise. Without talking, he motioned to a niche that held a bronze statue of a lady. In an instant, he had taken the few steps necessary to squeeze in behind the statue and hide in the shadows of the niche.

Gracie searched for another quick hiding place. Instinctively, she reached for a glass knob that opened a tall oak door. She was behind the door and inside a luxurious room in what would have been a swift and noiseless motion if not for the click of the latch on the striker plate as she closed the door. "Don't breathe. Don't make a sound," she warned herself almost fearing to look around the room where she stood. Slowly turning her head, Gracie saw that she was in a women's powder room. Mirrors encased in gold frames lined the walls. Boudoir chairs offered rest.

"Someday," Gracie promised herself as she took in the grandeur and dreamed of her own adulthood in a world where she could be pampered and loved. Softly, she moved under one of the dressing tables located near the door. Suddenly, Gracie grimaced as an odious smell filled her nostrils. She begged her eyes to focus in the dark. Could she see a shadow of movement in the small gap under the door? Listening to her own heartbeat for what seemed an eternity, she willed herself to breathe in shallow breaths while she waited until the air seemed again to take on the smell of the powder left behind from patrons of the opera. She lay her cheek against the soft pile of carpet.

Gracie bolted up, not even reaching a sitting position before she banged her head against the bottom of the dressing table. "Ow!" she ducked and reached for her head at the same time. In the darkness she could not determine how long she had slept beneath the dressing table. "I can't believe I fell asleep," she scolded herself as she crawled out of her hiding place. She remembered the pungent smell and knew why she had hidden. She remembered "the smell of evil," as Theo called it—the jaeger. He must have been right outside the door before she fell asleep.

Standing in the dressing room, she could see nothing. Fortunately, she also could hear nothing and smell nothing. She took two quiet steps to the door and turned the knob, prepared to throw her shoulder against the door if she sensed alarm. Smoothly, the door hissed as she pulled it across the plush carpet. The hall outside the door was as quiet and as empty as the room. Tentatively, she strained her eyes to see. A flickering bulb above a square light fixture was enough light to cast scant shadows after anything that stood out in the darkness. There were no shadows. Bolstered by the blank darkness of the hall, Gracie stepped around the doorframe, keeping to the wall. She side-stepped in a deliberately slow pace as she headed for the niche where Theo had hidden behind the bronze lady.

"Theo," Gracie breathed just beyond a whisper as she peered into the niche. "Figures." Gracie turned back to look down the empty hall, realizing that he was gone.

Think! she commanded herself. *Think!* "Okay. Herr Möeller said to take the tunnels. Well, it's a little hard to take a tunnel when I'm standing on the second floor of the Alte Oper!" Gracie snapped to herself. "I guess he headed for a tunnel." She retraced her steps past the powder room and down the hall to a staircase that made a sharp turn up five steps to a landing. "There's no use in going higher," she reminded herself as she continued down the hall to a flight of steps

bordered by a solid wood banister. Over the staircase hung a chandelier that was not lit but held dozens of glass droplets that refracted the
light from the bulb in the hall. Even in the poor lighting, the wooden
stair rail held a soft red silkiness rubbed smooth from the passing of
many hands. Gracie kept her imagination in check and denied herself the right to touch the banister as she mentally pictured so many
beautifully dressed opera patrons had done. She continued to side-
step along the wall as she moved down the steps of marble that had
poured from the carpeted hall.

The steps reached a landing, and Gracie recognized that she was
on the main floor. "Still no tunnel opportunities here," she assured
herself as she turned the corner of the landing and progressed farther down the marble staircase. Twenty more steps down were closed
in by a stairwell until the last two steps were freed from walls and
seemed to breathe with more air. The descent had brought back the
dark. Gracie knew from her days of living on the streets that her eyes
would need time to adjust to the deepened darkness. She remembered times of sitting curled up in dark alleys at night, staring at
a post or a bin on the sidewalks, allowing her peripheral vision to
remain alert in the unrelenting dangers of the night. Gracie lowered
herself on the last step while she sat and welcomed the dark.

Although the silent night seemed to hang for an eternity, within
a quarter of an hour, Gracie began to notice bulges in the dark. As
she sat at the side of the staircase, she noticed that the wall she had
slithered down had actually ended into a banister on both sides of the
steps. She had left the walls behind, and the stairs rolled out into a
grand hall. She could feel the tiny hairs at the nape of her neck tingle
when she realized how exposed she sat on the stairs. Ahead of her,
in the center of the room, she could make out a huge, round form.
Unsure of what waited in the darkness, Gracie crawled on hands and
feet toward the mass in the center.

"Oh," Gracie exhaled as she reached the large circular sofa centered in the room. It was covered with a deep velvet. Although the
red hue was imperceptible in the darkness, Gracie ran both hands
across the nap of the fabric as she knelt beside the soft mass. Giving
in to her wants, Gracie lowered her head to allow her face to lay

across the cushioned seat. The velvet, at first cool to the touch of her cheek, warmed quickly and begged her to stay and lie down. With her cheek on the cushion, she looked sideways and noticed another chandelier. It was big like the light on the staircase, but this one hung within reach directly above the round sofa. Gracie crawled to the top of the sofa and reached up to the light fixture. She couldn't believe what her touch was telling her. Besides many, many glass crystals, which would have caught the glimmer of lights, strands of diamonds dangled from various heights on the chandelier. Gracie touched and stared at the hanging glamour and then realized what she needed to do. "Oh, please forgive my violation of your beauty, but I know a diamond is a treasure to hold as well as a tool for a girl from the streets," she explained in a whisper to the hanging offering. Weaving a strand of diamonds through her fingers, she made a fist and gave a quick jerk as she pulled the gift away from the chandelier and deposited the gems into the pocket of her jeans.

Gracie wriggled off the top of the round sofa and moved across the floor until she was able to touch a wall and let her hands become the searchers for a doorway that could lead to a tunnel.

Theo squatted behind the statue so quickly that he didn't even think about how cramped he might be with such little open space in the niche. He realized it was good that Murphy wasn't in the backpack as he tightly smashed the pack between himself and the wall. His mind raced trying to plan ahead if the jaeger or anyone else saw him in the hiding spot. He couldn't keep his focus as his thoughts kept wondering where Gracie hid. Perhaps she too found a niche. He thought he had heard a door latch, but in the dark hallway, he could imagine all kinds of sounds. One sense was not imagined, and that was the strong odor that was becoming as thick as each breath forced into his lungs as he sat scrunched behind the statue. He realized that he needed to calm the rapid pulse that sent the oxygen coursing with the blood in his veins. He focused on taking as deep of a breath as possible with as little sound as possible. Each breath was challenged by the stench that filled his nostrils and threatened to enter his system with the oxygen he breathed. He closed his eyes. The pungent smell lingered. He could hear no sound, yet he could not escape the overpowering smell. *Breathe. Breathe. Breathe.* Theo forced himself into a pattern. *Breathe, Breathe ...*

An icy cold touched the side of his neck. "AUGH!" Theo lunged out of his hiding spot and knew that escaping the smell would be a matter of life and death. As he jumped, he pushed against the statue. Someone, something had a grip on his backpack. He knew he needed to escape, but he also knew the safety of his dad, the experiment, and getting back home was tied to the leather book in the backpack. Theo wrestled against the aggressor's grip while kicking out with one leg and then another. Adrenaline pumped. He could hear his coarse breaths giving him power to kick while trying to expel the smell being sucked in. With mechanical reaction, he kicked, holding tightly to the straps of his backpack. The jaeger could try to take him, but it would not get his dad's work, his life. With the exception of the arm and iron grip that had a piece of the pack, the bronze statue lay tipped between the two. His strength and balance from boarding kept his legs in constant motion against the odious growls emitting with impact. *Kick! Kick! Kick! Not my dad's work! Kick! Kick! Kick! Not from me, you don't! Kick! Kick! Kick!* Theo fell into a mental chant as if he were kicking a boxing bag in the gym back home. With a cry of vengeance and a force that came from deep inside, he kicked higher and felt impact. Whatever he kicked not only gave way to his kick, but the grip on the backpack released. Theo's own backward pull almost tumbled him to the ground as he caught himself with one hand and took off in a sprint down the black hall. He had come from this direction, so he knew a staircase lay ahead. Pumping his feet up and down, jumping onto the landing, spinning the turn to the next flight of stairs, he raced down the last ten steps, not even sure if he touched any or all. In a panic, he searched the wall and plunged behind a curtain.

His breaths were bursting from his lungs, punctuated by hoarse heaves that were left over from the struggle and escape. A quick scan of his surroundings surprised him to find that he had lunged behind a curtain only to find himself in an open auditorium. He looked up and saw the tiny stars of light sprinkled across the ceiling. "Oh, fine,"

Theo puffed. "This is just my luck to be out in the open!" Without losing any more time, he took off in a dead run down the sloped aisle. The stage seemed to loom in enormity. He didn't stop to plan but ran up the four steps and dove into the folds of the massive stage curtain. Theo knew he needed to think so that his next move would be his choice and not a reaction and flight. Even the musty smell of the thick curtains was more welcome than the stink of the jaeger. The weight of the curtains prevented much swaying even with the lanky young man tucked inside. He knew if he could stand quietly and wait, he could buy himself some time to look at his surroundings and visualize a plan.

Theo could move his eyes and his head without making any rustling in the curtain. He looked up and counted the iron ballasts suspended above the stage. "One, two, three, four counting mine," he enumerated to himself. He noticed the thick ropes that were strung from pulleys at the end of the curtains. The next curtain over didn't look as heavy as the one where he hid, but he noticed two large burlap bags tethered to the end of a rope. His curiosity encouraged him to quietly move out from the folds to the bags lying on the floor. He tried to lift a bag, but the loose contents were too heavy. He pressed his face against one of the bags. Theo squinted his eyes and furrowed his brow in an effort to recall the familiar odor. *I remember that smell from Dad's lab. He experimented after attending a lecture about how Henry Ford tried to convince scientists to use a plant to make a strong car body. It was—oh, come on, Theo,* he urged his mind. *Hemp! That was it! So these hemp bags must be weights to stabilize the curtain.* As Theo stepped into the curtain, his foot bumped a crank bolted to the floor. His eyes moved upward and followed the rope fastened into the crankshaft. The rope was threaded through a pulley attached to the ballast. From the pulley, the rope dropped back down and ended in a metal clamp holding the two hemp bags. He could not resist the urge to turn the handle of the crank. "Huh," he whispered. "Those bags might be heavy, but they're sure easy to lift with the pulley. I bet if they fell, they could knock out my teeth!" He pulled until the two hemp bags hung with a slight sway about two meters above the stage.

Theo caught his next breath when he heard what sounded like a door bolt being slid. Standing in the folds, he tried to look in the direction of the sound. "That doesn't make sense. There are no doors anywhere around here." Another sound of wood scraping wood came from the same direction across the stage. Nothing could be seen in the darkness, and only the lingering faint odor of the suspended hemp bags reached his nose. Whether urged by fear or confusion, Theo did not move. He knew the stage was too open for hiding and too flat for escape if he were detected. His ears almost ached as he tried to listen for the next sound.

"Uh!" Theo inhaled as a heavy thud came with a burst of blinding light from every light on the stage and in the auditorium. Someone had thrown a main breaker to bathe the opera house in light. For once, the light had become his enemy. "Still and quiet," he fought against the rapid increase of his heartbeat. With an impulsive reflex, Theo coughed as a stench wafted past in the wings of the stage. A heavy footstep hit the stage, and he knew the direction the unwanted smell and footsteps would take. Yet before a breath could fill his lungs, a black leather hand punched the side of Theo's face on its way to grasp his throat.

With impulse driven by a savage desire to survive, Theo lunged for the swinging hemp bag, heaving it above his head before releasing it to fall as dead weight behind him. A sickening sound of a dull impact came with a hoarse cry and splatters of blood that smattered the back of his coat.

Theo had no choice but to turn and run across the open and lit stage. He sprinted crossways to the back curtain. A sharp pain in his shin came just before he fell through a hole. Grimacing, he refilled his lungs with air and rubbed the back of his head where he hit a concrete floor. Theo rolled from his back onto his hands and knees. He felt like an old man as he used his hands and arms to pull himself up a ladder until he could stand. Braced against the ladder, he looked up through the hole. "Of course," he sighed, "a trap door. So that explains why I heard a bolt latch and heard the wood scraping but saw no door—which means …" Theo looked around the dark room where he stood. "There must be a room that has the light breakers."

One step and he just about found himself back on the floor again. "Owwww," he cried while grabbing his shin. He could feel a pretty good goose egg on his shin, but that had to be secondary to his getting away from the light shaft that filtered through the opening in the stage floor. "Buck it up," he huffed to himself as he limped away from the ladder, wishing the pressure in his head would ease up.

Theo extended his arms around him in a flailing sort of manner. He was reaching for anything—a wall, a door, a handle. He moved with two large strides. His arms were out to each side as his next step forward rammed his forehead into a steel doorframe. "Augh," he breathed through clenched teeth, "as if I needed to increase the pounding in my head!" Yet the doorway was welcome as Theo slid his arm around the doorframe and quickly slid with his backpack against the wall. Groping with his left arm extended, he was prepared when he met with the next doorframe.

"If only I had a light."

Slipping inside the open doorway, Theo sensed that he had entered a space as narrow as the hall. Just steps inside the doorframe, he extended both arms out to the side. Each fingertip touched something. This time without flailing his arms, he wiggled his fingers; he moved his hands with the slightest movement of his wrists. Yes, he was touching something, then not, then touching, then not—on both sides. He knew he must move closer to one side to understand what his fingertips brushed. He dropped his right arm and stepped left. His fingers touched and curled around something like a rod or a lever and another and another. "What panel of wall holds multiple and tiny projections? They feel like little levers that I can flip with one finger, little ... LIGHT SWITCHES! But there's too many to control what happened on stage. It wasn't a progression of lights. It was a ..." Suddenly with a passion for discovery, Theo faced the wall of switches and ran both hands lightly over the panel, fingering the tiny levers. He moved down the wall to a corner, across a wall just a little wider than the doorway. "So I'm at the end of the room," he reasoned, "but I haven't found a main switch." Remembering that both hands felt something just inside the door, he retraced his steps until he felt the doorway against his shoulder. Making a 180 turn, he faced the wall on the other side, held both hands in front of him in the pitch darkness, and stepped forward. Three steps and a large wooden handle was in his right hand. Sliding his left hand down the lever, he could feel where a metal bar attached the handle to a large section of the panel. "This must be it." Without hesitation, he pulled the lever down, heard the familiar clunk, and prayed that the stage lay in the same darkness that surrounded him. Listening, he heard heavy footsteps across the ceiling above his head—or did he just imagine? The deed was done. The jaeger had been to the power room in the dark once before; he would know how to return. Theo knew he had to get out of there.

Perhaps the greatest difference between the girl of the streets and the kid who played with technology was experience. She knew survival skills. He knew roads to tomorrow. What they didn't know was how powerful they could be together and how weak when they were apart.

Gracie used her hands to feel her way around the room while her eyes adjusted to the dark. "Okay, girl," she whispered to herself. "Use the skill that kept you alive on the streets and find a way out of here!" In the back of her mind, she knew she needed to find a tunnel to the Kaiserdom. In the depths of her heart, she didn't want to leave Theo. "Stupid boy. I don't even know where he is or if he's blown our cover and been taken. I don't need him. Herr Möeller told me what to do, and I'm going to do it for him," she decided with determination. She had spent her whole life letting her heart love someone and then losing—her father, her mother, Herr Möeller, now the boy from America. This was not different. She would survive. Her eyes seemed to swell in their sockets as she thought of her new friends, Theo and Murphy. "Poor little Murphy," she sighed. Shaking her head as if to shake off the sad thoughts of loss, Gracie moved along the wall with resolve.

She was beginning to wonder if she was trapped in a room with only a staircase for ingress or egress. "Come on," she breathed through her clenched teeth. "Come on!" Five more steps along the wall and her hand hit a doorframe. She could tell by the feel that it was probably wood. It didn't have the flat cold feel of a steel door. Cautiously, she opened the door to a sight of pitch darkness. Without going in, she leaned her head inside the doorway. "Whoo," Gracie gave a soft whistle. The sound hung in the air and dropped to the nothingness. "Whoo," Gracie gave a second call. "Terrific. Nothing." Gracie could tell by the muted sound that the door led into another carpeted room. "It would be too good to find a tunnel," Gracie sighed as she closed the door.

"Get going, girl," she urged herself back into motion of feeling the walls of the great hall in search of a tunnel. Two more times she found a doorway but each time had her hopes dashed as she determined the door only led to more rooms. Each time she resumed her search of the wall in hopes of finding a tunnel.

A fourth door frame stopped her progression of touch. Moving her hand across the frame, her heart gave a small leap as her hand met space instead of the touch of a door. "Uh," she inhaled and began waving her arm in the open space. "Finally!" With no door, she was sure she had found a passageway. Still standing against the wall in the great room, Gracie extended her arm around the doorframe, feeling inside. Her hand hadn't felt more than four inches before a wall was found. Gracie stepped inside the doorway and stood against the wall inside. Again she gave a small whistle, "Whoo." She listened. "Whoo," another whistle. She stood still with her emotions fighting her brain. This was not a room, her whistle had bounced off the close walls, but her steps had not promised anything new. Gracie slid down the wall until she was in a squat. She dropped her hand down beside her until she could feel the floor. Exasperated, she let herself drop on down until she was sitting in the corner. "Carpet." She wanted to cry. What kind of a tunnel has carpet? She moved her left arm in an arch up the wall. She felt smooth wall interrupted by patterns of soft texture. "Some tunnel," she said aloud, wanting to cry.

"Don't become soft now!" she scolded herself. Resigned to move on, she stood and stepped back through the doorway into the grand hall. Move. Feel. Doorframe. Another room. Over and over Gracie hoped she had found a passage only to find another room or hallway. The round shape of the great hall made her wonder how many times she had circled the room. In four places the wall had given way to a small niche where Gracie's hand had found a statue. "I bet these statues are having a good time watching me crawl around the walls!" Gracie laughed to herself as she reached a niche. Exasperated and needing to think, Gracie inched behind the statue and squatted in the niche.

"Whew. No wonder Theo didn't stay in the niche upstairs!" Gracie admitted. "It's cramped back here!" She let herself drop from a squat to sitting on the floor. She tried to extend her legs, but the best she could do in the three foot niche was put the toes of her sneakers on one wall, bend her legs, and put her back on the other wall. "I can't even think anymore!" she reprimanded herself. Gracie ran her left hand across and up the cold statue that stood between her and the great room. *I wonder if this is Mercury or Psyche or a nymph or a cherub.* Gracie let her thoughts fall away. She remembered the cold winter days on the streets when the docents would let her wander through the Alte Pinakothek museum of Munich. She loved the grand and detailed paintings—*Madonna and Child, Madame de Pompadour, Odysseus and Nausikaa,* and one of her favorites, *The Flea-Catcher (Boy with His Dog).* A faint grin softened Gracie's face as she remembered the museum while letting her hand feel the cold statue. A touch of something round on the base of the statue interrupted Gracie's thoughts. She let her fingers discern the round shape. Instinct and curiosity allowed her fingers to press on the round button shape at the base of the statue. The wall beside her left shoulder swung away from her. The pivoting wall left little room for her legs but that was no problem as Gracie stood up in a heartbeat with her back still against the wall but her head turned to the right as she looked down a passage that had been hidden behind the pivoted wall.

"Whoo," Gracie softly whispered, half afraid of being disappointed again and half excited about the possibilities of the new find. This time the whistle came back to her in a hollow sounding echo. "Whoo," again Gracie gave a soft whistle, and again the whistle returned to her in an echo. Reaching inside the pivoted door, Gracie moved her hand only inches before she contacted a cold wall. She extended her right leg through the new doorway and tapped with her foot. Even with her boot giving a dull tap, she could tell the path was not carpeted. Gracie's reaction was to lunge inside the pivoted door. "This is it!" Her excitement propelled her forward, not knowing where she was heading but knowing she was in a tunnel of the Alte Oper. "I won't fail you, Herr Möeller!" she breathed as she took off on a slow jog through the tunnel as she willed her eyes to give her sight into the blackness.

Theo turned and stepped out the door of the control room. "Now, where do I go?" he muttered trying to see both directions for any hint of a way to escape. In an instant, he turned right and headed back down the passage that had taken him to the lighting room. He kept his shoulder to the wall since his eyes had not adjusted to the darkness he had dumped on the opera house. He trotted down the passage, getting a periodic bump or snag from roughness in the passage wall. "Ugh," he caught his next step as the strap of his backpack snagged on an unrelenting disturbance in the wall. He reached up to free the strap and noticed it was hung up on something that felt like a metal cylinder. Theo hesitated and let his fingers talk to him in the dark.

"What's round, about a half inch in diameter, and four or five inches long?" He let his thoughts roam through the mental pages of his geometry book back home as he ran his hand up the wall. His hand hit another cylinder. Quickly, he dropped his hand down the wall and found a third cylinder below the first. *Hinges!* his mind snapped. Turning to face the wall, Theo used both hands to trace the crack in the wall that lay beside the hinges in an effort to find the opening for the door. He was frantic. He couldn't find a handle. "Talk to me!" he ordered his fingers as they felt the hinges and the crack and the wall. Then he remembered the wall had jutted out about four inches before he reached the door hinges. He stepped back to feel the jutted portion of the wall. "Cold air, this isn't solid wall! There's another passage! How do I get into it?" Theo growled at the wall. He pressed his fingertips into the crevice as if the squeeze into the crack would open his thoughts. "If this is a door inside a door, there must be another side." He moved his hand down the edge. His hand hit a lever, which he pressed with all his weight until he was awarded with a solid sound of the door latch giving way. Tugging the lever, Theo was able to slide the door along a track. *Go figure! We have fire doors in Dad's lab. Why didn't I realize?* He lunged through the opening. This time he hesitated long enough to slide the metal door closed. "Now, if this is like any of the fire doors at Dad's lab, if I crank this lever down, it will lock." Theo pressed down until a thud assured him that the handle had settled into a locked position. He ran his hand along the door and found the handle of the door within the door. "Good," he rationalized. "No one can enter this from the outside, but if I need to retrace my steps, I can get back out." He felt good with a plan of action. Without hesitation, he turned and began a fast walk through the passage.

Theo's eyes began to adjust, but there was nothing in the passage to see. "Ow!" He put a hand on the top of his head. Ceiling! He had not noticed the tunnel was closing in, but his leg muscles felt as if he were on an uphill climb. Confused, he stopped and looked back, not sure of his next move. Going back would only put him back under the stage of the opera house. No, he had to go on. He resumed his trek, but he slowed and held one hand above his head in an effort to keep his head from bumping the ceiling. The floor of the passage bent into a steep angle. The floor was moving up, but the ceiling did not turn upward. Theo found himself dropping onto his knees and crawling in order to move through the shrinking passageway. His hands felt the cold tunnel floor. He crawled several meters before he realized the floor was warming again. He stopped and swiveled.

"What would make the air in the tunnel get colder and then begin to warm again?" Returning to his hands and knees, Theo crawled backward until he felt the cold again. He stopped and ran his hands along the walls. He could find no cracks or breaks in the rough concrete walls. He rolled to a sitting position and lifted both hands above his head, feeling the rough ceiling. His fingers sent receptors back to his brain when his fingertips touched a crack. He tapped his fingers. The crack arched and circled. He inched his body under the round crack as he looked above his head. "Outside! I bet this is a manhole cover of some sort!" Theo mumbled aloud as he tried to think his next thought. He pulled his legs under his body until he was in a squat with his arms bent and ready to press above his head. He pressed upward. The round ceiling was unrelenting. "Okay, so I'm not the strongest person in the world, but I have to get out of here!" He pressed upward again.

"Augh!" He sat back down and put his head on his knees. He sat hunched over, berating himself for not signing up for any PE classes that would have built his muscular strength in his arms. He never felt the need to build up biceps when his quads were what helped with his skateboarding. His backpack slid to the side of his back. He reached for the sliding backpack. "Stupid pack. I can't even keep a backpack on my … hey!" Theo tucked the fallen backpack against his stomach as an idea surged through his thoughts. This time he stood as straight as his legs would allow with his back against the circle in the ceiling. Then, extending his legs, he pressed upward with his back as his leg muscles strained and straightened his legs. The circle above him began to move. Stabilizing himself and centering his feet under himself, Theo pressed upward and straightened again. The circle moved allowing a cold wave of air to rush down. Motivated, he let his adrenaline and leg strength fight against the metal circle until he was able to move it up and atop the stone pavement that surrounded the hole on the outside. Theo used both hands to lean against the circle and slide it open.

Slowly, he stood up enough to poke his head through the opening. *Where am I?* His eyes panned the night air. His eyes saw nothing in the dark. He turned, hoping to recognize a landmark. A black form in the night interrupted the view of nothingness. The obscurity of his surroundings made Theo continue to canvas the outside without moving from his stance in the hole. His peripheral vision caught something. He quickly turned his head to the interruption in the dark. Straining, he froze and held his breath, determined to see something in the dark.

"What did I see?" Theo strained his neck hoping his eyes were not playing tricks in the dark. Again, a blink. A blue blink. "Murphy!" The name caught in his throat.

"Murph!" a hoarse whisper came with a burst of breath. "Murphy!" The blue light moved upward a couple inches off the ground. "Murphy!" Theo huffed again. Suddenly, the blue light came to him unimpeded as Murphy jumped out of the bushes and ran toward his master. "Oh, Murphy!" He could not contain his emotions as he dropped the pack he had been holding and reached for Murphy. In one motion, Murphy was back in his master's arms and Theo was sitting on the floor of the tunnel. He buried his head in Murphy's fur.

Gracie slowed to a walk as she felt the air in the tunnel turn cold. "This concrete tunnel must either be descending farther into the earth or into some ice flow because it is freezing in here!" Gracie groaned, sure that her breath was coming out in puffs. She extended her hands out to her sides. She sidestepped to the left until her fingertips touched the wall. Then, she sidestepped to her right, counting her steps until her right hand felt the rough concrete on the other side. She had spent enough time in dark alleys to know how to figure the width even on the darkest night. With her short height, she knew the span of her arms would equal the same distance. Add in two sidesteps, and she could figure the walls were just under two meters apart. "Well, whether I'm in a tunnel or a small room, at least I don't have to worry about running into the wall if I can keep my bearing on a straight course," she muttered as she again picked up her pace. "If I keep moving, I can keep warm."

As she trotted forward, Gracie swung her arms out to the side. On one upswing of her left arm, her fingertips grazed a rough wall. Again she stopped and slowly lifted her right arm while keeping her left fingers touching the wall. This time her arm did not extend fully before the back of her hand scraped the wall. A feeling of uneasiness crept beneath her skin, and without moving, she tilted her head back as she raised her arm. The ceiling too was in reach. "Fine," she breathed. "Now I'm not only freezing but I'm also in a shrinking tunnel." Going back was not an option. She had been in tight places—both mentally and physically—before, and she was ready to face a challenge. Gracie continued at a slower pace, dragging her hands along the walls to either side. After a dozen steps or so, she would raise one arm above her head until she realized the ceiling and the floor were leaving less space for her to move. She couldn't tell if the floor was raising or if the ceiling was dropping.

"Ow," she was caught off guard as she was stopped by a wall dead in front of her. Her vision had adjusted enough that she could see her extended hands. Each hand reached out to an empty tunnel with a wall that now separated the two. "Well, I guess my surprise face plant into the end of a wall means I need to choose which tunnel to take. Hmmm. I'm tired of the cold, so this will be an easy choice. I'm headed for warmth." Gracie pivoted and walked into a warmer zone. She knew she left the cold behind her, but she didn't know the colder tunnel held a boy curled up with his face buried in the fur of the dog in his lap.

CHAPTER 13

Communication

Gracie plunged her hands into her jeans pockets to bring warmth back into her fingers. She felt the diamond crystal she had pulled from the chandelier. The touch of the diamond produced a memory of the velvet couch that seemed to warm her from the inside out. She walked slowly through the tunnel. The rods in her eyes were better adjusted and told her senses that the walls had widened again. Deliberately, she wandered to the left side of the tunnel to let her hand drag along. Her thoughts also seemed to drag along—not sad but not happy either. She tried to think what may have happened to Theo.

If only I could communicate with him. Think, Gracie! she admonished herself. Just like her emotions were tumbling, her thoughts churned, and one never stayed for long before being interrupted by another. Abruptly, her thoughts were again jolted but this time due to a change in the sensation coming through her fingers.

"I'm in a warmer tunnel, but my hand is feeling something cold." Gracie stopped in her tracks and placed both hands on the wall. "Smooth. Smooth and cold," Gracie concentrated as she used both hands to feel the texture of the wall. "Glass!" she gasped. "It's too dark to know if it's a window in the wall, but I know what I can do." Quickly, her hand dove into her pocket and retrieved the diamond crystal. "Ah, a diamond—a girl's best friend! I'll etch a message into the glass. Even if Theo never passes this way or never reads my message, at least I've tried!" She felt a renewed energy in doing something to communicate. *Oh, what to write? What to write?* Her heart was willing, but her thoughts did little to form into any communication. Gracie dropped the diamond crystal back into her pocket and wandered on through the tunnel.

Minutes later, she again felt the cool touch of a glass panel. This time she did not stop, however, as she was sure the tunnel floor tilted upward. She was anxious to see if the upward slant would take her again above the depths of the opera house, and she quickened her steps.

Gracie fought negative thoughts that swarmed in her heart as she realized she was, indeed, on an incline. The floor of the tunnel was giving her calves a bit of a stretch as she walked up the slope. Suspicious of the thicker air, Gracie swung both arms out to her sides. "Ow! Figures!" she exhaled as she rubbed her hands together to pacify the rapped knuckles where both hands had hit the concrete walls on either side. With her left palm facing upward, she extended her arm above her head and continued moving up the tunnel. Again, she found the tunnel closing in as the ceiling was within reach. This time, however, the air seemed to lighten and move in cool currents around her face.

"Wow. This almost feels like someone left a window open!" She saw a slant of light in the tunnel ahead. Gracie found herself bending over in the concrete box that threatened to trap her inside. But the glimmer of light ahead was tickling her curiosity. Gracie saw a metal circle in the ceiling where the shaft of light had entered the tunnel.

"Oh, my goodness! Where am I?" Gracie squatted under the metal circle in the ceiling, scarcely gathering her thoughts before she stood upright and extended her arms to press against the circle. The metal was cold and heavy, refusing to give way to the pressure of her arms. The more the circle refused to move, the more determined Lil Grey became. Pressing upward, she strained against the ceiling. "Ugh. Okay. Think, Lil Grey. If I were on the streets fighting for my life, I bet I could move this. Maybe I can lift one side and wedge it open to spin it out of place." Gracie felt in her pockets, along the dark walls, and along the floor for something to use as a wedge. She stomped her foot in exasperation. The heavy boot made a dull sound in the tunnel. "Wait a minute! My boot! Ugh! I hate you boots but if you help me, I'll love you!" She grinned as she unlaced her shoe.

Using the top of her head to help her arms lift the metal plate, Gracie slowly stood her full height as she pressed against one side of the round ceiling. The plate grated and moved enough that she could wedge the toe of her boot into the opening. Again, she pressed up and moved more of the shoe into the opening until she could stand and fit her shoulders into the opening to slide the plate open.

"Uh!" Gracie inhaled and almost choked on the cool night air that rushed into her lungs. Against the dark of the tunnel, the light from above was easy to see. However, Gracie slowly took in her surroundings to notice that the light was only a few rays of a three-quarter moon that had seeped down through a manhole cover. She carefully surveyed her surroundings and realized that the tunnel was no longer under the Alte Oper but was actually under the stone courtyard that surrounded the building. Gracie scarcely breathed aloud but let her eyes search intently to get her bearings. To her left was the edifice where she and Theo had entered as the jaegers closed in upon them. To her right was the grove of linden trees where the teens had last seen Murphy before his display of light and fireworks in the courtyard fountain. Even now, she missed Murphy and wondered if he had been caught by the sentries who wore the Schiffchen caps with the SS insignia. His plan to distract the evil men would only have been perfect if he could have escaped with Theo and Gracie. Squatting back down into the tunnel, Gracie let the manhole cover slip back down into its grooved position in the stones.

Again, Gracie's hands slipped into her pockets as she slid to the floor deep in thought. *If only I could see Theo or Murphy again. I just don't know where they are or how to find them.* She let her eyes close and her fingers roll the diamond from the chandelier.

What would I do on the streets? Gracie quizzed her exhausted mind. *Maybe I'd leave a trail, or set a trap, or whistle "Edelweiss," or write my name on the buildings in the alleys, or ...* Gracie felt like her mind had been clamped down with the metal plate that held her in the tunnel. Thinking clearly had become impossible.

"Maybe I can sell this diamond and buy our passage to the Kaiserdom so Herr Möeller won't be disappointed in me," Gracie whispered cynically into the air. "Lot of good it is to have a diamond when I'm trapped in a concrete tunnel with only a few glass walls … That's it! The glass! I can etch a message to Theo in case he's still in the opera house!"

With renewed energy, Gracie jumped up so quickly that she smacked her head against the low ceiling. "Augh! That wasn't my smoothest move of the day," Gracie huffed as she bent over and hurried back through the tunnel. She moved at a fast walk allowing her right shoulder to rub along the wall using her hands to search for the glass panels.

Nearly to the point of thinking she had missed the glass in the walls, she felt the cool, smooth change in the wall texture. In a heartbeat she pulled the diamond from the chandelier and began scraping the glass with deliberate letters, L-I-N-D-Y.

I wish I knew how far back it is to the other glass in the wall. Gracie mulled the thought over in her mind as she tried to remember her earlier trek through the tunnel. "Oh, I just need to go back and see if I can find it. Two messages have a better chance of being found!" she convinced herself as she resumed a quick pace with her right shoulder dragging against the wall while her hands searched as if they had eyes on each fingertip.

Within minutes, Gracie found the other section of glass in the tunnel wall. Again, she began her deliberate etching with the diamond, L-I-N, but her hand stopped suddenly as she was sure she heard noise in the tunnel. Gracie strained her ears to hear beyond the heavy silence and forced her eyes to peer into the blackness. She could see nothing, but her ears did not deceive her. What was it—a thud? a scrape? Gracie realized that she could not waste time trying to decipher the sound. She heard sound in the tunnel, and that meant danger. She turned and ran with her shoulder against the wall until she felt the rise of the tunnel floor. Gracie dropped to her knees and began furiously crawling toward the metal plate that promised her freedom from whatever was pursuing her in the tunnel.

"He needs the touch of love and an activity to get him out of the house." Theo could hear the words of his therapist bouncing off the walls of his mind just as clearly as when he struggled with his mother's death. Moving somewhere between survival and determination to retaliate, he had hardly slowed both mentally and physically since the explosion in the lab. Walking through the dark tunnel with his shoulder rubbing along the wall, Theo was left with his thoughts of how close he had come to losing both his dad and Murphy. The familiar thoughts of loss nearly overwhelmed him. He stooped to pick up the canine companion trotting along beside him.

"What would I have done if those stupid blue lights on your collar hadn't been blinking? You saved my life, Murph! You and your light show! You must have shocked the pants off those German SS guards!" Theo gave a good head rub to the dog he held in his arms while simultaneously fending off the tongue that threatened to lick his owner's face. Holding Murphy in his arms made him grin again and lightened his steps as he moved through the empty tunnel. Murphy squirmed in delight of being back with his master while the blue lights of his collar absorbed into the grey thickness of the concrete walls.

"Yeah, Murph, when we get outta here, I'm going to find you a huge slipper to chew ..." Theo's words stopped in midthought as his eyes were distracted by the tricks Murphy's blue lights were playing on the walls. The tunnel was dark, and the lights had done little to cut through the thick, almost palpable air. But there was something different as the lights seemed to bounce back from the wall ahead. The boy from America had matured during his time in Germany, and a young girl of the streets had taught him to be aware of his surroundings. Noticing the lights, he stayed his pace and stared at the wall. Murphy energetically wagged his tail, causing his body to shake and the blue lights of the collar to refract from the wall.

Cautiously, Theo inched forward with his left arm extended to the front as his hand felt along the concrete wall. His fingers felt a change from the rough wall to a smooth, cool texture.

"Look at this, Murphy. This must be a door with a glass window." Theo set the dog on the floor and felt around for a handle to verify his find. His fingers seemed to half walk half dance across the glass and down the metal door in search of a bar or knob to release a latch. "Ah!" Excitement reeled from his breath as he felt a lever just a little above waist high. Leaning his weight on the lever, he began to forcefully press down until the level gave way with the click of the door bolt. Theo pulled the door into the tunnel just enough to peer into the darkness that lay beyond. Nothing but dark and musty air seemed to lie within the door. Dejected, he closed the door and released the handle hearing the bolt reinsert into its original position in the striker plate.

"Fat-lotta-good that did." Theo looked down at Murphy as he rested his head against the glass. "I guess I was hoping for a way outta here." Murphy just sat with his tail whipping back and forth across the tunnel floor. The dejected traveler pulled his head across the glass window in the door as he pushed back to a standing position.

"Geez! That glass is rough!" Theo quipped as he put his fingers on his forehead where a slight trickle suggested a scratch oozing a little blood. Knitting his brow, he looked back at the glass and placed his hand on the section that had scraped his forehead. The glass felt rough.

"C'mere, Murphy." He picked up his companion and held him close to the wall so the blue lights would expose the roughness of the glass.

"Wow. Someone has been writing on this glass—in English! Let's see." Theo squinted to see the glass more clearly and held Murphy up as a light source.

"L-I-N. Well, that's a cryptic message. Maybe it's not English after all." Theo moved Murphy around in circles against the wall in an attempt to reveal any more letters, but none were to be found.

"A door with no good tunnel. Letters with no good word. Huh. We're batting a thousand, Murphy. Let's go." Theo set his dog back down to trot along beside him as they continued through the tunnel. Like a boy who clatters along dragging a stick along a picket fence, he let his left hand drag along the tunnel wall.

Too tired to care anymore but too hungry to stop, Theo and Murphy followed the left wall of the tunnel. Just as an eerie feeling made the dark walls seem to close in on him, he noticed Murphy's blue collar lights were reflecting off the wall ahead. "I suppose there's another door that wants to tease us and give us empty hope," he smirked. Murphy just continued his happy trot by his master's side. As Theo's hand felt the temperature and texture change in the wall, he again lifted Murphy to use him as a portable blue flashlight.

"Hey, more letters! L-I-N-D-Y. Hmmm. Murphy, do we know that word?" Theo moved Murphy around looking for more letters. "Figures. No more letters. Crud, I don't know that word. I'm not German! I don't even know any good Germans. Too bad IRIS isn't here to tell me what that means. Too bad your collar only translates speech. Too bad Gracie's not here to read it to me." He set Murphy back down onto the floor of the tunnel and started walking on up the tunnel.

"I don't even know where Gracie is." Murphy wiggled as if he understood his master's words. "You kinda like her, don't you, ol' pal? Huh? I saw the way you snuggled with Gracie out there in that grove of … That's it! Murphy! You're a genius! Lindy! When we were sitting in the grove of linden trees, Gracie said her mom was named Lindy—after the linden tree! You've found Gracie!!!"

Theo took off in a trot up the tunnel with a happy Murphy tagging along at his heels. As the floor of the tunnel began to rise, he remembered the tunnel where he found Murphy. The tunnel narrowed and closed in just as it came under a manhole cover to the outside. He held his hand over his head with the palm up and almost skipped when he realized the ceiling was closing in on him. Stooped and trying to hurry, Theo looked up trying to find any crack in the ceiling that would hold a metal plate. Not even a quarter of an hour had passed before he was rewarded with the sight of moonlight seeping through the tunnel ceiling where the metal plate rested in the round hole.

By the time Theo was tucking Murphy into his backpack and climbing out of the manhole, the dark sky was beginning to lighten enough to show silhouettes of the fountain, the opera house, and the gardens across the courtyard. He kept low to the ground and ran in a squat position, thankful that his tricks on his driftboard had helped his quad muscles strengthen and reject the burn of muscle held in the squat position. He ran toward the grove of linden trees knowing his and Murphy's lives depended upon stealth and speed. Theo knew the pat of his footsteps could be heard, but he dare not slow to try to soften his footfalls. Within minutes, the sounds changed to his own puffs of breath and the muted sound of his feet hitting the mulch path that extended into the grove. Again, the darkness blanketed his surroundings as the light from the promise of daybreak could not penetrate the web of trees.

Theo's feet left the path as something or someone grabbed his backpack and pulled him backward into the cover of the brush. Flailing, he reacted in fight. He had come too far to succumb to the terrors of the night. Thrashing with his legs, the strong legged teen tried to kick out at whatever had attacked him from behind. He was caught unaware, and his arms were being held to his waist.

"Umph!" Theo felt his face hit the mat of leaves on the ground.

"Stop! Stop!" Theo rolled over against the force that was attacking him and telling *him* to stop. Even Murphy's muffled yelps from inside the backpack revealed that he too was a victim of the attack. His skill on the driftboard had given him leg strength to push out from beneath the attacker and stand puffing and looking down at a mass on the ground.

Gracie looked up from the leaves where Theo's upheaval had tossed her.

"You!"

"Quiet!" Gracie retorted with a gruff whisper. "Do you want to be taken?"

"Why couldn't you just get my attention instead of attacking me from behind?"

"I didn't mean to attack you. I was half trying to get your attention without talking and half excited to see you. But don't worry. I'm over that!" Gracie breathed through her teeth, angry that a tear had slipped out with her words.

Theo fell to the ground beside Gracie, pulling his backpack around to see if Murphy had weathered the jostling. As he unzipped the backpack, he noticed Gracie drop her head to her knees as she sat in a tiny ball. Murphy crawled out of the backpack and lay on the ground beside the two silent teens. Impulsively, he wrapped his arms around the bent form sitting on the ground beside him. Reluctantly, then gratefully, the girl of the streets let him.

Although exhausted, the two teens knew they risked exposure by daylight.

"Theo, we still need to get to the Kaiserdom." Gracie pulled away and looked into his face.

"Right. But how?"

"We need to go through the tunnel."

"Um, we just came from the tunnel. I was at pretty much of a dead-end or at least in a very small space when I saw Murphy's blue lights on his collar shining down through a manhole cover. Then, I followed your path through another section of the tunnel and came out the manhole cover that's just across the courtyard from where we are right now. Neither tunnel leads us to the Kaiserdom."

"No, but I have a knot on my head to prove there's another tunnel." Gracie whispered with enthusiasm.

"I'll never understand girls. What the heck are you talking about?" Theo grunted.

"Oh, it's a little complicated to explain, but basically, I came to a fork in the tunnel and didn't know it until I ran head first into the Y. I'll bet you followed the tunnel by keeping the wall on your left."

"Uh, yeah, I guess so. But what does that have to do with you running into a wall?"

"We both took the left leg of the Y. The right leg of the tunnel will hopefully take us to the Kaiserdom! We won't know until we try it, and we need to do this for Herr Möeller."

"Okay. There's just one small problem getting to the tunnel," Theo warned.

"What?"

Theo gestured with a nod in the direction of the stone court-yard. Enough dawn was breaking that the silhouettes of the SS guards could be seen against the wall of the opera house.

"It's now or never," Gracie whispered looking Theo straight in the eye. "I'm game."

"Me too. But let's play it smart. I'll put Murphy back into my backpack. We can't have him running loose and take a chance on losing him again. One of us has to go first to remove the manhole cover so the other one can come after a minute or so and just slip in. I'll go first."

"Wait!" Gracie frowned. "Why should you get to go first?"

"Well, for one, it's dangerous, and two, I'm the guy, so I should go first." Theo enumerated holding up a finger with each point.

"Oh, don't be such an egotistical martyr! I'm going first because I can slide the metal cover even with the extra bulk of my backpack. Besides, I left the cover off once I was out, and I'm sure you did too. It doesn't matter who goes first. We are both in danger of being caught. I'm smaller and can get into the hole quicker if the cover blocks it in any way. Give me a minute, then you come and just drop into the hole. We can both slide the cover back into place when we're inside the tunnel."

There was something that just rubbed Theo the wrong way when he thought of himself being saved again by this girl. However, she was right. Who was to say which person had the most dangerous run? They needed to be as fast and imperceptible as possible.

They stood at the edge of the grove where the stone courtyard met the mulch path. In silence, they waited and watched as one of the guards sauntered around the corner of the opera house where two more guards stood in the arched doorway smoking cigarettes and blowing smoke into the morning air. When the guard rounded the corner, Gracie looked back at Theo, reached out and squeezed his arm, and took off in a low run toward the manhole cover. Gracie was nimble and quick first dropping her backpack and sliding her body down into the hole, then using her shoulders to move the cover farther off of the hole to make more room for Theo to quickly drop in with his backpack. Then, she ducked out of sight.

Whispering a prayer into the air of the breaking dawn, Theo dashed for the hole in the courtyard stones, dropped in, and the two slid the heavy cover back into place. The metal screeched across the stones, but the two didn't stay to see if anyone would come looking into the tunnel from the realm above ground.

"Wait!" Theo whispered and reached for Gracie's arm. "We can use Murphy's collar to help light the tunnel." In an instant, Murphy was unzipped from the pack and set down in front of the two teens where he happily trotted along as a guiding light. Gracie kept an eye on the wall as they retraced their earlier steps. She knew that they would pass both fire doors with the glass windows before reaching the place where the tunnel split in another direction.

As they passed the second fire door window, Theo glanced over his shoulder. "Hey, Gracie, that was a pretty good clue for me to find you, but it roughed up my forehead a bit."

"What?" Gracie was puzzled.

"Oh, let's just say it was just like you finding the Y in the tunnel—I *used my head!*" Theo chuckled remembering how he had scraped his head on the rough etched glass before he even knew it was a message from Gracie.

"We had better pace ourselves. We're far enough into the tunnel that I think we're safe. We should save our energy and only run when we need to." Gracie walked in front, running her hand along the wall so she wouldn't miss the turn they needed to reach the tunnel to the Kaiserdom.

Gracie's hand fell into nothingness and felt her heart skip a beat as she stopped in her tracks. "Murphy! Wait up!"

"What's the problem, now?" Theo snapped as he ran into the back of her.

"No problem! The wall ended."

"So?"

"So that means we've found the Y and the other tunnel." Gracie couldn't keep her voice from raising in excitement.

"Uh, yeah. Well, this is the tunnel where I found Murphy. Let me tell ya, it's a little narrow."

"So it's narrow. It's a tunnel! Whadda you expect?" Gracie didn't hide her exasperation.

"Look. The tunnel we've been in is under a building where there are stairs and manholes to get out. The Kaiserdom is at least a kilometer away. That means we'll be in a tunnel under the city. It just seems we might be able to move faster if we find a path above ground."

"Oh, so now you're smarter than Herr Möeller? Listen, if he said this is the path we need to take, I'm not going to look for some other way. Come on, Murphy." Gracie turned and rounded the forked tunnel before Theo could think of another response.

"When we get outta here, I'm going to make some of the decisions." Theo's voice trailed off as he hurried to follow Gracie and Murphy's blue lighted collar into the narrow tunnel.

CHAPTER 14

Kaiserdom

Time passed slowly as Theo and Gracie made the underground trek from beneath the Alte Oper to the Kaiserdom. The subterranean tunnel began to twist and turn after only a short distance of easy upright traveling. Murphy trotted ahead of the teens, seeming to enjoy his role of leading and using his blue collar to light the way. Theo tried to keep his bearings, but the constant turning and switchbacks disoriented him causing him to completely lose his sense of direction. The tunnel narrowed and expanded; it went from standing height to areas where both teens had to crawl on their hands and knees to get through. The confined space of the tunnel began to work against the young man's confidence. He had been less than fond of having to move through the closeness of the tunnel beneath the Alte Oper, but knowing there was an open edifice above gave him an assurance that he could not be trapped. Here, however, in the underground tunnel, Theo's mind began to suffocate him with thoughts of being trapped with the possibility of being buried alive with nothing but solid earth encasing the underground escape path.

"Do you think it's much farther?" Even in the dark, Theo could feel sweat dripping in runnels down his face. "I'm having trouble breathing. It's so hard to breathe down here."

Gracie stopped and called out, "Hold up, Murph."

Murphy obediently stopped, turned around, and trotted back to Gracie's side. He put one paw on her leg to show his presence.

Gracie could not help but smile as she reached down and gave her new hero a quick ear scratch.

"Murphy, can you shine your ocular light on Theo?" She lifted the dog into her arms.

"It really shouldn't take this long, should it? I mean, if we were above ground, it would take about fifteen minutes to get to the church." Theo complained as he wiped the sweat from his brow. He took long, slow breaths trying to get air to his heavy lungs. "What are you staring at?"

In the strange glow of light emanating from Murphy's eyes, Theo could see Gracie standing in the damp, dark tunnel with her eyes fixed on him. A smile began to form on Gracie's face as it dawned on her why he was sweating and complaining.

"You're claustrophobic." The smirk on her face didn't suggest compassion. "Just take it easy and breathe slowly."

"Thanks for the help." After a sarcastic retort, Theo leaned against the wall of the tunnel and slid down to sit on the ground. He laid his head on his crossed arms and took slow, labored breaths.

Gracie really did feel sorry for him. In her mind, she could understand how his problem could become her problem too. *This is not going to be good if he freaks out in this tunnel. We're too far in and too far underground.* "It shouldn't be much farther," she offered enthusiastically trying to help his condition and his mood. She leaned over and set Murphy on the tunnel floor beside his master. "Would it help if Murphy and I scout ahead to see how much longer we have down here?"

Theo lifted his head from his arms and looked at Gracie standing above him. The smirk was gone and concern had replaced it. "I'll be fine. Just give me a minute ... thanks, though."

"No problem." Gracie paused to collect her thoughts and choose her next words carefully in an attempt to restore his confidence. "If it makes you feel any better, I'm totally freaked out about being underneath the city. Do you want some water?" She started rummaging through her backpack.

Theo exhaled slowly then took the canteen of water that Gracie offered. He took a long, slow drink and then poured a little over his head to wake himself up a little. The lack of air, light, and any sense of direction was making him grumpy, nervous, and tired. "Thanks," he said as he handed back the canteen.

Gracie took a drink of water, just enough quench her dry throat, then replaced the cap. She slid the canteen back into her pack saving the rest in case Theo needed any more. She extended her hand, "Ready?"

Without reply he reached up and grabbed her hand and pushed off the ground with his free hand as she pulled with all her might. Standing in the tight quarters forced him uncomfortably close to Gracie, their faces only a few inches apart. Quickly, both looked away in embarrassment as if they found something else that grabbed their attention in the pitch black tunnel.

Assuming enough time had passed for the awkwardness to be over, Theo decided to give Murphy a quick check-over. He had not taken time to inspect his canine companion since his heroic reappearance after his fireworks display in the fountain of the Alte Oper. Theo looked down just as his dog took off running back down the tunnel to stand at their last turn. His front external light extinguished. Murphy stood in his protector mode, ears and tail sticking straight up.

Gracie followed the direction of Theo's intent look and noticed the change in Murphy's mode and position. She quietly slipped behind her tall friend. He stood listening for any hint of what was causing Murphy to stand on alert. A few moments of quiet had slipped by when Murphy's ears twitched. The teens looked at each other to silently acknowledge they heard a scratching noise from somewhere in the tunnel they had left behind.

"I bet it's stuck in the tiny crawl space."

"You could barely fit through there."

"We need to go before it gets through. We have nowhere to hide." Theo suspicioned the jaeger or Nazi guard must have found the opening to the tunnel.

"Well, I guess you can focus on that instead of the lack of space." Gracie slipped past him and ran her hand down Murphy's back. The dog's ears and tail fell as the motion gave him permission to come down from high alert. "Good boy, Murphy. Come on, this way." She pointed down the tunnel that still lay ahead of them.

Murphy gave a low growl in the direction of the tunnel behind them and then spun around and scampered past Theo and Gracie, his blue collar and forward external light springing to life, lighting the path ahead.

"Great, more tunnel," Theo mumbled cynically, looking over his shoulder as his gaze followed Murphy's trot.

Gracie just shook her head and smiled as she physically turned Theo around and pushed him forward.

"I'm going." He grunted as he started down the path. "Think I would rather just wait for whatever is coming for us." He shook his head and broke into a slow jog. Gracie followed closely behind.

After a few minutes of jogging behind Murphy's carefree pace, Theo and Gracie switched to a quick walk as the walls began to close in on them, forcing them to travel single file. The ceiling started to slope downward, getting closer and closer to their heads. Theo was glad Gracie could not see him well; the shrinking tunnel was really making it hard for him to focus. He reached down to grab his shirt and wipe his face, cleaning off sweat and dust.

"Do you hear that?" The inability to see far had forced Gracie to rely on her other senses.

"Hold up a sec, Murph." Theo closed his eyes and strained to pick up any new sound other than a faint but always present scratching noise of whatever was trailing them.

"Sounds like … sounds like running water. Like after a rainstorm when the water floods the streets as it pours off the roofs of neighborhood houses." Gracie hesitated as memories bombarded her mind. In spite of the fears of the tunnel, she smiled slightly at the scenes dancing in her mind's eye.

"Sometimes after the really bad storms, the drain pipes would be so full that the street would flood, and we would go out and splash in it. Papa loved to watch me splash around. Once he even "accidentally" fell into Mama, and they both fell into the stream of rain water. She was so mad at him, saying he had done it on purpose."

Gracie stood grinning, absorbed in the memory. "Papa proclaims his innocence even to this day."

Gracie's memory affected Theo. Without realizing, his breathing had slowed. Even his fear and anxiety had temporarily melted as he too visualized a young Gracie and her family having fun in a summer storm.

The scenes in his head shifted from Gracie's family back to a similar day when he and his mother had walked along the boardwalk and a storm rolled in. Everyone on the walk had dashed for shelter. Just as he started to run, his mother reached out and stopped him. "Feel the rain, Theo. Doesn't it feel wonderful, son?" Until Gracie's story, he had believed his mother was the only person who would stand in the rain and let it pour down on her. He could see her long hair stuck to her face. He remembered her smile as she laughed even as the rain fell harder on them. He would give anything to be able to share one more day in the rain with her.

"Theo, Theo … Hey, Theo!"

"Whoa, sorry, sort of zoned out for a minute." A sadness hit Theo in the gut as the memory of his mother faded away, leaving reality to rear its ugly face.

"You okay?"

"Fine, sorry." He rubbed his eyes and gave a quick shiver to shake the fog from his mind and focus on the problems they were facing. "So we've got a shrinking tunnel, water rushing in from somewhere, and oh yeah, forgot to mention something or someone chasing us down a tunnel that seems like it will go on forever."

"That something or someone is getting closer, I think." A look of concern had washed over Gracie's face.

"Right. Let's get moving." With each twist and turn in the path, the tunnel continued to close in. The two pushed themselves to keep up with Murphy and his guiding light. Theo's thoughts worked against him. *The only thing worse than being stuck in a shrinking tunnel is to be stuck in a shrinking tunnel in the dark.* His thoughts were about to form into words when Murphy's light that lit the tunnel vanished and punched them into blackness. "What the …" Theo moved in front of Gracie.

"Where'd he go?" Gracie gasped. "How is it was possible to vanish into thin air in the middle of an enclosed concrete tunnel?"

"I don't know." Theo tried to sound calm as he called out for his dog. "Murphy, where are you?"

They waited quietly in the dark for Murphy to reappear or bark or do anything to let them know he was fine. Theo reached back to find Gracie almost touching him. "We have to keep moving. Murphy wouldn't leave us unless he had a reason."

"What if he's hurt? You never got a chance to … to … what did you say you needed to do?"

"Check his operating system for damage."

"Yeah, that."

"I don't know, but hold onto my backpack, and *don't* let go." Once she had a firm grip and he could feel Gracie's tug on his pack, Theo started moving forward, his left hand on the wall beside him and his right hand outstretched in front of him.

Swallowed in darkness, more noises could be heard in the tunnel behind them. Nothing had been seen, but an undeniable feeling of something in the dark—something dangerous, something evil—motivated them to jog a little faster against the contractions of their tired muscles. The sound of rushing water grew louder as they moved deeper into the tunnel. Theo's lungs felt like they were being squeezed in a vise, and he fought back by taking shallow breaths. Not only was something terrible chasing them but the unknown ahead taunted them until they were unsure if it would be better or worse to go forward. The tunnel continued narrowing and lowering. At this rate, it would not be much longer before they wouldn't be able to move standing upright. Anxiety was suffocating him. He opened his clenched fist and put his open palm at the end of his nose. He saw nothing.

The concrete wall felt smooth and cool on his hand as Theo guided Gracie farther into the labyrinth. Within minutes of moving through the dark tunnel, he felt the roof of the tunnel brush his hair. He ducked defensively and lost his balance. He never had a chance to catch himself as he fell forward. His face hit the hard surface, causing him to groan much louder than he or Gracie would have liked.

The echo of his groan rolled down the tunnel. Noises behind them seemed to be getting closer at a faster rate. Something behind them must have sensed its prey was just ahead.

"Theo, what are we gonna do?" Gracie had an unfamiliar sound of panic in her voice. She was a tough kid who had been hardened on the streets of Munich, but the idea of being captured by a jaeger scared her more than she wanted to admit even to herself.

"Give me a minute," he shot back, the panic clear in his voice.

"We don't have a minute."

"Down here." Theo pulled Gracie down to the floor of the tunnel.

"It's not really a good time to take a break." Gracie scolded as she was yanked to the cold floor.

Theo ignored her jab. "Put out your hand ... Ow, that was my face not the wall, Gracie."

"Sorry, what am I feeling for?"

"Feel the bottom of the wall, just above the floor. This explains why it got brighter before Murphy and his light disappeared." Theo acted like Gracie should understand.

She didn't as she worked her hand down the wall. Her arm sank up to her elbow into an empty space. "Oh, no! Another crawl space!"

By the time Gracie understood, Theo had rolled on the floor and put his head into the opening in the wall before he sat up and tried to see Gracie's face in the dark. "Exactly, but that running water isn't up ahead—it's in the crawl space—possibly a river or spring or some way out! You can hear it really well when you put your head into the space. Hang on a second." He slipped his head back into the crawl space. "Murphy!"

"What are you doing?"

"Calm down. We're out of options. Whatever is following us will catch up soon. There's nowhere to hide in this tunnel. The most we can hope for—" Theo stopped midsentence as a soft blue light filled the tiny crawl space. "Come on, boy."

Gracie tried to stick her head into the space as well but slammed into Theo. She couldn't totally fit into the space but could see the blue light of the dog collar making its way quickly back to them. "Are you sure we should we go into this small hole?"

Theo sighed, "What choice do we have? You first. You shouldn't have any problem crawling through. If I get stuck in this hole, you're stuck in the tunnel too. Plus, you might be able to pull me through if you're already inside the hole."

Gracie didn't give Theo a chance to change his mind. She pulled his head and shoulders out of her way and started crawling like a rat into the tiny space. She was quickly greeted with a few loving licks from Murphy's wet tongue as he was able to traverse the crawl space much faster than either of them. He barked in excitement, then turned around and headed back the way he came, sure that the silly humans would keep up this time.

They crawled as fast as they could, but the space constricted, allowing less room for movement. Theo began to struggle to move his wide shoulders between the walls. "I swear, the next time someone gives me an option between a tunnel of earth and the Nazis, I'm taking the Nazis." He grunted in disgust and frustration. He was so focused on moving toward the sound of rushing water that he never heard his pursuers closing in.

"Theo, hurry!" Gracie rolled and looked backward as Murphy's blue collar shed enough light for her to see behind Theo. She didn't like the intense darkness that seemed to follow. Instinctively, Gracie began to move faster, fear taking hold of her and giving her a burst of energy to push on.

Theo sensed the worry in Gracie's voice. He did his best to squeeze himself forward, hearing his backpack scraping on the tunnel above him. He lifted his head as much as he could just in time to see Gracie and the light of his best friend vanish in a strange blur. He stopped crawling as the light that was his focal point dissolved into the darkness. The pitch black was wrapping itself around his throat as if to slowly choke the life out of him. Panic set in. His breathing became labored. The stifled air refused to enter his lungs. He tried taking small, short breaths, but his rapid breathing only made the suffocation worsen. Again, the scratching noise from behind and the sound of running water from ahead commanded his attention. *I don't want to die down here, not like this, not like this!* Fear started to take over. *MOVE YOUR BUTT, MOVE, THEO! NOW!* Another voice interjected into his brain. It sounded like a mix of his father and mother telling him to move, to take control, to stop being afraid, and to fight to live.

Theo inhaled through his nose and tried to collect his thoughts. He inched forward, but the effort was exhausting. His body was wedging in tighter each time he moved forward. He wanted to stop and rest, but the noises behind him and the voices in his head refused to let him close his eyes and rest. He twisted himself sideways and was able to work his arm over his head, then with a bit of effort, the other arm extended above his head. He dug both hands into the earth of the crawlspace and braced his feet.

Theo used his muscular legs to propel himself forward as he pulled with the tips of his fingers. He could feel the dirt under his fingernails and the tunnel of earth scraping both his flattened backpack and his stomach as he scooted forward a little at a time. He repeated pushing and pulling. The air being sucked in through his nostrils was earthy with a damp, musty smell. *Don't stop. Push! Don't stop. Push! Don't stop. Push! Don't stop. Push!* Theo used his thoughts to create a cadence for movement and to distract his thoughts of being buried alive in a hole away from the tunnel Herr Möeller had instructed him to take.

On his sixth or seventh reach forward to pull, his hands dug into a muddy floor. He pulled himself forward and felt the pressure of the earth around him lessening. The excitement of actual progress gave Theo a renewed burst of adrenaline to push harder.

Don't stop. Push! Don't stop. Push! Don't stop. Push! Don't stop. Push! Theo hung his hopes on the soft earth beneath him as the increased girth of the hole increased his hope. After a few more pushes and pulls, he was sure the tunnel was widening and getting muddier with increased sound of rushing water. His eyes teased that he could see light ahead, but the light seemed cloudy and distorted. *This is not a time to let my mind wander and play tricks on me! Don't stop. Push! Don't stop. Push!* He felt a drive to keep moving toward the mysterious light and, hopefully, find Gracie and Murphy.

Exhaustion began to threaten as Theo discovered he could move freely enough to get into a bear-crawl position on his hands and knees. The dirt of the crawlspace had absorbed water causing mud to cake all over him. A spray of water splashed onto his face and neck. The light wasn't getting any brighter as he moved forward, but he could see something moving behind a cloudy veil and hear what sounded like distorted voices shouting.

After crawling a little farther, Theo could feel water splashing down around him. The muddy mess of crawlspace emptied into a wider cavern. He moved into a kneeling position and slowly reached out his hand. The sensation of rushing water caused him to jerk back his hand and laugh. He began to pull his feet under him when he noticed a ball of light shining through the down pouring waterfall. He froze, not sure what to do or think. He sure as heck wasn't going back into the crawl space—it didn't matter what he was about to face. He reared back his fist ready to swing first and ask questions later.

Theo stood up from a squat position and readied himself for the worst. He was about to swing as a hand holding a lantern emerged through the water, just as a hand wrapped around his ankle. Glancing down, he screamed at the sight of a black gloved hand holding his ankle. Another scream ended with the wind knocked out of his chest as the clenched hand pulled his leg out from under him. Against the muddy ground he rolled to his back gasping for air and kicking wildly. Another hand emerged from the crawlspace grabbing his leg as he kicked. "Help me!" He screamed to the ball of light as he looked away from the leather clad hands and back to the waterfall.

Theo's vision was blurred by what looked like two lanterns suspended above him. The mud gave way as the powerful hands dragged him back into the tunnel. He reached in desperation to hold something solid. A hoarse cry lodged in his throat as a pair of rough hands grabbed his arms. A man emerged from the blurred light, gripping Theo's arms, doing his best to pull the boy to safety.

"Nina, trow the cocktail, now!" came a voice from in front of him.

"I haven't got it lit yet, Fritz. This waterfall has complicated matters a great deal," a feminine voice replied with a calm tone. She was frightened for the youth but not scared about the situation. Her steady voice suggested this was not her first time to save a life from being sucked into a black abyss. "There we go, love," she shouted. Theo watched as two liquor bottles with flaming rags were tossed past his feet into the crawl space.

A combination of flame and alcohol from one of the bottles exploded around Theo's feet in the dark tunnel. He screamed with a force from the depths of his lungs as he felt the air around his legs heat up like an oven. The heat moved up his body. He felt the hair on his legs singe. As the flames swept back into the crawl space, he felt the grip on his ankle weaken. He seized the moment to kick both legs, hoping they weren't on fire. With the help of the man pulling him away from the hole, he was able to pull his legs from the crawl space and free himself. The second bottle exploded in the muddy tunnel, shooting flames where Theo had been just moments ago.

The stranger with the funny accent practically lifted Theo to his knees. He took a moment to wipe off mud that had caked onto his clothes as he had rolled around trying to get away from his assailant. He swiped his hands on the side of his legs then extended his hand toward the small-framed man.

"Thank you. I hate to think what would have happened if you two hadn't shown up when you did."

The woman called Nina was the first to reply. "Gracie said you were having a bit of trouble. Seems like she wasn't exaggerating."

"Ve need to be on our vay. Tat von't keep tem down for long." The small stranger named Fritz had bravely stepped in to help, but the tone in his words let Theo know that he was worried.

"Wait, you mean those things in the tunnel aren't dead?" Theo was shocked that anything could survive the assault.

Nina and Fritz looked at each other and tried to hide their smiles. "Theo, dear, I'm honestly surprised that these," Nina said holding up another liquor bottle with a rag sticking out of the spout, "even slowed them down. The lack of space in that section of tunnel must have amplified the blast. Fritz is right as usual. We need to get outta here now. Grab your pack, and let's be on our way."

"All right." Theo turned to get his pack. He caught a glimpse of something coming through the waterfall and ducked in reaction.

Murphy exploded from the water with his ears pinned back. Gracie followed just steps behind the possessed dog. Murphy landed on the muddy tunnel floor, then without any wasted movements, sprang over a kneeling boy in one fluid motion. Theo rolled away from the crawl space entrance as a badly burned arm reached out to grab him again. Murphy's mechanical jaw locked down on the arm, viciously twisting and turning it, attacking to protect his master. As Murphy struggled with the ferocious and inhumanly strong arm of the emerging jaeger, Gracie looped her forearms under Theo's arms and pulled him farther away from the immediate threat.

"Fritz, give it to me!" Nina ordered holding out her hand for something.

Fritz frantically searched his satchel and smiled as he found what he was looking for. He pulled out a thick red stick of dynamite and handed it to his companion.

"Let tem have it. Dis tunnel has already been compromised." Fritz pushed the girl back through the waterfall. He looked at the young man crouched on the ground, wide-eyed in shock from the attack on his life. The boy's body fell limp as Fritz started to pull the stunned youth to safety through the waterfall. "Call your dog, boy. He needs to get away from the tunnel!"

"MURPHY!" Theo screamed with emotions of the tunnel and the attacks pouring out of his body at once. "Come on, boy!"

Murphy gave one last strong yank then released the attacker's arm to run to his master's side. Murphy turned to face the attacker as he slowly backed through the falling water.

Nina waited until Theo, Fritz, and the dog made their way through the cascade of water then lit the shortened wick and held it for a moment as it quickly burned closer to the stick. Her eyes widened in horror as arms emerged from the crawl space and a badly burned head with a look of sheer hatred in its dead eyes poked out of the opening. She shivered as the eyes focused on her. Repulsed, she threw the stick of dynamite over the burned head and into the narrow space where the creature was wedged. "Run!" Nina screamed at the top of her lungs and dove through the waterfall. In front of her three figures and a dog ran through another tunnel toward safety.

Seconds later, a deafening explosion rocked the cavern and tunnel causing the world around them to shake and tumble, knocking them to the ground.

"Please tell me that the creatures in that hole didn't survive!" Theo rolled to his back to lie on the cold floor of the tunnel, taking long deep breaths.

"Ve vill have to hope so." Fritz used the wall to lift himself up off the floor where he had been thrown by the explosion.

"Seriously, what the heck are those creatures made of?"

"If we knew that, we would be further along in our fight." Nina expressed the disgust of not knowing if the massive explosion had in fact done anything but bury the jaeger for a short while. She knew that most likely it was already digging itself free, but she kept that to herself. She shot a quick glance of frustration toward Fritz who nodded, knowing exactly what she was thinking.

CHAPTER 15

A Cause

The group walked silently down the tunnel. A waterfall plummeted from the ceiling and veiled the path before them. Nina continued her pace, undaunted by the waterfall, but stepped to the side of the tunnel and within seconds emerged on the other side of the falls. The tunnel opened up as they crossed through where two could easily walk side-by-side. Theo began to breathe easier as the ceiling gradually rose farther above their heads. With a few more twists and turns of the tunnel, the sound of falling water faded.

Theo realized the ground under him had gone from a soupy mess to firm earth and they were walking on a solid stone surface. He hoped they were close to the end of this personal nightmare. He noticed his breathing had returned to a steadier pace in the lighter air. Even, with the expanding tunnel, he shivered and rubbed his chest. His mind still convinced him that he could feel the walls of the crawl space crushing down on his lungs, robbing him of air. Theo looked down and pretended to examine the stone floor with great interest as he tried to gather his thoughts and fears before they exploded out of his skin. Theo wondered if Gracie and their rescuers could hear his heart pounding as it rattled off his ribcage.

Murphy trotted along beside Theo, keeping in step with his master. His tail was wagging with the excitement of the tunnel still coursing through his mechanical wiring.

The woman called Nina began to slow their rapid pace as the group made one last turn and faced a heavy steel door intricately decorated with various religious scenes. Theo only got a quick look before Nina opened the door, slipped inside, and slammed the door shut behind her. He exchanged glances with Gracie then went back to scanning the artwork of the door. He couldn't imagine how much care and precision must have been used to create something like this. Who had the ability to manipulate the hard material into beautiful scenes from the Bible? He recognized a small boy defeating a giant in one scene and a man and a woman under an apple tree in another. He walked closer to the door and noticed the handle on the door. He ran his hand gently over three ellipses that were all intertwined. He thought they looked like arms locked to hold together in a circle.

Theo turned to mention the symbol to Gracie just as a strange clicking noise echoed through the tunnel. His immediate reaction was to turn and prepare himself for the worst. Terrible thoughts and scenarios flashed in his mind. Fritz noticed the look in Theo's eyes and put a reassuring hand on the boy's shoulder. Theo looked past Fritz in time to see part of a seamless wooden panel open and reveal a hidden exit.

Emerging from the hidden passage, Nina smiled at the trio then pointed to the door. "If the explosion didn't stop them, hopefully it will take some time for them to navigate that labyrinth. However, we must go."

"Cool," Gracie mumbled as she took Nina's outstretched hand to help guide her up through the slightly raised threshold. "I never would've found this secret door in a hundred years!"

"In our line of vork, it pays to be as sneaky as possible." Fritz grinned as he motioned for the young man and his excited dog to enter the hidden passage.

Theo grabbed the side of the opening and lifted himself inside then turned to watch as Murphy sprang effortlessly up to the landing. He smirked at his dog's boundless energy. He looked ahead and could see light dancing on the walls and floor at the next turn. He took a deep breath, positive that was the sign he was hoping for. *Light equals salvation from these tunnels,* he promised himself, eager to get to the outside world once again.

Nina navigated the group to the turn in the tunnel which opened into a beautiful lawn beginning to awaken with sprouts promising spring flowers, shrubs, and stone statues. The sun was just rising over the eastern sky and shone down on morning dew, causing the yard to glisten. Theo was too excited to worry about the beauty of the garden. He'd had his fill of tunnels and dark crawl spaces. He just wanted to be in the open again and almost knocked Gracie to the ground once Nina finally unlocked the gate to motion them into the sunlight.

Murphy ran stride for stride with his master who couldn't wait to soak in the early spring's warm rays. He closed his eyes and let the morning sun warm his cold, tired muscles. After a good stretch with arms extended high, Theo found a stone bench and sat down to rest. The sun's rays bolstered his spirits, but he was a long way from feeling like himself again. Murphy found a rabbit in a nearby bush and playfully chased it around the yard, making sure never to come close enough to actually hurt the rabbit. The weary teen laughed and wondered how that animal, regardless of what it was made of, could possibly have the energy to run around.

Gracie sat down beside Theo. "He won't hurt it will he?"

"Honestly, you need to ask that?" Theo was a little surprised by her question.

"I know. He might still be excited from all that commotion down in the tunnels." She immediately felt badly for even thinking that Murphy was capable of hurting something so innocent.

Murphy slowed down to a trot once he noticed the rabbit was panting and frightened. He padded back to the two sitting very close on a rather large bench. With a plop onto his rump in front of them, Murphy looked back and forth at the two teenagers. Theo looked down and slapped his leg. Murphy sprang from his squat position and landed lightly in his master's lap, then curled and rolled for easy access to his tummy. Even as a robot, he knew how much Theo liked to scratch and laugh as Murphy's hind leg would kick uncontrollably as his master tickled his belly.

For the first time in days, Gracie and Theo took turns petting Murphy and laughing out loud like carefree teenagers. The shadow of the Kaiserdom lurking in the background gave each of them a sense of serenity and safety that they hadn't been accustomed to feeling lately. Neither of them noticed that they were being watched closely by the man and woman who had just rescued them from the jaeger and the possibility of being lost in the network of tunnels that ran beneath the city.

"Gracie, Theo, we really need to get you two out of the open and away from prying eyes," Nina offered softly, not wanting to make them worry.

"Okay, sorry, we just really haven't had much time to thank Murphy for saving us." Gracie stood up quickly, embarrassed, and added "or you two!"

Theo, who hadn't stopped petting Murphy, jumped up in response to Gracie's words, knocking Murphy off his lap and down onto the new grass with a light thud. "Oh yeah, thanks. Sorry— didn't mean to be rude," he added with a grimace on his face as the quick standing movement taxed his body. He sat back down and rested his head in his hands, the weight of the world and exhaustion crashing down on him.

Fritz laughed as Murphy quickly rolled over and stood up, head-butted Theo on the back of the leg then trotted away to find his bunny friend again. "I tink your dog is mad at you, my dear boy." Fritz led them all in a brief chuckle.

"You two have been through a lot the last few days. You've got to be exhausted. Let me show you to your rooms. This evening we can worry about saying *thank you*." Nina flashed a beautiful smile at both teens.

"I'm not sure what we're even doing anymore," Theo complained uncharacteristically. "I am exhausted and my dog needs …," he hesitated as he almost slipped with the word *repaired*. "He needs rest."

"Theo, you're being rude," Gracie scolded him as if he were a child, embarrassed by his outburst. "We're safe now. We can rest. You'll feel better in the afternoon."

"Safe, are you kidding me?" Theo looked up at the girl, the shock and embarrassment evident on her face. He immediately felt badly for snapping at her, but he had never been this tired or scared in his life. He didn't hold back even though he knew he probably should. "Safe? Did you see that thing? Well, I did. When it had ahold of me, I gotta real good look at how we're both probably gonna die!"

"Hey! Get ahold of yourself! You're being incredibly rude!"

Theo looked from Fritz to Nina. "Don't get me wrong, I am very thankful for both of you. Had you not shown up when you did, I'd probably be getting dragged back through that suffocating tunnel, or maybe I'd already be in front of Brack being interrogated!" Theo knew he was yelling, and his voice was getting louder and angrier with every breath.

Fritz looked down at the young man with pity. Although it seemed like a thousand years ago, he could remember his own personal battle. The emotions coursed through his body as the memories of his first brush with death flashed vivid images in his mind. He could almost taste the dry bitterness of fear he had once experienced. He could feel the sweat on his brow and his heart pounding in his chest. He could feel the cobblestones under his feet as he ran with reckless abandon through the alleys of Prague. He never looked back; he just pushed forward. He pushed against the strain in his legs, the screaming of his lungs. He ran and he ran. He knew that he had to escape, no matter how badly he was hurting. If they caught him, it would be far worse or even final.

Closing out the past, Fritz shook his head allowing the memories and the emotions to slowly fade. He tried to recall how he had felt rescuing the youth from the jaeger in the tunnel earlier. He couldn't remember even being afraid; he should have been. He realized that invincible monster was probably digging its way out of the rubble as they stood there talking. Fritz knew he had been in complete control of his breathing and emotions. Now he wondered if that was a good thing or bad thing. How many times does a man have to face his own possible death before he can stare it in the face and not feel the fear of dying but rather feel the fear of not completing the task he had set out to accomplish.

"My dear Nina, vhy don't you show Gracie to her room. I'd like to have a few minutes to spend vith this fine young man if you don't mind." Fritz asked in a most polite manner, but though it was a question, Gracie knew he wasn't asking. He was telling Nina to leave him with Theo.

"Ah, that sounds like an excellent idea!" Nina clasped her hands together as if Fritz's suggestion was a wonderful and much needed relief after a long day. "Gracie darling, will you follow me? You can catch me up on your journey and let me know what dear old Jahile has been up to these past few months."

"Will you be okay, Theo?" Gracie's voice was soft and concerned.

"Yes, I'm … I'm sorry," he mumbled, never looking up at his dear friend. He knew that he didn't want to see the disapproval of his behavior in her eyes again.

"Ah, don't vorry about Theo. He'll be fine. He just needs a minute to collect himself. A jaeger encounter can have a profound effect on a person."

"Fritz is quite right. Those bloody things still give me the shivers when I see them or even think about them, for heaven's sake." Nina shivered for effect. She gently took Gracie's hand as they started across the yard toward the towering church.

Theo sat on the bench, head and shoulders slumped, exhausted, defeated, and most importantly, scared. *How can something like those jaegers actually exist?* He didn't try to pull his thoughts away from what had happened in the tunnel. He knew no matter how this adventure ended that anytime something went bump in the night he would be looking over his shoulder waiting to catch a whiff of what smelled like fear. He would never be the same. Nothing in his Holo-Games or zombie movies could have prepared him for facing a jaeger.

Fritz watched as the women made their way across the yard then disappeared behind the beautifully crafted double doors on the west entrance of the Kaiserdom. He sat down beside the dark haired boy and waited, giving him a few more minutes to collect his emotions and let the early morning sun warm his tired muscles. He liked to give any problem a few minutes. It always seemed a little less tense or scary once the adrenaline faded.

"So, Theo, have you been enjoying your stay in Deutschland so far?" Fritz attempted to ease the boy into talking.

Theo wanted to scream *NO!* but he had to laugh. He slowly lifted his head and looked at the man sitting with an infectious smile spread across his face. "Well, I've been beaten, left for dead, almost stuck in a cavernous coffin, and nearly had my leg ripped off by a smelly monster or man or whatever the heck those things are. So off the top of my head I'm gonna say no, I haven't really been enjoying my time in Germany."

"*Ihr Gestank,* er, um, das odor is quite off putting, I must say." Fritz chuckled as he stumbled over his use of the English language. "I'm not sure vhat causes it really, must be they don't like to get bath. Blasted things are afraid of vater, you know."

"Isn't that something—killing machines that can't swim," Theo scoffed.

"Maybe I shoult buy a small island und stay avay from die cveatures forever." Fritz grinned.

"Now, that would be nice. We could just leave this … this fighting behind us." Theo stood and stretched his back, then reached down to touch his toes without much success.

"Vell, ve can't simply valk away from this var. Vhat vould happen if the goot guys couldn't stop der bad guys, Theo?"

"Is that what you are? The good guys?"

"That's vhat *ve* are, Theo," Fritz replied emphasizing the plural and waving his index finger between the two of them.

"You may be the good guy. I'm just some stupid kid who got mixed up in all this." Theo didn't like the pressure of being the good guy. Sure, it was fun in Holo-Games and in the movies where good guys always won. But this was real life. He remembered climbing out of the pit filled with bodies. Good guys didn't always win and the losing was painful. He looked up at Fritz. "Besides, I'm not even sure what you're fighting for."

"Ah, my boy, an excellent point. Sometimes I vonder …" Fritz paused and rubbed his head. He opened his lips to say something then stopped. He looked over his shoulder and up to the top of the highest tower of the beautiful church looming behind him—a reminder to the people of Frankfurt of what good man is capable of doing. "I guess I could show you vhat *you* and I are fighting for,

Theo. Vhy I have committed the last tirty or so years of my life to the cause? Follow me."

Theo quickly realized that Fritz wasn't really giving him an option. While speaking the words, "Follow me," Fritz stood and started walking across the manicured lawn, headed straight for the double doors the women had entered. Theo shrugged his shoulders then gave a soft whistle to get Murphy's attention. He walked as fast as his sore legs would move, trying desperately to catch the shorter, older, yet at this time, much quicker man who disappeared around a hedge and up a set of stairs.

The boy and his dog found Fritz Malleczewen speaking with a man dressed similarly to how Father Kolbe had been. A breath momentarily caught in Theo's throat at the sight of the priest. The robed man wasn't who he had hoped to see. Theo silently scolded himself for getting his hopes up. What were the chances that he would ever see Father Kolbe again? He was probably still in Munich or off somewhere helping more kids who needed him.

The priest looked past Fritz's shoulder to see the young man and his dog climbing the stairs to where he stood. The man slightly raised a hand to finish talking with Fritz and turned to walk back into the church. By the time he reached Fritz's side, the brown-robed man was gone. Theo tipped his head back to look at the massive doors that opened into a room with a huge vaulted ceiling. The beauty of the entryway made him want to look without talking, without moving. He realized Germany had offered a lot of wonderful sights amid the chaos since his travels through the light of a star a million miles away. This entryway, though simple, was awe-inspiring. He couldn't imagine how long it must have taken the artist, woodworkers, and engineers to create, design, and build this magnificent church.

"Breathtaking, isn't it?" Fritz asked rhetorically. He knew no one would criticize such a work of art. "Stay close, Theo. This church has seen many new additions over die years and can make for a confusing journey trew its hallways, rooms, and antechambers."

"Where are we going?" Theo's youthful curiosity kicked into full gear at the wonder that surrounded him.

"You'll see. As much as diese place has to offer die senses"—he waved his arms around, trying to point at everything in the church at once—"it has vone more trick up its sleeve tat you must see vith your own eyes." Fritz left the mysterious comment hanging in air as he headed across the ornate, tiled floor with the sound of his footsteps echoing throughout.

Theo jogged a few painful steps to once again catch up with Fritz, then fell in step behind him as they zigzagged through hallways and, eventually, made their way up a few flights of stairs. The stairs ended at a wall bracing a ladder that looked like it could quite possibly go all the way to the heavens.

"You okay to climb, Theo?" Fritz didn't wait for an answer but scurried up the never-ending ladder.

Theo shook his head in disbelief. *Why bother asking?* He began his own climb up the ladder when he heard a familiar growl below him. He looked down to see Murphy sitting at the base of the ladder, his head tilted and his big brown eyes looking extraordinarily pathetic. Theo climbed down a few rungs then jumped down to the floor and gave his best friend a long ear scratch. "Can you go find Gracie?" he pleaded, feeling guilty for not having the energy to carry him up the ladder. He was already tired from the stairs they had come up just to get to the ladder.

Murphy let loose another low, angry growl and promptly turned around and trotted down the hall. He bobbed his head from side to side, looking for the pretty girl who was always so nice to him. "Sorry, boy!" Theo yelled down the hallway, the guilt really getting to him. He turned and grabbed the highest rung he could, let out a long, loud sigh, and started climbing back up the ladder.

Theo's arms started to feel very weak, and he was having trouble stabilizing himself with his legs as well. He looked up, exhaling hard through his nose and redoubled his efforts as the end of the ladder was only a few agonizing rungs away. He struggled the last few rungs, moving slowly and sluggishly until he emerged through an opening. Fritz's outstretched hand was waiting to lift him to the top of the tower.

"It's qvite a climb, isn't it?" Fritz heaved the heavy teenager up to the landing.

"You have no idea." Theo looked at Fritz with a half smile, half grimace on his face.

"Vell, I promise you tat it vasn't a vaste of your time. Come see!"

Nearly as soon as he raised his eyes, Theo saw that the climb was worth the effort, and Fritz had not undersold the proverbial gold at the end of the rainbow. He was pretty sure the entire city could be seen from his vantage point on the roof of the Kaiserdom. The sun was making its way higher into the sky, and the people of Frankfurt were already busy moving about the city. In a slow turn taking in the panoramic view, he could even see movement in the fields far to the south and west of the city.

"Look at all das people down there, Theo. They have no idea vhat ve do, but vithout us how different vould tere lives be each day? Vould sie have die freedom to go to vork, go to school, fall in love, und create beautiful vorks of art? Or vould sie be slaves to der men und vomen tat vant to see the vorld in chains?" Fritz spoke passionately as he gestured toward the people moving below them.

Theo stepped beside Fritz as he looked out over the people and the city. He took a long hard look at the surrounding areas and then looked at Fritz, who still had the fire in his eyes. "I understand ... but ... but, Fritz, this is an entire city. How can you ..." Fritzed frowned at the word *you*. Theo caught his mistake. "Sorry. I mean, how can we help them all?"

"Theo, ve can't help tem all. But ve can help tem make decisions for temselves und families. Not everyvone down tere ist goot und honest. Some are not goot people at all. Ve can't ... ve *don't* have das right to change voo or vhat sie are. All ve can do ist give tem die freedom to make decisions." Fritz paused and looked directly at the youth. "Und be tere to stop anyvone or anyting that vants to take tat from tem."

Theo couldn't find the words, so he vigorously shook his head in agreement as he plunged his hands into the pockets of his jacket.

Fritz chuckled at the boy's silence. "It's a lot to take in, Theo, but every time I start to feel defeated or vonder if ve, if I, am making a difference, I spend some time up here. Vhy don't you sit down over tere for a few minutes. I'll be back." Fritz motioned to the wall around the roof as he walked back to the ladder. "Just take it in, young man. Also, remember, up here, you are safe!" Fritz slipped down the doorway in the rooftop and made his way down the ladder.

Theo eased himself down on a narrow bench that had been constructed into the side of one of the smaller steeples on the tower. He leaned back and rested comfortably on the bench. He realized his hand in his pocket was rolling something through his fingers. A saddened memory crossed his heart as he pulled a soft yellow star from the pocket of his jacket. He stared at the star until a face emerged from the wool fabric. Theo tilted his head as he looked at the star, not wanting to lose the image of the boy who died as they escaped the pit of death--a memory that seemed to have happened years ago..

"I said I wouldn't forget you." Theo spoke to the imagined face on the star. "I won't. I won't forget you--or Yari, or any of the other kids while…" His head rolled back to look up at the fresh morning sky as the tears rolled down his face and a hoarse cry caught in his throat.

"I think I understand, Fritz. I think I understand." Theo whispered into the air as he tucked the yellow star into his palm and closed his hand into a fist. With arms crossed, he closed his eyes and felt the sun warm his face. When he opened his eyes again, the sun was not where it had been a few hours earlier.

EPILOGUE

In 2016, we stand on the cusp of advancing technology that may have already made the fiction of Part I into a reality. How wonderful that what is written on these pages as futuristic may already exist as the tomorrow of our world.

Although the episodes in *TimeWorm* are fictitious in nature, people such as Viktor Brack, Oskar and Emilie Schindler, and Father Maximillian Kolbe were very real and very much a part of the stories that need to be told. From the architecture of buildings to the layout of city streets and rivers that flowed through the heart of country and city were true elements that give a visual foundation for the story. The beauty of cities such as Munich and Frankfurt need to be seen from both the spiritual light of the cathedrals and through the evils of the night and Third Reich.

Stories of the Holocaust have been told by survivors, by museums, and in classrooms dedicated to educating youth around the globe. Pictures, accounts and stories told and retold, and writings do all they can yet may fall so short in capturing the truth and horror of the victims of the Third Reich. Although the characters and location are different in the novel, the inhumane event of the death pit was real. May the brutality and pain of the shortened lives of the children of the boxcar be scars from which we learn and reminders for our hearts to direct our paths with compassionate humanity.

As high school teachers, we realize that we sometimes present history to our teenagers as dead as the people about whom we read. We want readers to become excited about history—no, not all of it, just bits and pieces that they can tuck away into their memory-- about real people and real life that have shaped the world today. It is our hope that this novel will cause history to waft past the readers' mental visions and create a yearning to know more.

Jimmy and Brenda

ABOUT THE AUTHORS

JIMMY ADAMS joined the US Army immediately after high school and served two years in the infantry. He went on to college to earn degrees in political science and history. Now married, he resides with his wife and animal family in the heartland. He is currently a secondary social studies teacher doing his best to ignite a fire for learning and understanding history in all his students. Outside the classroom, Jimmy coaches cross country, track, and the swim team. He enjoys competing in triathlons, obstacle course races, and cycling. He is very excited to bring his love of history and storytelling to the pages of TimeWorm.

BRENDA HELLER is a retired schoolteacher who spends time with five grandchildren and outdoors with animals and gardening. At age 6, she wrote her first book for her friend Nancy, but it wasn't until college that she published her first work. She and her husband have spent most of their married life in Kansas, where they cherish the sunsets across their country fields. Her hobbies include four-wheeling, hiking, camping, water and snow skiing, and traveling. Her thirty-four years in high school and college classrooms fulfilled her passion for working with teens and encouraged her love for storytelling. When she is not writing, she looks for opportunities to volunteer with her church family. For Brenda, a great day ends by in the satisfaction that being busy brings, and she's ready to weave more stories into her dreams.

CPSIA information can be obtained
at www.ICGtesting.com
Printed in the USA
BVHW04s2148170418
513695BV00001B/36/P

9 781640 278585